ROOTBOUND

ROOTBOUND

GRACE NOSEK

LOLLYPOP PRESS

ISBN-13: 978-1-0689816-1-6 (Paperback edition)

ISBN-13: 978-1-0689816-0-9 (Ebook edition)

ISBN-13 978-1-0689816-2-3 (Hardcover edition)

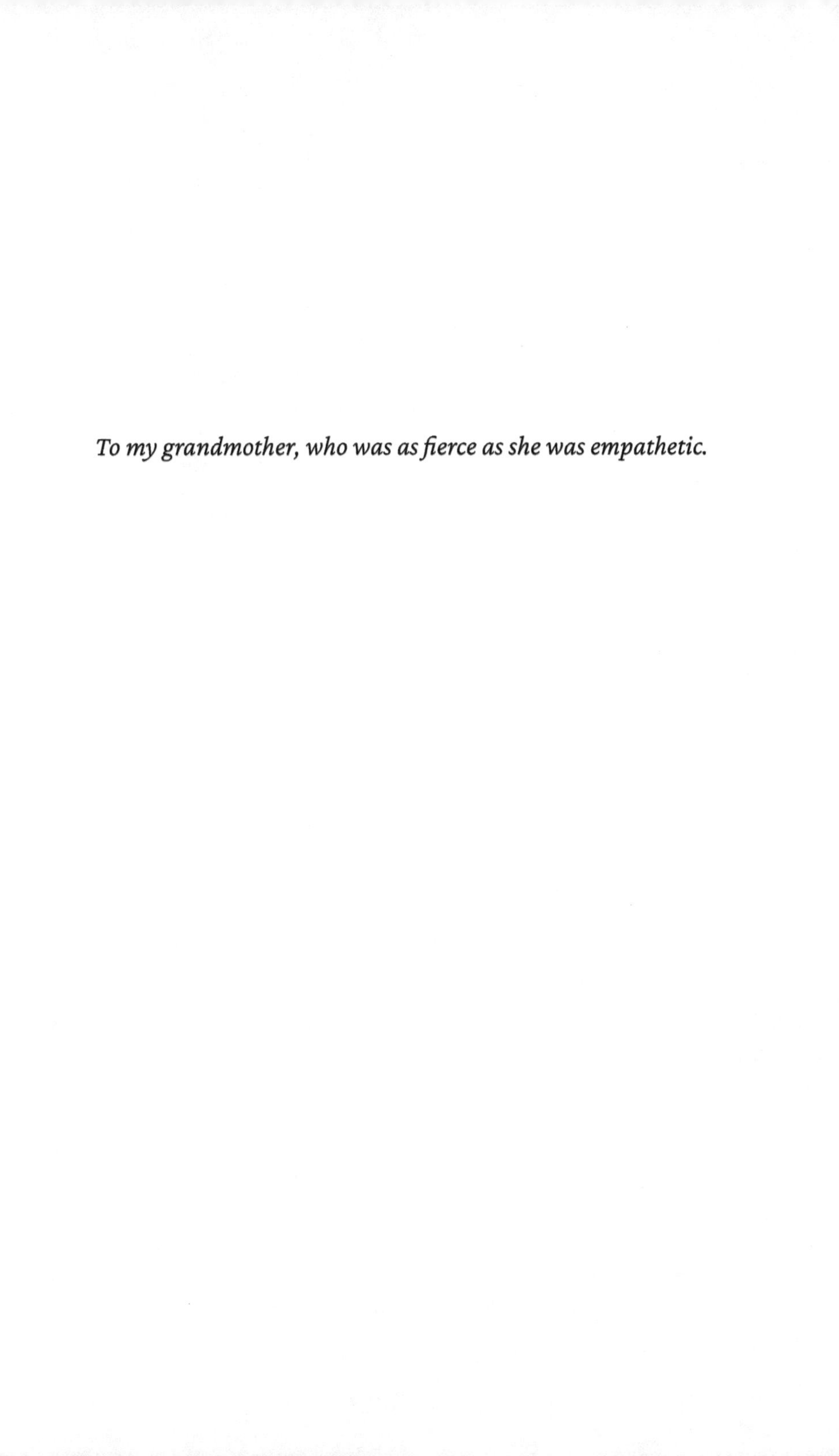

To my grandmother, who was as fierce as she was empathetic.

The pain started the day after my sister disappeared, nerve ends blistering as if being torched by invisible flames. "Complex regional pain syndrome," the doctors told me. But I knew what it really was—grief burning through me, making me desperate, restless, compelled to keep searching, searching, searching.

Where are you, Aspen?

My parents had given up after a year but I hadn't stopped. I couldn't—not with the wildfire raging through my limbs. I papered neighbourhoods with flyers in an ever-widening circle. I messaged celebrities begging them to share a picture of Aspen on social media. I went on any podcast or livestream or TV show that would have me, reminding an uncaring world about my sister. How good, how kind, how passionate she was.

How *gone* she was.

It was that fire in my limbs that drove me to the protest today. Aspen would've gone; she never missed a protest. Climate justice, labor strikes, gun control—Aspen was there, always with some new, shimmering banner she'd painted draped around her shoulders. This morning Canadian police had arrested dozens of people from an Indigenous-led rally peacefully opposing a pipeline being built across many First Nations' territories. Thousands of people were marching in solidarity through downtown Seattle, the June drizzle doing little to dampen their spirits.

I tried to trail along the outskirts but somehow the vortex of people swept me into the center. A high school marching band dueled with an old-school ska band and the protesters swirled in something that resembled a mosh pit. I ran a finger over the faded half-moon scar bracketing my right eye and a memory overtook me. I saw Aspen whirling in the neon vest of a protest marshal, leading the crowd of youth strikers in a belted rendition of Rihanna's *Umbrella*. Aspen had been mid-scream, mouth wide, when she'd accidentally collided with me —teeth-first. It had been one of our favorite party stories, how Aspen had bitten her little sister—*at seventeen*. I'd needed ten stitches.

I stared mesmerized at the dancing group, holding back the urge to throw myself at their swirling mass, to fall to my knees and be trampled by their stomping feet. Intrusive thoughts— that's what the school guidance counsellor had called them— these wild, fleeting urges to hurt myself. Apparently everyone got them. Some part of me knew I would never give in to the urges, especially when they were chased by the image of my parents' faces as the police told them it was unlikely Aspen would be found alive. I'd never even seen my dad *cry* before that moment, and he'd howled so loudly for hours that I'd had to wear headphones over earplugs to block out the sound.

I turned my face to the rain, catching a few drops in my mouth to soothe a throat hoarse from a thousand urgent repetitions of, "Have you seen this woman? Have you seen my sister?" The pain flared and I promised it I would rest as soon as I'd given out my last handful of missing person flyers. The pain didn't let up. It was used to my lies.

The crowd took up another chant of "System change not climate change!" Despite the sandpaper feel of my throat, I joined in. But what I was really saying was "I'm sorry." The day before she disappeared, Aspen had begged me to help her make posters for the divestment sit-in she was organizing at a Seattle U Board Meeting. I'd promised to come but flaked at the last minute.

Sry, sis, not gonna make it.

The last words I said to my sister. With a sad face emoji.

My foot caught on something and I tripped forward. I flailed my arms in a useless struggle against gravity. With a wet thud, my body met the ground. I lay there, face pressed into the pavement, feeling like this was it. There was no getting up.

"Are you OK?" a gentle voice above me asked.

I let out a sob, shaking against the ground.

"Can I help you up? Wiggle your fingers if you'd like me to."

I wiggled my whole body and someone hauled me off the ground, holding me upright as the crowd of protesters streamed around us.

"Are you OK?" the stranger asked again, fixing their dark eyes on me with a warm, steady gaze. They handed me the last of my flyers, which were torn, soggy, and covered in shoe prints. But I could still see Aspen's face grinning up at me, as if she knew how uncomfortable I was in the presence of this beautiful stranger.

I know they're hot, but c'mon, sis, at least say thank you.
"Thanks," I mumbled, looking at my feet to hide my blush. I saw something weird.

A root.

A root that had burst right through the asphalt. Like it was trying to trip me.

You're losing it, sis. Why would a tree want to trip you? Or how, for that matter?

"Are you OK?" the beautiful stranger asked for the third time, as if they really wanted to know the answer.

I held in the hysterical laughter the question stirred in my belly. "Do you...uh...do you know how I got on the ground? Or I mean, I guess it doesn't matter but did I like kind of dive at the road?"

"I didn't see. Is that something you're in the habit of doing?" There was an undertow of kindness in the teasing.

"You'd be surprised." The ground was one of the few places that felt safe anymore.

"I bet I would. I bet there are many surprising things about you...?"

"Mira," I said. They smiled and held out a hand to shake mine but didn't offer their own name. "Don't let the blue hair fool you. It's way more interesting than I am. Sorry for the false advertising." I shrugged.

Steady Gaze ducked so they could look me right in the eye. "There's nothing false about it. I was drawn to you from across the crowd, seeing the grief and love crashing out of you like a tidal wave."

I blinked, too stunned by the stranger's words to speak. I forced myself to meet the dark eyes in front of me and saw they shone with unabashed sincerity. Something moved out of the corner of my eye—a tiny silver thread emerging from a crack in the pavement like a self-inflating spiderweb. "Did you see that—"

"Can you walk?" they spoke over me, gently. Their demeanor was still warm, but seemed more guarded, and I wondered if I'd imagined the last few minutes.

I nodded. "I think I might go sit down for a moment." Or forever.

"There's a bench over there." Steady Gaze pointed at the sidewalk on the next block, past the major intersection the protest column was crossing. "I think it'll be dry, that giant maple is blocking the rain."

"Oh. Yeah. Cool," I said, remembering it was raining. My brain had been far more focussed on the arched eyebrows in front of me, the fresh smell of oak and lavender, the undercut I was so tempted to run my hands across.

"Do you want company?" Steady Gaze asked, following my diagonal shuffle through the protesters.

Yes, screamed my brain. *Yes!* screamed my heart. *YES!* screamed my body, goosebumps running across my skin at the thought of being near such kind, such calm. "No, that's OK," said my mouth. "Don't want to slow you down. Plus I kind of wanna be alone right now." As if I wasn't always alone.

"I understand. I'm sorry for..."—they shrugged—"*every-thing*. I hope you find your sister. *Aspen*."

I ducked away, not wanting Steady Gaze to see the new flood works at the sound of someone else saying my sister's name. "Thank you," I whispered.

A policewoman stood in front of the oncoming traffic, blocking the intersection while the protesters streamed through. A few drivers shouted encouraging messages out of their windows: "People over profit!" "No consent, no pipeline!" But a middle-aged man in a black SUV leaned on his horn and hurled obscenities at us.

"Sheeple! Morons! Dumb cow, dumb ugly cow covered in dirt," he yelled, and I realized he must be talking about me. I tried to ignore him but ignoring things was not my brain's strong suit. I clutched my hands into fists, resisting the urge to brush the mud off my shorts. The pain roared in my forearms like the engine revving behind me. The jerk was trying to scare us with his pathetic imitation of a Formula 1 driver.

I was almost at the bench when I heard the shriek of the policewoman's whistle.

Then screams.

The SUV was barrelling directly at the column of protesters. Without thinking, I took off in a sprint towards the car, hands up as if I could somehow push the speeding metal away from vulnerable flesh. Something yanked me out of my pursuit—*Steady Gaze*. They held my wrist, and I swung around clawing my other hand into their chest. "We need to help them. *Help them.*" At my command, the muscles in the stranger's neck stood out like vines on a tree and those gentle eyes flared in surprise. Their body convulsed and silvery light spun out from where I dug my fingers into their skin, growing more and more solid.

The screams got louder, blending with the roar of an engine directly behind me.

Steady Gaze shoved me to the side but something hard blocked my path. There was a thunderous crack, the horrible crunch of shattering glass, and then I was face first on the damp pavement for the second time that day. The pain spiralled out from its thousand tiny hiding places, fusing, burning my whole body in its embrace. I heard the echo of my dad's sobs when he was told Aspen was presumed to be dead. Then everything went dark.

TWO

Just like my brain couldn't ignore, it couldn't forget. Not the things that caught its attention. And apparently Steady Gaze had caught its attention—bad. My guidance counsellor had stopped all subtlety in suggesting that I find new people to talk to or hobbies to try, and straight up begged me to make a friend. Any friend. I felt for Dr. Zhang; I could imagine the difficulty of getting loner teens to hang out with one another in this wired world. But I wasn't a natural loner. I just had the terrible (wonderful) misfortune of sharing the same house with the best person on the planet since my very first day in the world. And after Aspen, nobody else really stood up. I tried to explain it to Dr. Zhang; I was so porous to the world, to other peoples' energies, that they actually had flavors my mind could taste. And at the moment, none of my offerings were very nourishing. My parents were like day-old coffee—stimulating anxiety without providing any warmth. My friends had the trace of Aspen about them, but cloying, fake, like chemicals masquerading as sugar.

But Steady Gaze tasted good, tasted real, like home-made

sorbet. Something I hadn't felt since losing...I pushed the thought a way, sinking back into the memory of meeting the mysterious stranger. The loud beep of something cold and foreign forced my dazed, drugged mind to attention and I realized I wasn't dreaming about Steady Gaze, but *looking* at them. What were they doing here? Where was here?

"You," I rasped, trying to sit up, but the motion caused my head to swim so I gave up. A bleach stink of industrial strength disinfectant. The scratch and rustle of a paper gown whenever I moved.

I was in a hospital bed.

"Careful, you're pretty banged up," Steady Gaze said. "I brought you to Seattle General after the crash."

Oh my gawd—this is like the cutest meet-cute ever, sis, Aspen whispered to me.

"Did I get hit by a car?" I croaked

"A tree actually. But I don't think the tree was trying to hit you. I'd say it was trying to rescue you."

"Uh huh," I said, skeptically. I felt the bandage on my head. "Heck of a rescue."

"Do you remember what happened? How you literally tried to stop a thousand-pound metal missile with your bare hands?"

The violence of the day rushed back to me—the speeding car, the screaming youth. But the final moments were hazy, dream-like. I had a vague memory of silver thread spinning out of the stranger's chest, a sense of commanding them like a puppet. But that couldn't be right; the fall must have jarred me. "Wait...sorry—I realize I don't even know your name."

"I'm Kes," they said with a warm smile. "And you're Mira the hero. It kind of rhymes."

"No," I said sharply. Aspen was the hero. I was just the sidekick, the one who couldn't even be bothered to make it to my sister's final protest. Pain stabbed at my temples. I realized how vulnerable I was—alone in this dark hospital room, naked but for a paper gown, and struggling to move. Where were my parents?

As if their eyes could bore right into my brain and read my thoughts, Kes said, "I called your parents from your phone, so they'd know where you were. They're on their way over now." They looked at their watch. I could tell they were trying to hide their impatience but it was hard to hide those things from my brain.

"You don't have to wait," I offered. "I'm sure my parents will be here any moment."

"Unfortunately not. Traffic is a nightmare." Kes peeked through the blinds. Why were the blinds closed? "They haven't found the man who rammed his car at the protesters, so police have shut down a bunch of roads."

"They...they haven't found him? But wasn't there a police-woman right there?" I squelched the irrational fear that he was looking for me. After all, I was just another teen in a crowd full of young people protesting. "Still, it's OK, you don't have to wa—"

"I want to." Kes let the blinds clatter shut and sat next to me. "What I'm about to say is going to sound very strange. But can you listen with an open mind?"

"Sure," I said. "I'm not going anywhere. *Clearly*." Kes was nervous. I could see it now. They hid it well but there was no masking the dilation of their pupils. The little tap of their foot. The tension in their shoulders. I realized they were younger than I'd thought, no more than a year or so older than I. "What is it? You're making me—"

"They're coming for you," Kes burst out. "Bad, powerful people. They must've seen what you did back there. Maybe they've even been watching you for a while, testing you. I don't know how they'll come or what they'll try, but there's no way they'll leave you alone now. Don't trust anyone. Got it?"

Unsure how to respond, I decided to go with the laughter bubbling up in my stomach. "What *I* did? Was my fall that spectacular? Thanks for keeping me company while my parents get here; truly, you are very good at distracting people from their problems."

"Yeah, that's how I thought this was gonna go." Kes cursed under their breath. "Why did we have to find each other like this?"

Find each other? This interaction was getting weirder by the second.

"Can I show you something?" they asked.

"Yes please! Is it a wand? An enchanted sword? One ring to rule them all? Gawd, I hope it's that."

"So you've got jokes—even when seriously concussed."

"Ah, I have a concussion—this is all making so much more sense."

Kes held out a muscular arm so I could see their phone screen. "Just FYI—it's gonna look and sound pretty intense, but nobody was seriously injured or killed, *thanks to you*."

Instead of eyeing the video queued up on the screen, I fixated on the black lines of a tattoo pooling out of Kes's sleeve. The lines formed a dense web.

The sound of screams pulled my attention to the video. I watched the black SUV explode out of the traffic and screech onto the sidewalk. As protesters panicked and scattered, a lone figure—me—rushed towards the car. Now, the video was much blurrier, its filmer running with the crowd. I made out a figure colliding with me, heard a rumble, saw concrete ripple as something dark—roots!—pushed out of the ground. Then the whole huge maple fell, right onto the speeding car.

"I've never seen anything like it; the maple *threw* itself in front of you." Kes's voice was thick with grief. My head swam.

"It *is* wild timing," I said. "Maybe it was struck by lightning? It was raining today."

"You don't understand." Kes got up and paced the little room. "The amount of energy, the *power* the maple must've sensed in you to sacrifice itself like that. You might be the strongest treetalker in a generation."

Treetalker? Now they were really spouting nonsense. "I mean, I remember that something weird happened right before the crash, but it had nothing to do with the tree. It was like I electrocuted you, like we were fused together at the cellular level for a second. Or maybe I'm just concussed and desperate for connection." I inched away from Kes, darting a look at the shut blinds, the closed door.

Kes sighed. "I'm sorry. I'm gonna go now, cause I can see I've freaked you out. But in the unlikely event that even the tiniest part of you believes me, please try to lay as low as possible in the coming days. You're safest if nobody knows who you are or what you can do. Play the concussed innocent for as long as possible. Say you don't remember anything about today if anybody asks."

"Uh thanks. I think I need to sleep now."

"Of course." Kes looked like they wanted to say more but I squeezed my eyes closed like a toddler pretending they've nodded off. When I opened them, they were gone. I blinked— did they just jump out the window? There was no way they'd opened and closed the door without me hearing it. My parents always teased me for my bat ears.

You're magic, Aspen hissed. *Knew it—didn't I always say?*
It was ridiculous. All of it.
And yet. That root tripping me. The tree falling just at the

right moment. The silvery substance pouring out of Kes's chest.

Does that mean I'm magic too?

As a rule, I tried not to talk back to my brain's projection of my missing-probably-dead sister, but I was too tired. "You've always been magic, Asp—if there's anything good and right with this world that magic is keeping you safe."

Speaking of safe, I think you should get out of here. Something feels wrong—Hot Kes was right.

Something *did* feel wrong. But something had felt wrong every day for the last eighteen months, so how was I supposed to know the difference?

Mira, I'm serious, get out of this place.

Ignoring the protest from my ribs, I heaved myself into a sitting position. My brain moving at the speed of honey, I scanned my surroundings. The worm of an IV slithered from the crook of my left arm. My backpack hung on the clothing rack next to the window and my clothes were folded on the chair. I tried to get out of bed but I felt heavy. So heavy.

"It's fine," I muttered. Who was I even talking to? "You're just flipping out cause we're in the hospital. Once I get some sleep, we'll both feel better, safer." I fell back in the bed and let the heaviness overtake me. But my sleep was restless, filled with shadowy figures and dark eyes.

CHAPTER

THREE

I woke up to gentle humming and the feel of something warm against my forehead. There was a soft-faced woman in scrubs dabbing my face with a washcloth. She looked vaguely familiar but I couldn't quite place where I'd seen her before. Her name badge read "Kirsten."

"Funny," I croaked. "You don't seem like a Kirsten to me."

"Oh?" She raised an eyebrow. "What do I seem like?"

"Sorry," I mumbled. "I'm really out of it."

"How are you feeling? Does anything hurt?" She dabbed again.

"Trick question. Might be easier if you ask me what doesn't hurt. I've got complex regional pain syndrome."

"Oh, I'm sorry," Kirsten said. "That's really tough."

She didn't sound sorry. She didn't even sound like she knew what it was.

I tried to move an exploratory hand over my aching ribs but couldn't; both my wrists were bound by some kind of restraint. Those hadn't been there earlier, had they? "Wait, what are these for? Why are my hands tied?" Not wanting to be the "hysterical girl," I tried to keep the panic out of my voice.

Kirsten frowned. "Didn't the doctor tell you when he was here?"

I shook my head. "What doctor?"

"Dr. Vermeule came to check on you a little bit ago and said you needed restraints—you were thrashing in your sleep and he wanted to make sure you didn't hurt yourself, especially with the concussion."

"Can you take them off now? Since I'm awake and obviously not hurting myself?"

"Deep breaths, Mira—I need you to take some deep breaths. You're hyperventilating."

"No I'm not!" I shouted. "OK, I realize that didn't help my case. But it's been a long, weird, scary day and I really, really want these off." I tugged at the restraints, feeling bruises blooming on my wrists. What was one more ache to a body that was practically a strobe light of pain?

"Calm down, Mira, *calm*—"

"I AM CALM."

"I'm going to give you something for the anxiety. Hold on a sec, just one sec."

She rummaged for something out of my line of vision. I glared at Kirsten's profile helplessly. And then I froze, as realization overtook me. I had seen Kirsten before. In a different uniform.

The policewoman.

Kes's warning came back to me—powerful, evil people would be coming for me. Adrenaline shook me out of my stupor. I scanned the room for means of escape. I needed to alert someone else to my predicament without tipping Kirsten off to my plan.

Forcing calm into my tone and posture, I said, "Sorry about

being such a drama queen. I've gotten kind of claustrophobic since...since my sister disappeared last year."

Kirsten held up a syringe, flicking the tip. "Aspen, right?" she said, casually. So casually. Too casually. "I saw your posters. Do you have any idea what happened to her?"

"Well..." I drew the word out, noticing the tension in the fake nurse's body. *This* is what she was here for. She wanted to know about Aspen. But why? "She disappeared without a trace. The day of one of her biggest climate actions yet. She never got to see the change she pushed for."

"Oh, that's so sad," Kirsten said. But her eyes were cold. She sounded almost bored. "Do the police think her disappearance has anything to do with that extremist cell?"

"Extremist cell?" I said, forgetting to keep my voice calm.

"Yeah, total cultists. They swear some kind of blood oath."

"Blood oath?" I shook my head. Was I still lucid?

"To the trees. They claim the trees are directing them to kidnap, torture, *murder*. There was a whole exposé online."

Kes. Kirsten thought Aspen was connected to Kes and their tree magic. "Oh my God. The police never mentioned anything."

"Apparently they were behind the attack at the protest today. Did you see anything? You were *right* there." Kirsten leaned towards me, the syringe seemingly forgotten.

"There was something...*someone* strange. I'm trying to remember, but everything from today is a blur." I feigned a shiver. "My *head*. It's like somebody's jamming a screwdriver into my skull."

"Stay with it, Mira. Think—for your sister," Kirsten cooed, all softness and warmth again.

"Do you have any ice?" I whimpered, trying not to overdo it.

Kirsten didn't budge.

I scrunched up my nose in faux concentration. "There was a person...I thought they were following me. I couldn't seem to shake them."

"That's it. What did they look like?"

"Ice, please. My brain is on fire—the pain syndrome is flaring."

"Right, let me see. I'm sure we can find something to help that poor head of yours."

As soon as Kirsten turned her back, I snuck a look over my shoulder. I almost screamed in relief at the sight of the red emergency button on the headboard. Holding my breath, I strained my neck, pushing my head back and into the button as hard as I could. Kirsten turned around before I could relax back into my slumped position and I blurted out, "I remember. I remember what they look like!"

"That's a good girl. Tell me and I'll tell the authorities."

Why hadn't anyone responded to the emergency call? Had I missed it? I wouldn't get another chance. Stalling, I rambled, "Have you seen the first *Matrix*? Such a good movie. The two leads? Keanu Reeves and that woman who looked amazing with her hair slicked back and those tiny sunglasses. They kind of looked like a cross between the two of—"

A sharp rap came on the door, cutting me off. "Excuse me, did anyone ring the nurse call button?" Someone rattled the door handle. "Why is this door locked?" There was muffled shouting, something about "maintenance" and "emergency."

Kirsten met my eye and without warning lunged at me, syringe aimed at my heart. I threw myself to one side as hard as I could, kicking the IV stand at the charging woman, and grunting as the needle was ripped from my vein. The metal pole of the IV stand landed with a thud against Kirsten's collarbone and the syringe flew out of her hand.

Something slammed into the hospital door like a battering ram. I screamed, "Help! Help me! She's locked us in and I think she's gonna hurt m—"

A hand clamped over my mouth, squeezing my cheeks together like a vice. "Shut up, now," Kirsten hissed. I gnashed my teeth, bucking and writhing against the grip, uncaring as the restraints bit into my skin.

"Shut up and stop struggling or you'll never see your sister again."

I stopped moving. Stopped breathing. Stopped thinking. *Aspen. They had Aspen.*

Kirsten kept one hand clamped on my jaw while reaching with the other. The sharp whine of metal cutting metal came from outside but my rescuers wouldn't be fast enough. Kirsten was turning back around, a needle clutched like a knife in her hand.

Glass shattered and sprayed across the room falling over me like rain, as a blurred shape hurtled though the window and knocked Kirsten over. Something rough scraped across the skin of my wrists and I screamed, before realizing my restraints had been slit. Freed, I pushed myself out of the hospital bed to see the nurse impersonator pinned to the ground by a tree branch. A maple from the courtyard was leaning through the hole in the wall where the window had been, like a little kid punching their arm into a dollhouse. Neon green leaves shook violently as Kirsten battled the maple, grasping for the syringe, which had landed a few inches from her reach. I threw myself unsteadily at the needle and held it to Kirsten's neck. "Where is my sister? What have you done to her?"

A hand gripped my shoulder, this one gentle. "She doesn't know, Mira, trust me. We've gotta get out of here. *Now.*"

Kes. They were back.

"She said they had Aspen—"

"She lied, dug into your deepest pain to manipulate you. It's what they do."

There was more banging at the door. The grating sound of a saw.

"We've got twenty seconds before that door gives. *Come.*"

"But I called for them. I think they're here to help."

"As long as you stay in this hospital, on *their* radar, you'll be vulnerable."

I hesitated, Kirsten's words about murderous cults and blood oaths flashing in my mind. But Kes had helped me—three times today. I dropped the needle, letting them pull me up and away.

"Can I carry you over the glass? I've got your clothes and shoes in the backpack."

I nodded and Kes crouched in front of me. I climbed awkwardly onto their back, nuzzling my head into the warmth of their neck without thinking. They scrambled over the windowsill. I held my breath, wondering if we were about to jump. But there was a makeshift ladder of braided tree branches waiting for us. As we descended, the branches above us unbraided. I wondered what other patients looking out their windows would make of the scene. Then I saw that all of the windows were covered by a thick curtain of leaves. The maples looked like they were standing on tiptoe—branches stretched wide and to the sky in an unnatural pattern. *They were blocking the view.*

Kes jogged across the hospital courtyard to a door marked "No Entry." They grabbed a swipe card from their pocket and opened the door into a dark stairwell. Not even breathing heavily, they took the stairs down two at a time with me still balanced easily on their back.

We reached the bottom of the stairwell and Kes set me

down gently, handing me my stuff. "Hold on a sec." They darted through another door and I caught a peek of a cavernous underground parking lot. Hurriedly I tore off my hospital gown and shoved uncooperative limbs into my t-shirt and shorts.

Kes appeared a moment after, their tall form now clad in a navy blue EMT uniform, complete with radio. They tossed me a bundle of blue fabric. "These should be big enough to put on over your clothes. I'll go grab our ride and have it waiting outside. Come out as soon as you're dressed. There are other EMTs and staff around, so try to look as confident as you can when you walk out of the stairwell. Got it?"

I nodded, fisting the rough cotton. Look confident. Don't die. They made it sound so easy.

FIVE MINUTES later we were barrelling through traffic blockades and closed streets, gaining easy passage with the blaring sirens and flashing lights of the ambulance we'd stolen from the hospital.

"I'm sorry," Kes said, flicking off the sirens.

They slumped in their seat, not meeting my eye. I wanted to scream *you just saved my life*! Instead I blurted, "You couldn't have shown up *before* that nurse pointed a needle the size of a nerf gun at me?"

Kes caught the smile on my face, and a faint one of their own appeared on their lips. "Blondie blocked the door with some kind of chemical sealant. I was just climbing the fire escape to your window when you let out the scream heard round the world. Thanks for that by the way—makes the whole covert exit thing super easy."

Were we *flirting*? I strained to catch a glimpse of myself in the rearview mirror. I took in my round face and hair that went from brown to bleach to faded blue. The bruise blooming on my jaw made my cheeks look even more full, especially next to the sharp angles of Kes. My hair looked tousled and voluminous, exactly how I'd imagined it when I'd let Aspen talk me into dying it, but could never quite achieve in my rushed mornings before school.

"I like it—the hair," Kes said.

They'd caught me staring at myself in the mirror. "Erm, uh..." I started, as my brain ran through ten different responses.

When I didn't continue, Kes asked, "What'd you do to make Blondie so angry?"

"Honestly, that's just my natural charm."

"No seriously. What happened?"

I shrugged. "I wouldn't tell her what I knew about you. And that made her really mad. I think she would've killed me if she needed to." I felt the truth of the words as I said them.

Kes reached to put a hand on my knee. "*Thank you.*"

I stayed very still, hoping they would keep their hand where it was.

"Where can I drop you to lay low for a few weeks? Not your house—that would be too obvious. But an old friend? A cousin of a cousin?"

"I'm not...I'm not coming with you?" I asked.

"No, you've already done enough. You were amazing today, Mira. But you're right—that nurse would've killed you, without a second thought. So we need to get you somewhere safe. I'll send someone to keep an eye on you and your family. I won't let you down again."

"What? No. You didn't let me down. You saved—"

"Think hard," Kes interrupted me. I have to make a quick stop to grab my friend and then we'll drop you off—wherever you want." They turned the ambulance into a strip mall and parked in front of a laundromat with a sign missing several letters so the store name was indecipherable. "My friend might ask about what happened today. If she does, can you...can you not mention the moment before the crash?"

The moment where I somehow electrocuted you with my voice and had full control over your body? Sure I won't tell this literal stranger about something I barely believe happened and have absolutely no understanding of. "Why not?"

"I want you to have a chance to join..." Kes trailed off, distracted by a woman charging out of the building. Tall and muscular, she could've been Serena Williams' teenaged stunt double. "Scoot over—Ramaya's getting in," they said, pressing their long frame into me. The woman opened the ambulance door and swung herself easily into the driver's seat. Seconds later we were speeding down the road. Ramaya swerved around a red Tesla, throwing me into Kes as a crashing noise came from the back.

"What's with the plus one, Kes?" Ramaya asked casually, as if we were not rocketing down the highway at a hundred miles per hour.

"*Mira*, here, was the one who threw herself in front of the car speeding towards the protesters."

Ramaya whistled. "Right, of course. I recognize the hair. Brave move, Mira. Stupid, but brave—we owe you one."

"We're keeping her safe for a moment while she thinks of a place she can hide out until this whole thing calms down."

"Please. This 'whole thing' is not going to calm down. Like a thousand people saw a tree throw itself onto a speeding car to protect Blue Hair over here. There's video evidence."

"Already wiped from the internet. Even the version I downloaded to my phone. They don't waste any time."

"They?" I interjected.

"Did you tell her anything about us?" Ramaya asked. "Give her the chance to join?"

"That's not how we do things, Ramaya. She's concussed, probably still in shock."

"Give me a chance to join what?" I asked, louder this time.

Ramaya shot me an appraising look. "We're part of a… community. An ancient one—"

"Not now, Ramaya. Not yet. It's not fair to put Mira in that much danger without her consent."

Ramaya laughed but there was no humor in the sound. "As if they haven't put the whole world in danger without our consent. You can't protect her, Kes. It's too late. The only way out is through."

"It's not the time or the place," Kes said firmly.

"Fine. For the record, Blue Hair," Ramaya said, turning to me, "you seem like a stone cold legend, and if it was up to me you'd be coming with us today." She turned back to the road just in time to perform a complicated figure eight around two vans going the speed limit. "Kes, any youth missing from Seattle?"

"None."

Ramaya whooped and high-fived her friend. "And what about Berlin? Dakar?"

"All safe. The extra security measures worked."

The named cities scratched something in my memory—they were all the sites of big climate protests this weekend. "Wait, are you two talking about teens missing from climate events?"

Kes shot Ramaya a warning glance.

"You are. You *are*! My sister went missing just before a climate event. Is somebody targeting climate leaders?!"

"Our enemies are kidnapping youth climate strikers from

protests around the world," Ramaya announced as Kes glared at her.

"What did you just—" I was cut off by a trill from Kes's phone.

"What is it?" Ramaya asked as Kes scanned their device.

Kes clenched their jaw, digging their hands into fists. "They snatched a teen in the chaos after the collision today."

FOUR

Ramaya swerved around a merging semi-truck, knocking one of its mirrors off with a metal *thunk*. The truck driver laid on the horn. It had been like this for the last twenty minutes, the tension increasing with the ambulance's speed as more intel on the missing teen trickled in.

"Slow down," Kes called through gritted teeth. "You're drawing too much attention."

"Is that an order, *boss*?" Ramaya's hands tightened on the wheel. "You know she'll be dead, or worse, within the day if we don't find her. Fourteen, Kes, she's fourteen."

"We don't even know if she's at the airport—"

"She's at the airport! I'd bet my life on it. It's their MO. They always go to the closest private airfield, there's always an unregistered jet waiting for them, and once it gets in the air, we can't track them. They're the ones with the satellites, not us. If that girl gets on that plane, she's gone."

Kes sighed, turning from Ramaya to me. "Alright, your ride's cancelled. We'll have to drop you somewhere public." They offered me a wad of crisp hundred dollar bills. "Here's cash for a bus or a taxi or an e-bike. Just please get yourself somewhere safe."

I crossed my arms, refusing the cash. "I'm staying with you."

"No. You're not. This is not a game, Mira. Ramaya's definitely gonna get us all killed."

"Two people have already tried to kill me today, and look—I'm fresh as a daisy." Without thinking I ran my hands over the deep bruises on my wrists. "What if my sister is one of the youth climate strikers kidnapped by these powerful enemies?"

"Mira—" Kes started again, speaking as they would to a small child.

"You heard Blue Hair. She knows the risks and she wants to stay. Plus I'm not pulling over to let her out unless you *make* me."

Kes threw their hands in the air. "I hate you."

"You love me." Ramaya grinned and stepped harder on the gas.

I tried to catch Kes's eye but they stared fixedly out the driver side window. Finally, they called, "Turn here!"

"On it!" Ramaya skidded the ambulance into an awkward left turn, almost knocking over the small sign that read *Falcor Premium Aviation*. "I clock two rent-a-cops at the entrance. You ready to charm the pants off them? There won't be any time to waste."

"I'm ready, Maya-Bear."

"Call me that again and I'll kill you myself."

They were putting on a brave front, but I could see it clear as day—they were afraid. And we were hurtling closer to the source of that fear.

"Mira, gimme your uniform quick," Ramaya ordered. "And then duck down—we don't need airport security asking about you."

I hurried to obey, tossing the clothes over and crouching below the dashboard. The last thing I saw out the window was a long stretch of chain link fence topped by barbed wire and sleek white jets trapped like doves behind the metal.

The ambulance pulled to a stop and I held my breath. From above me Kes said, "Evening, sir, we got a call about a teenager in cardiovascular distress. Fourteen. Petite. Do you have any idea where she might be?" Their voice was different—soothing, sneaking around me like soft scarves, pulling, tugging. I fought the urge to climb towards them.

There was a garbled exchange and then a voice said, "The only ones who've been in or out are headed to runway number seven. Didn't get a look in their van, the higher-ups told us to wave them through, but she might have been in there. I don't think you'll catch them in time—HEY!" A gruff male voice shouted.

"*FREEZE!*" Kes yelled and this time the words constricted around me, the soft scarves pulling tighter than the hospital restraints.

The ambulance swung wildly, knocking my head against the door. Kes pulled me back up to the seat and whispered, "Hold on," bracing their arm across my midsection like the safety bar of a rollercoaster just in time for Ramaya to swerve around a parked jet.

"That's gotta be them. Tinted windows, reinforced body, discrete." Ramaya nodded towards a black SUV in the distance.

"What's our plan, here? Gonna run them off the road?"

"Their jet's already in position on the tarmac. If we don't catch them before then…" Ramaya swerved around a rent-a-cop ramming a golf cart towards us. Gun shots rang out and the ambulance pitched to the side. With a screech of metal grinding against pavement we shuddered to a stop. "They shot out our tires. They're getting away! Do something!"

Kes put a restraining hand on Ramaya. "There's nothing we can do now. They're armed, and we're sitting ducks, miles away from the closest entry to the Rhiza. We have to get out of here."

Ramaya shook their hand off. "NO. I will not let another teen die on my watch. She's fighting, Kes, *look.*"

In the distance, the SUV had pulled to a stop. I could just make out a small figure being bundled towards a jet by two men in black tactical gear. The figure let out an anguished scream.

Without warning, Ramaya shoved the door open and jumped out of the ambulance. I moved to follow, seized by the idea that the scream was coming from Aspen even though the figure was far too small to be my lost sister. Kes also flung themself after Ramaya and we tangled together, crashing out of the open door to the pavement below just as a hail of bullets shattered the ambulance windshield. Kes shoved me under the vehicle and rolled after me.

"Are you hurt?" Their face loomed next to mine.

"No," I lied through gritted teeth, unable to feel anything in my body.

"Can you help me? Ramaya and that girl might have a chance if I can just get into the Rhiza."

I nodded even though I had no idea what they were talking about.

"Look for a crack in the pavement!" they urged and started commando-crawling around the space under the ambulance, hands trailing over pavement. I followed their example, trying to block out the shouting and gunfire, trying to focus only on the slick tarmac in front of me. *There*—was my mind playing tricks on me? I followed the barest shadow of a line to the back tire of the ambulance, where I saw the line fan into a series of cracks. "Here!"

In a moment Kes was lying next to me, throwing what looked like handfuls of air at the cracks, and letting out a guttural plea for Ramaya's safety. Something frothed out of the cracks, like a mass of maggots churning and growing, faster and faster. The crack widened against the pressure and Kes rolled out from under cover of the ambulance and plunged their fist into the split pavement, burying it almost to the elbow. A pop of gunfire came from somewhere nearby and I screamed as Kes knelt in the open, completely vulnerable.

And then the ground erupted.

I closed my eyes and threw my hands up against the spray of dirt and rock. As soon as the ground stopped shuddering, I scratched at the mud caking my eyes, and felt along the ground in what I hoped was the direction of my friend. My hand hit air instead of pavement and then I was tumbling down what felt like a steep slope. As I came to a stop, I forced myself to a crouch and opened my eyes, ignoring the sting of debris.

I was at the bottom of a crater the size of a cellar that hadn't been there a moment earlier. Kes stood sentinel, body tensed and eyes closed as what looked like silver wire spun out of the ground and around their legs. Their arms were scratched and bleeding, their t-shirt torn, and dark bruises bloomed on their cheeks, but they were *alive*. I dragged myself upright and shuffled to them, throwing my arms around them with a sob. Their eyes flew open and they hugged me tight.

A burst of gunfire came from the distance and they whispered urgently, "However you were feeling back at the protest when you stepped in front of that car and commanded me to protect the bystanders—I need you to do it again. Command me to help Ramaya."

I wanted to laugh at this ridiculous request. But I could still feel the lingering power I'd lashed like a whip at Kes earlier in the day, forcing them to obey my words. So I did what they asked and turned inwards. The pain and the fear and the rage that I'd been holding at bay to survive the day—to survive the year—I let it flood out of me as I shouted for Kes to protect their friend and the kidnapped girl. Kes shuddered in my arms as if they could literally feel the power of the emotions sweeping through their veins. The earth rumbled, louder and louder, like it was being torn asunder by an excavator. I couldn't see what was happening on the airfield beyond but I could hear the screams.

"To the jet, Mira! Now!" Kes half-dragged me over the wall of dirt, easily keeping their footing on the shifting ground. I turned to catch a typhoon of dirt sweep over another rent-a-cop in a golf cart, but Kes kept pulling me forward. We scrambled between chunks of tarmac as if they were paving stones in a river of mud and sprinted the final stretch to the jet. Kes clambered up the boarding stairs, and burst into the plane. I paused at the top, torn between a desire to stay close to them and a sudden dread at what we would find.

Primed by a slew of RikRok videos by gazillionaires, I'd expected the plush leather seats and the soft lighting of an upscale spa. I had not expected to see two men in black combat gear bound by a thick vine slumped unconscious against the door of the cockpit. A third man in military garb crashed through a partition at the back of the plane, jerking and bucking wildly. Ramaya stepped through the wrecked doorway after the figure, seemingly unconcerned by his behavior.

"Call off your zombie ants," Kes said. "We don't want him eaten alive."

I shivered, peering closer and saw an ant the size of a cockroach skittering over the man's leg. It sank its mandibles into the man's calf, and he groaned, kicking his leg uselessly. Another ant drilled into his neck.

Ramaya held up what looked like a tube of lipstick,

spraying a cloud of something the length of the man's body. The ant burrowed in the soldier's calf twitched and withdrew its head. It marched straight for Ramaya, and dozens more fell into line behind it. The killer ants snaked up Ramaya's foot, disappearing under her pant leg. She caught me gaping and winked.

The soldier lay strangely still, his eyes darting between Kes and Ramaya.

"The ants injected him with a temporary paralytic," Ramaya explained.

"Do you have the flower ready?"

"Of course."

Kes knelt next to the figure, heaving him into a sitting position and forcing his mouth open. Ramaya stuck something under the man's tongue and his eyes turned suddenly docile.

He spoke dazedly, "Ah, the flower of truth. I always wondered what it would feel like."

Ramaya held her watch up, showing a running timer. "Two minutes before it blooms."

Kes held the man's face to theirs. "What are you doing with the youth climate strikers? Why are you kidnapping them?"

"I don't know. I don't like it—today's target looked just like my niece. Too young to be dragged into this. But The Confessor ordered it—one hundred thousand dollars for every striker acquired. A hundred grand for a day's work." His eyes widened as he said the last part.

Ramaya cut in, "Who is The Confessor? What do they want?"

The man began to sing, in a surprisingly pleasant voice, "The rich man in his castle—"

"Not this again." Ramaya groaned. "Enough. Who. Is. The. Confessor? A Huntsman?"

The man beamed and began his song again, "The rich man

in his castle, the poor man at his gate. God made them, high or lowly, and ordered their estate—"

"Thirty seconds," Ramaya warned. I found myself talking before I even realized, "Aspen Bracken. Was she one of the strikers you acquired?"

"Aspen Bracken," the man murmured, considering. He opened his mouth to speak, but instead began to gag. His eyes bulged and his face turned red as he choked. A bruise-colored flower burst out of his mouth, its petals unfurling like tentacles across the rest of his face, and the man slumped over unconscious.

"Did you see that? It looked like he recognized the name? Didn't it? Didn't it?" I looked between Kes and Ramaya but neither met my eyes.

"*Selfish*," Ramaya hissed under her breath.

Kes put a hand on Ramaya's shoulder. "I couldn't have neutralized the reinforcements without Mira. It's been a long day."

They looked at me expectantly, clearly waiting for me to say something. "I'm sorry," I murmured, even though I wasn't. The man had recognized Aspen's name—I was sure of it.

Kes's expression hardened. "Rama, we've got company." I followed their gaze out the nearest window and saw a convoy of black vans turning into the airport entrance. They reminded me of the ants marching towards Ramaya, moving as with one mind and one purpose. "Do you need a co-pilot?"

"No, stay with the girl. Make sure she's comfortable." Ramaya kicked the unconscious Huntsmen aside, stepped through the cockpit door and settled herself into the pilot's seat. Kes disappeared into the back of the plane.

"Buckle up, Blue Hair," Ramaya called as the plane jerked forward. "I haven't flown one of these in a minute."

I was an anxious flyer at the best of times. Now I huddled

into a plush leather seat, scrambling to find the seat belt. Trying to distract myself from the plane's lurching progress, I looked out the window in time to catch a wave of soil collide with the two closest paramilitary vans, scattering them like toy trucks. Black-clad figures swarmed out of the overturned vans, each carrying a gun bigger than the last. I thought again of Ramaya's ants as the black figures fanned out in easy coordination—who was their queen? This 'Confessor' person?

I felt suddenly freezing. Teeth chattering, I closed my eyes and wrapped my arms around my chest in the self-hold my counsellor had shown me, rocking back and forth. "Please don't hurt me; please don't hurt my sister. Please don't hurt me; please don't hurt my sister," I whispered over and over again, matching the rhythm of my rocking.

Eventually a warm hand wrapped around mine and Kes whispered, "We'll protect you now. *Promise*." I let out a rush of breath, stopping my murmured pleas. Why was it so easy to believe them?

"Kes, a little help," Ramaya's voice called from the back of the plane.

"Is no one flying?" I asked, alarmed.

"The plane has an autopilot." Kes gave my hand a squeeze. "Wait here."

They moved down the aisle, through a half-splintered door. Over the hum of the engine, I heard what sounded like an argument. A growing sense of dread forced me up and I tottered to the back of the plane and pushed my way through what remained of the door.

The scene was like *Sleeping Beauty* gone terribly wrong. A petite girl with a tumble of dark hair lay perfectly still, draped across the bed in the jet's master bedroom. She was covered in bandages and a shiny salve that smelled like herbs. Blood seeped through the cloth like rose petals. I strained to see her face from under the tangle of her hair, searching for Aspen's thick eyebrows and sharp chin even though I knew I wouldn't find them.

"Mira," Kes warned. "You don't want to see this."

I ignored them and pushed closer.

Something was sticking out from the teen's neck...some kind of foreign object with legs. Too many legs. It looked almost like a tick, but not like any tick I'd seen before. This one was the size of a quarter, made of obsidian stone, with a blood-coloured jewel where the body should have been. The creature's legs began to tremble and its jeweled body lit up, casting a red glow across the room. The girl's eyes flew open in a silent scream.

My stomach heaved and I swallowed against the bile in my throat. I pitched sideways, slumping to the carpeted ground.

"What's wrong with her?" I heard Ramaya's voice from far away.

Kes grabbed my hand and looked deep into my eyes. "You can sleep now, Mira Bracken. Sleep long and deep—*you're safe*." The words held that same echo of power as before. I had the sensation of hot water streaming down my back and then my world went dark.

FIVE

I opened my eyes to a whispered, "You can wake now, Mira Bracken, you're safe," feeling the same strange sense of emerging out of nothingness as I had after waking up from my wisdom teeth surgery. The compulsion of Kes's words lingered and my ribcage sank in my chest in a way my body had forgotten it could.

"Did you...put me to sleep?" I rasped.

"I did," Kes said. "You were having some kind of panic attack. You're safe now."

"Safe...I feel safe." It was a startling revelation. I couldn't remember the last time I'd felt safe. Certainly not after Aspen disappeared. I was lying in a four-poster bed in what looked like a palatial room at a ritzy hotel. Somebody had written "Welcome, Mira!" on a whiteboard stuck to the door and a wild laugh clawed its way out of my throat. Welcome, indeed. The gold wallpaper was covered in posters and flyers for various rallies, protests, and concerts across the world. In addition to a crystal chandelier, the ceiling was criss-crossed with dozens of strands of twinkling LED lights. Inexplicably there was also a toy kitchen complete with a miniature shopping cart and perfectly detailed cooking implements in one corner. The tiny fridge hummed as though it actually worked.

The trauma of the day before flooded back. I grabbed Kes's forearm. "The girl on the plane—"

"She's OK, she's OK," they soothed.

"But that thing on her neck..."

"She'll heal, Mira. We have the best healers in the world." They shifted in my grip and I realized how tightly I was holding their arm. I snatched my hand away and busied myself looking for my shoes and backpack. "And my parents. Are they safe?"

Reading my mind, Kes handed me my things. "Yes. We've scrubbed their digital connections to you, and activated the trees in your neighborhood to red alert."

Right. The magical warrior trees. The zombie ants. The black vans full of powerful enemies. It should've been a terrifying new reality. But I was already living in a waking nightmare, at least this nightmare was exciting. And had turned up the first and only real clue to Aspen's fate. "The 'we' you keep mentioning, that's the ancient community Ramaya wanted me to join?"

"Yes, we call ourselves rootbound."

Rootbound—I repeated the word in my mind, strangely drawn to the sound. "How did my parents take the news? Are they worried about me?"

"Not yet. We can be very convincing when we want to be," Kes said cryptically.

"You mean you did the Jedi mind control thing on them? Like you did to the security guards at the airport?"

Kes nodded. "We call it 'leeching.'"

Leech. I'd always been afraid of leeches. Those slug-like bodies, hooking themselves into your skin, draining your blood. During our summer lake hangouts Aspen had loved diving deep into the murky water and tickling my feet, making me scream.

"They think you just left for a summer program in Oxford."

"And that's what I did to you, back at the protest? Leeched you to tell that tree to sacrifice itself for the protesters, to throw itself in front of the speeding car."

"About that." They traced their collarbone with a finger, a nervous tell. "I've told everyone that *you* called that tree down to protect the protesters. And...let's just say it would be very much to your advantage if people continued to believe that you treetalked the maple."

"So you want me to lie?"

"I want you to be safe, Mira." After a moment they added, "I promise everything will make more sense soon."

The fake nurse's warning about blood cults sprang back into my mind. What had I gotten myself into? To cover my unease I rustled through my backpack, fishing out my sunglasses along with a shower of old candy wrappers.

"You don't like the lights?" Kes asked.

"I guess I didn't realize the revolution would be *so* bright."

"Let me guess—neurodivergent?"

"Um, yeah. ADHD. How'd you—"

"Most of us are. It's connected to our abilities. We can sense and feel things others can't. What others hear as a whisper, we hear as a scream."

What others hear as a whisper, we hear as a scream—yes, that was my whole life summed up in a sentence. "Great. I've joined a band of fellow overly-sensitive weirdos and their army of pet trees with anger management problems."

Kes snorted. "I believe you mean *our* army of pet trees with anger management problems. And please don't let anyone else hear you say that." They leaned in closer, their breath warm on my neck, adding, "And please try to control your impulses while you're here. They might not let you stay if they think you're unpredictable and...I want you to stay."

OK, Hot Kes, laying it on a little thick here, Aspen whispered.

"Ready to go meet our fearless leader?" Kes put a hand out to help me stand.

"Definitely not, but..." I shrugged. When you're looking at me like that, I'd follow you to a root canal.

Kes led me out of the hotel room into a wide, tiled corridor with dozens of doors branching off of it. It had the same shiny, fluorescent feel and disorienting size of a shopping mall, and I couldn't help but think it was a weird place for magical hippies to set up camp. I strained to see out the windows set high in the wall. I caught a glimpse of pine trees but had to look away. The sunlight was too bright. It was always too bright for my brain that processed everything but especially so today. I did a double-take. "Did that window just flicker? Are the windows television screens?" Kes grinned; they'd been waiting for me to notice. "Is this some weird abandoned mall?"

"Better. Well, worse. Much worse. But the irony is delightful. We're underground."

"This is all underground?"

"Did you ever hear about the billionaires prepping for the end of the world?"

"I've mostly heard about them causing it."

Kes's grin widened. "Well, to bring you up to speed, a bunch of billionaires have spent their riches building lavish underground estates to survive the apocalypse that they're creating. And we've stolen them out from under their noses. Isn't the irony delicious?"

"Yes, a million points for irony. Or should I say...a *billion*?" I wiggled my eyebrows. Kes didn't smile. "OK, I got it, no joking about the evil billionaires. But I assume there's some strategy behind the takeover of the bunkers? Or are you all just in it for the '*delicious*' irony?"

This time I got a grin out of Kes. I tried to ignore the way it made my stomach flip like I'd gone over the top of a roller coaster.

"Being underground, we're close to this massive, interconnected network of roots and mushrooms we call the *Rhiza*. Or the wood wide web. It's why I had you scraping your belly on the asphalt while being shot at. The closer rootbound are to the Rhiza and the longer we spend with a local Rhiza, the more powerful we are. Powerful enough to make this entire bunker disappear from the minds and eyes of anyone who could possibly know about it."

"And what exactly do you do down here?"

"We throw sick ragers." I couldn't tell if Kes was teasing or not. "And organize against those trying to drag us towards climate apocalypse."

"Isn't it creepy being underground?"

Kes put a hand on my shoulder. "Another thing not to say in front of anyone else. This crew *loves* being underground—remember, the closer to the roots the better. That's why you really have to temper your impulses. You don't want to accidentally tap into the power of the Rhiza and not be able to control it."

Our conversation was interrupted by a strange whirring sound. I looked up and noticed two thick wires running the length of the corridor. One of them vibrated like a suspension bridge at rush hour.

"Oh right," Kes said. "I forgot to mention. We've uh, made a few adjustments to the billionaire bunker."

"Are those ziplines?"

"Yeah, this place is the size of a small city; there's a tram but it's kind of impractical when all of us are at the base. By the way, welcome to Salish Sea Hub." They gestured in a wide circle. "It's the rootbound headquarters of the Pacific Northwest."

The whirring sound came again, much louder this time. Kes pointed at a slender teen swinging nimbly off the zipline. "Ah, there's our fearless leader now."

"*She's* the leader? She barely looks old enough to drive."

"It's 'they,' actually," the teen said, walking towards us. "And just FYI—I led my first protest against armed para-military guards when I was fourteen years old."

"This is Zo," Kes said. "Zo's grandma was one of the Elders arrested for leading the march peacefully challenging the pipe-line yesterday."

"Wow, uh, thank you, Zo. And thanks to your grandma. I'm Mira, and as you can see, I'm amazing at first impressions."

"Don't sweat it. Walk with me," Zo said, turning down one of the branching tunnels. We passed signs for a Japanese garden, a sauna, and a candy store (did billionaires have to label their aboveground mansions too?) before going in a door marked "Chip's Corner Cinema." We were in a rectangular room with a high ceiling and more than a dozen black leather recliners, but where the screen should have been was instead a wall of soil. A root the size of my arm jutted out of the wall like a worm and then burrowed its way back in. I suppressed a shudder.

"Been making some home improvements?" Kes nodded at the soil.

"Just a little light decolonizing."

I snorted and Zo turned sharp eyes on me. "Sorry. I just... that was a good joke."

Zo smiled. "Grab a seat."

Kes practically dove into a chair, immediately cranking the foot rest up to make themself as horizontal as possible. The dark circles under their eyes had only gotten more bruise-like. I wondered for the first time what they and Ramaya had gone through to get to the bunker while I'd slumbered blissfully. I wanted to sit next to Kes but instead I joined Zo several chairs over.

"So, Mira," Zo said. "Kes and Ramaya have told me some remarkable things about you. Remarkable *and* unusual. Do you mind if I ask you a few questions about what happened in Seattle?"

While Zo had framed it as a question, their tone made it clear I didn't have much choice in the matter. "Of course."

"Do you like trees?"

"Um...yeah trees are great. Except for Bonnie, the cherry tree in my backyard. Refused to bloom on my birthday—old cow." I laughed but Zo's face didn't change.

"So you have a history of talking to trees?"

I felt Kes's eyes boring into the back of my head, willing me to take this seriously, to say the right thing.

"Yes," I answered simply. "Sorry, I'm a little nervous after a rough few days."

"Understandably. I heard what you did to protect the protesters. And about the nurse-imposter's assault on you at the hospital. We are all indebted to you for your selfless act of courage. I can see how you could make a powerful addition to the rootbound. But here we value community even more than individual power and courage, and our siblings the trees are wary of you, Mira Bracken. They do not like to speak of you for some reason. Yet one of the oldest trees in our network, a total stranger to you, threw itself out of the earth at your command. How did you treetalk this ancient maple into such an act?"

I was a terrible liar. I could feel my cheeks redden; my eyes widen in guilt. But Kes had warned me not to expose the truth —that they had treetalked the maple after I compelled them to

—and I sensed my fate with the rootbound hinged on what I said next. "It's a little fuzzy. I hit my head when I fell. But I remember a man yelling at me from an SUV. The sounds of an engine gunning. The shrieks of the crowd. Running to intercept the speeding car. Silvery thread spinning out of the corner of my eye. The feeling of overwhelming grief and fear. And then..." I trembled as the memories rushed back.

Zo nodded, their eyes suddenly far away. "Thank you. Violence against peaceful protesters is a terrible thing." A root stretched out of the wall, gently nudging Zo's shoulder the way a cat might. The hairs on the back of my neck stood on end. Zo sighed, returning from whatever memory my story had triggered. "How old are you, Mira?" they asked.

I thought about lying and saying I was eighteen. But something about the root now wrapped around the teen's arm reminded me of a lie detector and I chickened out. "Sixteen. I just finished my second year of high school."

"And what do you want in life?"

I panicked, trying to remember my old dreams. But all I got was a full-body longing to laugh with Aspen, to feel my shoulders fall down from where they hunched beneath my ears. "I uh...I want to go to Berkeley. And study brains. Maybe psychology, maybe sociology..." I petered out, hearing the lie in my own words. "I want to find my sister. That's it. That's all. And you're the only lead I've turned up in months."

"Kes told me—I'm so sorry about Aspen." Zo paused, giving me a meaningful look. "But what if staying with us doesn't help you find your sister? What if you get hurt? Or worse? Or see terrible things—things you can't unsee, no matter how hard you try? What if this path leads you far from your other family, from your other dreams? Would you choose it, even then?"

My brain spun out the possible futures, dozens and dozens

of them. I caught glimpses of myself watching a movie with my parents, meeting the other freshmen on my college dorm floor, examining a slide under a microscope, wearing a blue cap and gown...they were all missing Aspen. All of them but one.

"I would. I *do*. I have to stay with you. Have to. Please." I grabbed Zo's wrist—and something stabbed into my hand like a drill. I looked down to see the root that had been around Zo's neck now piercing my palm.

Before I could even scream, the root withdrew and Zo took my hand in theirs. Their hands moved quickly, as if stitching my skin together with some kind of invisible thread. I squinted and caught a glimpse of silvery substance, no thicker than a strand of hair. After a moment of Zo's strange hand flourishes, the pain receded, and the skin knit closed. I flexed my fingers in front of my face in amazement. There wasn't even a scar.

"What just happened?" I asked.

"Scilla—the tree—must've thought you were threatening me," Zo explained. Their voice was calm but their wide eyes betrayed surprise.

"I'm so sorry. I shouldn't have—"

"No, *I'm* sorry. I've never seen anything li—" they paused, exchanging a quick glance with Kes. "That was quite unusual behavior."

That word again. Unusual. I was different. Weird. One pea in a pod all my own.

"I wish I had more time, but I must go prepare for the arrival of some honored guests. Kes, I'm asking you as one of the most powerful willbinders in our order, as a master in reading not only the mind, but the heart—do you still vouch for Mira?"

"I do," Kes said without hesitation.

"Then she can stay. For now. But it's the responsibility of

you and your motley little crew to keep an eye on her. We've been preparing for this rootbinding for months—don't let me down."

"Never have, never will," came Kes's easy reply. They sprung up to pull Zo into a tight hug, their tall frame swallowing the petite leader.

A new root emerged from the wall, and I drew back from it without thinking. It seemed to have the same reaction, stopping well short of where the three of us stood. Zo nodded absentmindedly at the root and it began to windmill faster and faster, carving out a tunnel in the dirt wall. "Until next time, Mira." The teen crouched to step into the newly formed tunnel, tugged along gently by the root. After a moment, they were gone, the soil filling in behind them.

"Did that tree, Scilla, did she tug Zo along? Like a weird distorted version of a tree zipline?"

"Something like that," Kes said. "Only a few of us can pull that one off, but the trees will do pretty much anything for Zo. What's this?" They brushed my shoulder and I shivered. Actually shivered. Why was I like this? "Some of the paper gown from the hospital is still bunched under your shirt. Do you want me to get it out for you?"

I nodded, trying to focus on something, anything other than the warmth of their arm on my upper back.

"How's your hand?" they asked gently.

"Fine, totally, completely, magically fine." I held my hand up as proof.

Kes grabbed it, lifting it triumphantly. "And you can stay!" They tugged me towards the door. "C'mon, let me show you around."

"Wait, wait, wait. Why did I just lie through my teeth to your leader? And am I lowkey a prisoner? Is that what Zo meant by having your 'motley crew' keep an eye on me? And who's your motley crew?"

Kes laughed. "I assume Zo's talking about my weirdo friends. Tai and Adrian would *die* of delight at the idea of somebody finding them scary. I can't wait to see their faces when I tell them."

"OK, so I'm not a prisoner. But *why* are we lying?" Kes stared longingly at the door. I pulled my hand out of theirs, crossing my arms over my chest. "I'm not going anywhere until you tell me."

"Fair enough. The truest answer is...I'm not exactly sure. I hate lying, especially to Zo and Ramaya."

And yet you did it so easily.

"My gut tells me that your place is here, amongst the rootbound, and willbinders trust their guts above all else."

"I'm still not getting it. If you think I belong here, why not tell everyone that I was able to leech or willbind you or whatever?"

"Rootbound are very skeptical of people who can influence other people. We have been for centuries."

My brows furrowed. "But Zo just said you're one of the most powerful willbinders—"

"Yes, I know, but I'm *also* a powerful treetalker. We have a rule against allowing anyone into our order who can willbind but not treetalk—essentially anyone who can commune with humans, but not with trees. So we just have to keep the secret until you learn how to talk to the trees."

"What if I can't—"

"You can. I know you can. You just need a little time. And rest."

They looked at me with such warm certainty. I tried to smile back but in my mind I flipped through a montage of the many plants I'd killed over the course of my childhood. Aspen had managed to nurse a few of them back to life, singing sweet lullabies to their wilted petals. I thought of all the times I'd messed up as a climate activist—sleeping in rather than making signs or caring about a crush more than an election—how disappointed Aspen had been. She deserved to be here, not me. No doubt she'd be treetalking up a storm. But if I didn't learn, I couldn't stay. And if I couldn't stay, I'd lose my best lead at finding my missing sister. Not to mention, the first friend I'd made in years.

CHAPTER
SIX

I wanted to start learning more about the rootbound and treetalking right away, but Kes insisted I take a few days to rest before diving in. Apparently I was nearing something gnarly called OS, or oversaturation, and couldn't do anything taxing until I'd nourished myself "body and soul." So I binge-watched bad reality TV from my huge bed while the roots delivered me delicious homemade meals and treats. Kes popped by when they could to catch an episode, but refused to talk about anything other than who they most wanted to see voted off.

I opened the newest treat, a basket of warm blackberry muffins, to find a small note rolled like a scroll tucked in a corner.

You are cordially invited to...
A very fun party!
(If you're feeling up for fun parties, and totally no worries if not)
The dress code is JOY.
Rootbound from all over the world are arriving at Salish Sea Hub

for an upcoming ceremony and tonight we're throwing them a welcome dinner.

I smiled at the absolutely lawless grammar of the note, and rifled through the pile of clothes that had been gifted to me from other rootbound. I was just pulling on a neon floral jumpsuit when I heard a tinny honking sound echo outside my door.

I ducked out of my room to see Ramaya and Kes pulling up in a tricked-out golf cart. Kes leapt up to offer me their elbow. "Your chariot awaits, Mira the Hero. People are so excited to meet you."

Ramaya waved from the front seat. "Kes, don't oversell it, you charming menace. Nobody calls you 'Mira the Hero.' And people are way more focused on our honored guests. But *we're* excited to see you."

"It's cute, this old married routine you two have going on."

Ramaya laughed. "You'll fit in perfectly."

Beaming at her words, I climbed onto the bench at the back of the vehicle and Kes slid in next to me. We lurched forward as Ramaya jammed her foot on the gas—apparently she only had one speed. Scenes from the "windows" melted together, the endless blur of pixelated trees making me feel stuck on the shabby virtual reality ride at our local fairground. My stomach flipped and I wondered if I was about to puke on the only two people I knew in this new life I'd agreed to.

A life that seemed to be defined by chaos.

We whirled past scene after scene of teens that looked less like they were saving the world and more like they were dead set on having as much fun in the dumbest way possible. Two teens spray-painted the walls with filthy words in dozens of different languages. One of the spray cans was wielded by a root; I tried to decipher what it was writing and realized it must be the tree equivalent of cursing. Another group—preceded by tinkling bells and barking—romped through the halls with a gaggle of puppies, kittens, and even a piglet. While waiting in the traffic generated by the animals I noticed a teen intently pressing their fingers into a wall, penetrating the stone with their nails. From each of the holes sprouted a blue flower, forming a pattern that looked like waves.

"What kind of magic is that?" I asked.

Ramaya rolled her eyes. "It's not magic; it's equisymbiotics."

"We really don't use the term, 'magic,'" Kes said. "Or 'equisymbiotics.'"

"Sorry. What kind of...rooting or rootwilling or binding is that?"

"I know it's a lot of jargon," Kes said with an apologetic shrug.

"The key thing to understand," Ramaya jumped in, "is that every living being on this earth is connected to every other living being. Like the algae in corals. Or the bacteria in roots that fix nitrogen. Or a baby growing in a parent's womb. Some are more skilled than others at seeing and amplifying those connections. Rootbound tend to have a strong connection, or symbiosis, with plants or fungi—what we call treetalking, although it should be more like tree-and-mushroom-and-moss-and-fern-and-flower-talking. And so on and so on. You get the point."

"I really don't," I mumbled.

"Ramaya takes a very clinical view of binding," Kes said. "But all you have to remember is this"—they put up three fingers, counting off—"Plant. Human. Animal. Most of us can connect to plants in some way—*treetalking*. A few of us can connect to humans—*willbinding*. Or *leeching*, if the connecting is done without consent. And a very few of us can connect to animals. So few that we don't really have a name for it."

Ramaya mumbled under her breath, "It's called anim-imicking."

"So I'm a willb—I mean a treetalker." I blushed and added hurriedly to cover my mistake, "Could I learn to talk to animals, like you and your ants, Ramaya?"

"Oh, I wasn't talking *to* the ants. I bio-engineered a fungus to attack the ants and highjack their motor control, and I was talking to the fungus," Ramaya said, as if this was the most natural thing in the world.

"Obviously," Kes said, grinning.

"*Obviously*," I repeated.

"But we can teach you all kinds of cool treetalking skills, like winterseeding and springwalking and lichenarmoring..." Ramaya said.

"To be honest, I don't have much of a green thumb."

"Says one of the most powerful treetalkers in a generation." Ramaya shook her head.

"You just need to practice," Kes assured me. "You'll love connecting to the Rhiza soon—won't be able to live without it."

"And I can practice willbinding too?"

Ramaya shot a look at Kes through the golf cart mirror. Kes shook their head slightly, as if to discourage their friend. She shook her head right back and launched into an explanation, almost gleefully, "These idiots kicked most of the willbinders out of the order in the 1980s."

"What. Why?"

"A few of them were caught leeching other rootbound without their consent and then the order went full McCarthy on them. Total witch hunt. But lucky for you Kes is one of the most formidable willbinders in the order. And I dare say they'd be more than happy to give you private lessons…"

I expected Kes to toss back a reply but instead they grinned at me and flushed, making the freckles across their collarbone stand out.

"What are they doing over there?" I blurted.

Ramaya slowed so we could get a better view. To our right in what had once been a bowling alley, rootbound tended to rows of rich black soil along the alleys. They knelt as if in prayer, whispering into their palms. Ramaya pulled alongside one of the rows of dirt and I saw clusters of seeds, quivering and faintly glowing.

"They're seedsinging," Kes said. "Learning how to heal and nourish ancient or injured seeds and germinate them into strong healthy plants. Those who excel at seedsinging usually garden for the collective and produce most of our food."

"They also have the ability to arrest the growth of a plant before it germinates," Ramaya said. "That's what they're doing here."

"Uh, cool, I guess?" I said. "Is that something that you need to do a lot?"

"May I?" Ramaya asked one of the rootbound, who wore a frayed straw hat despite the fact that we were many hundreds of feet underground.

Straw Hat grinned. "Knock yourself out. Just be careful where you throw it."

Ramaya took a small black seed and squeezed it into a ball of dirt before chucking it at the far wall, where it struck a framed photograph of a skyscraper with an underwhelming plop. I studied her face, trying to see if she was pulling my leg or not—and then a mass of thick thorny vines exploded out of the clump and consumed the wall.

"Whoa," I said.

Ramaya grinned. "Seedsinging can store all the potential growth of the plants—the energy it would take them to grow to many hundreds of feet—without making the seeds actually germinate. Then when a rootbound activates them, all of the growth is released in an instant."

"A literal seed bomb," I said.

"I've seen Kes chuck one of these at an enemy helicopter— oh man, the looks on their faces when they went from taking off to being suddenly stuck in a fifty-foot maple. Priceless. Which reminds me. Let's check in on our less welcome guests."

Ramaya pulled away from the bowling alley and set off again at max speed. With a fishtail slide she pulled down a narrow, utilitarian hallway barely wide enough for the cart and then screeched to a halt in front of a heavy metal door.

"A meat locker," Kes said. They pulled the door open and beckoned me to follow them inside. There was no meat, or hooks for it; it wasn't even cold. Instead, the far wall had been replaced by soil...and something else. In the dim light I made out several tangled figures pinned to the dirt with thick roots.

"What the—are those the dudes from the plane? Did you turn them into *compost*?" I stepped away from them in horror.

"Compost?" Ramaya said, laughing. "What are you blabbering about?"

"No, no. We don't kill—*ever*," Kes said at the same time. "It's part of the rootbound oath."

"So the trees killed them?"

"I wish," Ramaya said. "But no, if you can believe this turn-the-other-cheek nonsense, the trees are healing those goons, who, by the way, are *exactly* the kind of sadists who would murder two people and turn their bodies into compost."

"Come back to us," Kes urged, but their voice seemed very far away. "You didn't accidentally join the bad guys. Tomorrow

I can show you what it feels like to be healed by the trees. It's like a float tank, but a hundred times better."

I stared at them, trying to focus on their words, to push away the image of roots feeding on flesh like worms. "You're safe, Mira," Kes whispered again, grabbing my hand. The echo of their earlier words washed through me, bringing that sense of infinite safety. My eyes fluttered and I leaned against Kes's shoulder.

"So what," I said. "You're just going to keep them locked up here?"

"No, we're going to leech them," Kes said. "Give them new lives based on their dreams and ambitions. We won't change their personalities—leeching only works when people are convinced to do something they already want to do in some way. Then we'll give them IDs and money and release them somewhere they can't hurt us and hope they make better choices."

"Flipping stupid if you ask me," Ramaya grumbled. "They try to kill us and then we help them go off and follow their dreams of being amateur potters and anime collectors or whatever."

"This has been a lot," Kes said. "Why don't I take you back to your room to rest?"

"No," I pulled away and forced myself to stare at the bodies tangled in the dirt. Their faces were drawn, but their eyeballs moved rapidly under the lids as though they were in REM sleep. "I want to go to the 'very fun party.'" I want to pledge your witchy sorority.

"Mira," Kes said. "You don't need to overdo it."

"I'm fine," I said. "I can handle it."

"Great!" Ramaya said, clapping me on the shoulder. "She said she can handle it. Let's go!"

We piled into the golf cart and Ramaya zoomed away at light speed. I stared through half-lidded eyes as the cart struggled up a steep ramp towards what looked like cathedral doors made of steel. Graphic signs warned of the risk to life and limb of getting stuck between the elevator's closing doors. Somebody had graffitied the word "capitalism" over an image of a figure getting crushed. I hugged my limbs to my body as we rode the golf cart onto the elevator, which was easily the size of the first floor of my house. The elevator started upwards with a thunderous rumble.

"Are we in some kind of missile shaft?" I shouted over the noise.

"Some billionaire bunkers *are* built from decommissioned cold war military stations," Ramaya answered. "But not this one. This idiot built his directly under one of his above-ground mansions. Lucky for us."

The elevator shuddered to a stop. I sat tense, willing the doors to open.

"One of those yoga pant tyrants," Kes said, shaking their head. "Getting grossly rich by stirring up fat phobia and pumping microplastics into the ocean."

The doors slid open and a red blur shot through the crack right at Ramaya. I blinked as a muscular man with stop-sign-red hair grabbed the woman in a headlock.

"Got you!" he exclaimed, gleefully.

"Sheldon, if you don't let go of me right this second, I will flip you over so hard you won't even be able to remember the only ten words you know."

"OK, OK," the redhead said, releasing Ramaya, only to grab her back into a headlock.

Kes helped me disembark and ushered me through the elevator doors. "Trust me, we don't want to be part of that."

Banging and yelling ensued, and then a solid *whumpf*

echoed through the space as if the golf cart had collided with the elevator wall.

"Are they going to be OK?" I asked.

"They'll fight for a few minutes, one of them will win, then they'll heal each other and laugh about it."

"It sounds like she's killing him," I said.

"I'm serious—we don't kill, not even annoying redheads. Ramaya pretends to hate the vow but she's actually intense about enforcing it. And anyway, Sheldon can grow lichen on his skin and make his limbs harder than rock. That boy can take a heck of a punch. And give one."

"Should we wait for them?"

"No, let's give them some privacy." Kes blushed. "Here, come with me while I grab some libations for the party." They led me through a cedar door into a high-ceilinged room lit with stained glass "windows." It looked like a library, but instead of books the walls were lined with bottles of wine. Kes grabbed a few bottles from the hundreds of racks in the space and ushered me down the hallway to another, smaller elevator. There were over a dozen buttons; Kes pushed the penthouse button marked with a star and we started to rise. "Are you sure you're up for this?"

"Ask me one more time and I'm going to take it personally. If you don't want me around you can just say it. And you don't have to babysit me or anything."

"Sorry, sorry—I do want you around. I can be a bit *intense* about looking after my friends. It's kind of a family trait." Kes shrugged, and in the gesture, I saw the weight on those shoulders. "My family is old...ancient. My flesh and blood have known the Rhiza for a long time. The trees take care of me...and I feel like I need to take care of them. Of the other rootbound. Of everyone. Of you."

Ooh. Ask them more, ask them more, Aspen chanted. But

before I could, a loud beep sounded from somewhere above us. I jumped.

"It's OK," Kes said. "The elevator's just whining cause we've been stopped for too long without getting off."

I hadn't even noticed we'd stopped. Kes pressed the open button and I steeled myself for another magical spectacle, trees tossing dancing teens through the air or a house made out of moss and mushrooms. But the doors opened onto a white kitchen. A very *fancy* kitchen, with all kinds of marble and steel, but just a kitchen.

Ripples of laughter drifted over from somewhere close. We followed the sound to a deck nestled in the tree tops. I breathed in the fresh air greedily, glad to be back above ground, and took in the glowing orbs strung across the space like tiny moons. Clumps of people, maybe four dozen total, laughed and chatted, some standing, some dancing, some huddled in hammocks. Most of them looked to be about my age, and they were all...beaming.

Oops, I think we might've joined a cult, Aspen said.

Oh yeah, and whose fault is that? I shot back.

"Can I take you to the food?" Kes asked.

"Always," I answered, happy for the excuse not to talk to any of the smiling people. Kes led me to one side of the deck where long tables were piled high with food. It was just like the divestment potlucks Aspen used to host at our house. All of the food was labelled: vegan, vegetarian, sustainably harvested, picked by a friendly neighborhood dormouse, etc. I grabbed a corn chip and dragged it through a tub of hummus the size of my forearm. "You know this looks a lot like a cult, right?"

"We're not a cult." Kes popped bruschetta bites into their mouth like they were popcorn.

"But I mean, does anyone in a cult actually know they're in a cult? Why does...why does everyone look so happy?"

"They do, don't they?" Kes scanned the assembled crowd, a matching smile coming to their face. "Imagine, if you will, that this samosa was a glowing ball of string, and that I held one end of the yarn and threw the rest to you." Kes looked earnestly at me, clutching the fried treat. "Then you did the same thing, holding a piece and tossing the rest to Wongi—the girl with the pink hair—and she tossed it onwards, through the crowd, and then around and around again until there were hundreds of glowing threads connecting everyone here. Now imagine that string could transmit energy or emotion—joy, fear, hope, happiness—between us all. Those bonds do exist between people, trillions of them, invisible to the naked eye. Or invisible to us mere mortals. Apparently the most potent willbinders can actually see the threads."

Kes's words jolted me back to the day we'd met. Hadn't I caught a glimpse of silvery thread connecting us, unspooling from the spot where my hand clutched their chest? Or was it just the concussion? I pushed the memory away. "That's how leeching works? Manipulating those invisible links between people?"

"Exactly. But nobody's leeching anyone here. We're all sharing energy through the connection, freely, consensually, happily. A rootbinding is like a wedding, but like the Super Bowl of weddings, if that makes any sense. It's when two people pledge to share each other's lives so completely that the Rhiza binds them together. People who are truly rootbound can share thoughts, feelings, and even their abilities. It's a big deal. And it's super rare for so many of us to be together, friends and allies from all over the world. So, tonight, in this community bound so tightly together, it's almost too easy for one emotion to jump through everyone on the deck."

"Everyone but me." I grabbed a handful of candied ginger and shoved them all into my mouth.

"Do you want to feel it?" Kes asked, holding out their hand.

"Totally a non-culty thing to say," I gummed out, my teeth stuck together by the ginger.

Kes laughed and started to pull their hand away but I snatched it before they could. I didn't feel anything. I knew it—I was still alone. So painfully alone. I dared Aspen to contradict me, but she didn't. "Anything?" Kes asked.

I shook my head. "Sorry."

"Don't be sorry. By the end of the night you will...promise. I just have to introduce you to a few more people, add some links to your chain. Speaking of, here come the twins. Adrian, Tai, it's been too long!"

I turned to find two teens beaming at me. The one Kes had called Tai was tall, thin, and Black with high cheekbones. The other one, Adrian, was white with freckles, sandy blond hair, and a round face, and he had what looked like a wheelchair crossed with a motorcycle.

"Kestrel!" Tai called.

Adrian winked at me. "Forget Kestrel—I want to talk to the girl who took on the robo-nurse."

Oh, Aspen said. *Kes is short for Kestrel. That's hot.*

"You heard about that already?" Kes rubbed their chin. "Ramaya's gonna have my obituary circulating before I even know I'm dead."

"Ouch, morbid, Kes. *You'll* never die," Adrian said.

Kes laughed with the newcomers but their eyes looked sad. They pulled me into a side hug. "Tai, Adrian, meet Mira, the newest member of our team."

"Pronouns, Kes," Tai prompted. "Also WELCOME."

"Right, Mira uses she/her—actually, I just assumed..."

"I do," I said. "And you folks?"

"We use he/him," the twins said simultaneously. Tai added, "We're trying to move away from the gender binary in the order, but as you can imagine, with a thousand-year-old institution called the Seven *Sisters*, it's not easy. Men weren't even allowed to join until like a century ago."

"The Seven Sisters?" I asked, confused.

Adrian guffawed. "Don't tell me you don't know. *We* are the Seven Sisters. You've literally just pledged your life to us and had your parents' memories erased...and you don't even know our name. You're comedy gold, Mira the Hero."

My cheeks burned. I could hear the echo of my school counsellor telling me to breathe and sleep on it before making yet another impulsive life decision. Like joining a cult of tree warriors without even knowing their full name. Or history. Or enemies.

"We heard you made the land rise up like a serpent," Tai said, shooting a glance at his twin. "That might be the coolest Awakening yet."

"I wish it was that epic," I said. "But really I just...tripped."

"Tripped you say?" said a woman with a lilting accent, bursting into our small group. I had a second to take in her auburn hair and the wide scar across her bicep before she threw an arm around me. Pulling me close enough to smell the cinnamon on her breath, she whispered, "Gotta be careful where you trip these days."

"Harriet!" called Kes, throwing their arm around the woman's other side. "Old friend, you came all the way from Wales just to do the same tired bit? Scaring the new recruits with your stories about the man-eating bog in the forests of Ceredigion?"

"It's not a *bit*," one of Harriet's friends insisted, joining our circle. "One of our magpies went to ground there last year and we haven't seen him since. That was after four different hikers disappeared. *Four.*"

"Oh, spoo-ooky." Adrian waved his fingers in the air. "Want to bet they all walked straight off the side of a hill with their noses glued to their phones? And that your magpie deserted for greener pastures."

"Greener pastures than the Welsh countryside?" Harriet asked dryly. "Samiron would never. Why isn't the Council taking our report seriously? Kes, we need more magpies to investigate. Trained magpies, not the wide-eyed little hippies the Council keeps sending."

"I know, Harriet, I know. Everyone's overwhelmed since the kidnappings accelerated. Let's talk about it later."

"Will you plead our case to the Council?" Harriet demanded.

"I'll try, I promise. Find me tomorrow." Kes flashed her their patented Steady Gaze, but it looked more tired than usual.

"I'll hold you to that, Kestrel."

"You always do."

"Well, somebody's gotta *hold* you down. And I'm just the gal for the job." Harriet winked and strode away, the Welsh contingent trailing after her.

"Was that hot or scary?" Adrian faux-whispered.

Kes frowned and murmured, "I'll be right back," disappearing into the crowd.

I stared after them, willing them to turn again. The twins caught my eye and giggled.

"What?" I asked, wiping a hand over my mouth without thinking.

"It's just...you have the classic Kes-hangover face," Adrian said.

Tai added, "Don't worry; we all get it—it's kind of unavoid-able. Kes is like the sun."

"Yeah, if the sun was six feet of queer Japanese-American snack," Adrian added.

I laughed, spitting out the sip of rhubarb cider I'd taken. Adrian joined me. Tai gave us a look and I stopped laughing abruptly, sure he was going to reprimand us for being inappro-priate. "Kes *wishes* they were six-feet tall."

"Wait, dearest brother, you don't think you're taller than Kes do you?" Adrian asked.

Tai scoffed. "Of course I'm taller than Kes. I know depth perception can be tricky from all the way down there, but it's not even close."

"Really—you're gonna make fun of how short I am in my wheelchair?"

"Love, your wheelchair makes you *taller*. That's how short you are."

"Magpies, to my rescue! My rootbound brother is attacking me. Ugh, I wish I got to be a magpie like Kes, disappearing into the fray looking all cool and mysterious."

Tai swatted his twin lovingly. "As if you could handle the stress. You can't watch a scary movie without covering your face with a pillow."

"I take it the magpies are the action-hero-type people of the rootbound?" I asked.

"Ding, ding, ding."

"So if you're not magpies, what do you two do?"

"We're larks, the rootbound comms team. Think Kerry Washington in *Scandal.* Or Tree Paine."

Tai raised an eyebrow at his twin. "Are you really putting Taylor Swift's publicist in the same breath as the thousand-year-old storytelling tradition of the larks?"

"You're right, we don't deserve to be in Tree's company.

Maybe we could recruit her to the rootbound—she's certainly got the name for it."

I soaked in their affectionate teasing while drinking my cider, which tasted like fizzy shaved ice, and worked my way through the food offerings—hand-rolled sushi, samosas, seaweed salads, curries, and vegetable stir-fries. Everything was delicious.

"You two are so lucky," I said. "To have each other."

The words hung awkwardly a moment, and then Adrian said, "Hey, maybe you can be our triplet?"

"I wish that's how it worked," I mumbled into my cup, drinking deeper.

Tai put a hand on my shoulder. "It can work like that. We're not bio twins; we're chosen family. Here, chosen families are just as important as bio families. The Seven Sisters we're named after? They weren't *actually* related, they just vowed to love each other as kin. You'll see at the actual rootbinding."

"It's the best. Maybe you'll even find yourself a sister—"

"You know what?" I interrupted. I put a hand over my heart, feeling the skin, afraid the words had pierced me like a nail, but I only felt fuzzy, kind of far away. "I think we need to dance. Yep, Rihanna's on. Now's the moment."

Tai grabbed my hand, pulling me towards the dance floor. Adrian had already shot ahead. He shout-sang the Billie Eilish song that came on next. Someone in an iridescent cape pulled Tai away. They raised their arms to twirl, their cape painted to look like the wings of a monarch butterfly. Inspired, I flapped my arms in wide circles. Someone threw a glowing hoop in the air above me and I jumped towards it, catching it around my neck with a whoop.

"They're real flowers," Tai shouted over the music. "Still very much alive." More glowing hoops spun through the air and others caught them around their necks, their waists, their wrists. We looked like those glow-in-the-dark stars little kids put above their beds, but dancing, swirling, laughing through the cool night air.

"But…" I started, trying to puzzle out how a flower could shine brighter than neon, before Adrian tapped my shoulder.

"Fancy a dance?"

"Uh…how do I—" I fumbled, unsure of how to interact with Adrian in his wheelchair.

"Just grab my hand. I'll lead."

I did as Adrian directed and soon he had me spinning around him in a wide arc. Tai laughed and clapped, and I felt a matching laugh rise in my throat. Eventually, our hands grew so sweaty they slipped, and I fell out of Adrian's orbit. But I didn't want to stop spinning. I couldn't. I closed my eyes and threw my head back, the world dissolving around me until I was only aware of the pulse of blood through my veins, the wild beating of my heart. *I'm alive.*

An arm caught me around the waist and I spun into the solid warmth of Kes's chest. "You're feeling it, aren't you? The affection of the crowd?"

"Sure am, Steady Gaze."

"Dance with me?"

"We are dancing."

"Technically we're standing. Swaying, at most."

I laughed and turned so my back was pressed into Kes's front. "Is this better?"

Before Kes could answer, Tai and Adrian sandwiched us. "OK, she's grinding. New girl is *grinding*," Adrian called, like an announcer at a baseball game. Stuck together in a sweaty, handsy tangle we danced and danced. I felt completely in my body, but also completely out of it, enjoying the beat, the warm breath, the press of skin against me. After eighteen months without touch or affection, it felt like breaking a fast.

I drifted to sleep like a cat who'd spent all day basking in the hot sun, the safety and warmth settling deep into my bones. I woke to fresh berries and granola on my bedside table, and the delightful thought that I'd get to do the whole joyful thing over again at the rootbinding ceremony this evening.

Look at you beaming like a little kid with a cotton candy the size of your head, Aspen whispered. *This is the happiest I've seen you since...*

I shoved a handful of blackberries in my mouth, trying to distract myself from the searing pang of guilt in my chest. "I haven't forgotten about you, Asp, I promise," I whispered back.

No, it's good. I miss it—your happiness. It used to feel like you might burst right out of your skin from the force of it. Even over the littlest things. Baking a Christmas brunch masterpiece. Watching a corgi trot. Making a new friend in Spanish class.

I tried to remember that version of myself. A girl who laughed easily. Who made new friends at the drop of a hat. Was it really true? My journal had lots of evidence of that girl

—breathless stories about sleepovers and crushes and stupid dance routines. My parents had tried to tell me about her, reminding me how much fun I used to have at improv and debate club. But I dismissed the evidence as fake, planted, corrupt. It wasn't just my mind that rebelled, but my body. My knees burned at the mere thought of dancing. My eyes couldn't focus on those of my peers' trying to console me. My arms refused to mold to their embrace. I had failed Aspen in every way imaginable, as an activist, a protector, a sister. And this was my penance. A hollow life. How dare I flourish while she suffered?

"Get it together, Mira," I hissed to myself. "You're here for Aspen. That's it, that's all. Go through the motions—make the rootbound like you, make the trees like you. Turn up every lead you can. But no more fantasies about Kes whisking you off to the rootbinding for a dreamy night beneath the stars."

I rummaged through the room for something to write with, and after finding a notebook and pen in my beside table, began to jot down everything I knew about the rootbound so far. Hours and pages later, I squinted at my scrawled notes and realized how little I really knew. Ramaya and Kes seemed genuine and good. Tai too. Adrian...Adrian was a lot. The robo-nurse had warned me about a murderous blood cult obsessed with trees, and for all their righteous talk, the rootbound still kind of seemed like they fit the bill. I thought about the two men bound and gagged in the dark room, held prisoner by the roots.

I jumped as a different root burst out of the wall, plunging a grimy note right into my bowl of granola. I fished the sodden paper out, recognizing Kes's handwriting.

Sorry I can't personally escort you to the rootbinding this eve—I'm needed for prep.

But I'm very much looking forward to seeing you again...
The roots will point you in the right direction if you get lost.
Trust me, you won't want to miss the beginning—don't be late!

With that somewhat ominous warning urging me on, I rifled through the closet looking for something to wear to the mysterious event. After a few moments of indecision, I settled on an emerald green velvet suit, running my hands up and down the fabric to calm myself. I paced the room, trying to work up the courage to walk through the underground bunker alone, at the mercy of the roots.

A sharp knock came at my door and I opened it to find Ramaya dressed in an exquisitely draped scarlet gown. I looked down at my suit, which was slightly too big for me, and felt suddenly ridiculous for thinking I could really do this. Infiltrate a coven of magical tree warriors.

"Ramaya! What are you doing here?"

"What do you think, Blue Hair? Collecting you for the root-binding ceremony. We've gotta hurry—we don't want to miss the beginning."

"So I've heard. Dare I ask how come?"

Ramaya grinned. "I don't want to ruin the surprise. C'mon!" She strode down the hall, somehow moving at twice the speed of a normal walker.

I hurried after her. "No golf cart today?"

"Needed for the VIPs. No offense."

"None taken. Thanks for coming to get me."

"Honestly, I wish I could say it was my idea, but my plan was to sprint to the deck so I could grab a seat with the best view."

"Oh, I get it," I huffed out, trying to hide my disappointment. "You're part of the 'motley little crew' Zo was talking about, the one that's supposed to be keeping an eye on me."

"I mean, can you blame Zo? You have a terrifying amount of power, guts of steel, and an axe to grind with the world. Plus I see the way you look at the roots. You're scared of them."

I didn't answer.

"Sorry, but it's the truth."

"You're right. Well, except about the guts of steel part. But I am afraid of the roots. Since you're obviously so fond of the truth, tell me, do you think I can befriend them? The trees? Get the Rhiza to trust me, to talk to me? Kes keeps saying I will, but..."

"You're not so sure?" Ramaya finished for me. "Most new recruits are obsessed with treetalking once they Awaken. They're in the dirt so much they look like kittens rolling in a field full of catnip."

"But I can learn?"

Ramaya slowed her pace so we were walking side by side and gave me a serious look. "Put it this way. I didn't do very well in science when I was in elementary school. My teacher used to say it was like trying to teach an elephant how to swing dance. Mrs. Smith-Williams, what a...*gem*. So I built myself a lab. Took things apart. Entered a science fair. Won a prize. Won a bigger prize. Won all the prizes. And well...you saw what my ants can do."

"Yeah, but you're...well, you."

"Do you know there's research showing that how teachers talk to students before a test literally changes how those kids do on the test? If girls are told they're good at math, they actually do better at math. Stories are powerful things. Be careful about the ones you're telling to yourself. If you think you're going to fail at treetalking before you even start..."

"Why is that so much scarier than the man-eating bog of Ceredigion?"

Ramaya groaned. "Don't tell me they're still trying to pull

that corny prank on the new recruits. The forest that eats its prey."

I glanced at the healed skin on my hand. "I mean a tree root did stab me in the fist the other day."

"Yeah, forests are predators. But so are we." Ramaya smiled, flashing her teeth.

"Rewind a second, did you say you built a lab in your room in *elementary* school? God, you're just like my sister. She built a greenhouse in hers. Or more like a forest. Even let a family of ravens swoop in and out of her window whenever they wanted. That's where my parents tried to draw the line, but you didn't really draw the line with Aspen. Any line."

"And what was your room full of?" Ramaya waved me onto the industrial elevator that would lift us out of the bunker.

I blushed, grateful for the rumbling as we ascended so I didn't have to answer. As we exited and wound through the underground wine cellar to the other, smaller elevator, Ramaya asked again, "OK, Blue Hair, I see how flushed your cheeks are. Redder than my dress. Now you *have* to tell me."

I thought guiltily of the trove of dead succulents I'd hidden in my closet so Aspen wouldn't chastise me. I could only imagine how much the trees would hate me if they knew— would they think me a murderer? "Just pictures of my friends. And...maybe a few Tessa Thompson posters. A shot of Paul Mescal playing rugby."

The elevator opened to Tai and Adrian. "Where have you been—"

"Shhh. It's starting. I can hear them," Ramaya whispered, her eyes wide. The trio hustled me through the kitchen and out to the twilit night air, to a deck filled with people dressed in an explosion of sparkles. As loud as the clothing was, the crowd was silent

An eerie moan pierced the quiet, making the hair on the

back of my neck stand on end. I turned to look for Ramaya but she was gone. Adrian and Tai looked transfixed, like they were taking in the Sistine Chapel for the first time. The haunting sound came again. It tickled a memory in the depths of my mind—I'd heard it before, but where? I focused on the hint of ocean visible beyond the thick forest surrounding the deck, catching movement in the waves. "Whales! I see whales! It sounds like they're singing."

Tai nodded reverently. "They make up a new song for every rootbinding ceremony at Salish Sea Hub."

In tenth grade we'd listened to the famous recordings Carl Sagan had sent into space decades ago with sounds from across the globe. At home I'd played the song of the humpback whales over and over, vowing to hear it in real life one day. Apparently that day was here. Adrian saw the wetness in my eyes and grabbed my hand, hugging it to his chest. The tears fell faster. I wasn't just hearing the song of humpback whales; they were singing for us, *to* us.

A low buzz started. The gathered crowd was humming a response to the whales. I tried to match their tone, but just as I'd gotten the hang of it, they stopped, parting to reveal Kes, Zo, and four other people standing in a half-circle. Two men stood in the center, trading nervous glances. They were flanked by Kes and Zo and two women—one tall and imposing, one short and jolly.

"Sisters, brothers, siblings, it is a joy to see you today," Zo proclaimed. "Tonight's ceremony is about time. Honoring the past. Celebrating the present. Protecting the future with a life-long commitment between two humans, witnessed by their community, and sealed by our sacred kin, the trees."

"Our Hub is grateful to welcome so many rootbound siblings from around the world, including our beloved, unofficial rootbound archivist—Teddy." Kes gestured at the shorter woman, and the crowd whooped and stomped their feet. Petals rained down from the sky like confetti as the trees joined in the clapping. I studied the tiny woman at the center of the hurricane. She had an athletic frame softened and rounded with age. Her grey-white hair was cropped in an asymmetrical pixie cut and run through with purple. Oversized glasses, also purple, framed warm brown eyes.

When the noise quieted, Kes continued, gesturing at the other woman, "And the only one in our order who our animal kin have chosen as their confidante, the woman who can talk not just to the trees but to the birds, the bats, and the bees...our very own First Magpie, Naomi Squall."

The crowd roared its approval. Owls hooted in a chorus and squirrels began somersaulting overhead. Naomi didn't react to the applause and her pale eyes emitted none of the warmth I was so used to with the other rootbound. She was dressed in a black trench coat with a high collar and only more black underneath. First Magpie—was this woman Kes's boss? She looked a little older than I, but still far too young to carry such a heavy title. Whoever she was, the other rootbound were giving her a hero's welcome.

Adrian whispered to me, "Don't worry, it's almost time for the good part. You won't believe the spectacle that's about to go down. Last rootbinding we found Tai snoring in the top of a hundred-foot cedar the morning after—had no idea how he got there."

I smothered a giggle.

Naomi, the First Magpie, stepped forward and I felt my new friends stiffen. "For as long as people have sought to plunder the earth, there have been those who rose to resist such plunder. We are but one of many who resist—some are newer than we are, some far older. We call ourselves the Seven Sisters, or the Seven for short, to honor the ancestors who founded us. We were born out of the same breath as the Huntsmen and we have sworn to be a thorn in their side since that very first moment—"

"Sometimes more successfully than others," Kes added wryly, breaking the spell.

Naomi gave Kes a frosty look and continued, "Would you grace us with a story, Teddy? Nobody knows more about Godda than you."

Teddy blushed and stepped forward shyly.

Adrian groaned. "We're never going to get to the good part."

Tai elbowed him.

"Perhaps I'll start with the tale they tell today. It never fails to make me laugh how wrong they got it, and I bet we could all use a laugh this evening." Teddy turned twinkly eyes on the two men in the center who looked noticeably more anxious.

"Edric the Wild is both heralded and reviled where I'm from—the southwest of England. Some say Edric bravely resisted the Norman takeover of England under William the Conqueror, harassing Norman forces in ever more violent ways. Some say he betrayed his countrymen, joining forces to attack Scotland in 1072. For this betrayal he was imprisoned in the rocky mines of Shropshire and cursed to ride the skies forevermore, feeding on the lives of other lost souls in the Wild Hunt. Most agree that Edric came upon a gathering of seven otherworldly women, fairy folk in the lush forests of the countryside. Entranced by the beauty of the seventh woman, Godda, he stole her away from her sisters and kept her as his fairy bride. Of course, all of the early stories are written by men. And all of them are wrong." She winked at the crowd, drawing giggles. "I'm never sure, even after all these years, whether to start with grief or with joy. They are so deeply intertwined, are they not?"

"Like one breath and the next," the crowd echoed back.

"Well, this story has much grief and much joy. A millennium ago Edric and William circled each other as enemies. But each was the same—burning and pillaging, the land and the women taking the brunt of their violence. Seven women escaped the violence of William, of Edric, of other lords and masters, and sought refuge in the forest. Each had been training in plant lore and they banded together as chosen kin to live among the trees, growing and learning in peace. They were the true wild ones. These women, already trained to pay deep attention to the land, to read the landscape, learned to listen so closely to the trees that they realized the trees were listening back. And so began a new friendship, halting, sweet, full of laughter and misunderstanding.

"Working with their friends, the trees, these women did what no one thought possible of women—lived through hard winters cozied up in burrows in the hills. They found kinship with all creatures of land, air, and water. One Sister, Edeva, even learned how to read the secret messages coded in bird-song, and it's said that she was never without a warbler on her shoulder.

"On their fourth summer solstice together, the women were out dancing in celebration, flowers strung through their hair and draped around their waists, when they heard the horns of the royal hunt. They did not know it, as they had cut themselves off from the outside world, but William had taken most of the forest land for his own, claiming forest law, and anyone found in the royal woods risked forced blinding, or even death.

"Edric and William, and their baron friends, found Godda a little way off from the others, alone in the woods, and stole away with her. The birds alerted Edeva to the treachery and she led the other women in a charge through the forest, wielding whatever they could grab for weapons, stones, sticks, and little else. They did not ask the trees to join them; it was not their fight. But the trees came to their aid, driving their branches like stakes through the hearts of the intruders. Edric and William were lucky to make it out with their lives. Some of their companions did not. And thus the Seven Sisters and their ancient alliance with the trees was cemented, on the blood of those wishing violence against women and the land."

The branches began to creak and whip like helicopter blades. The other rootbound hollered back at the trees, pounding their fists to their chests. I watched in astonishment as Sheldon grew lichen armor and then disappeared it, flashing it on and off in rhythm with the trees.

After the uproar had finally died down, Kes continued, "Tonight we celebrate the rootbinding of Torin and Hassan. They have our full support, but it is up to StarLeaf"—a root burst over the edge of the railing, making the most dramatic entrance I'd seen yet—"to decide if the rituals of promise ring true, and to seal the two together forever."

"Let's get to it," Zo chirped, breaking the tension and bringing smiles to the strained faces of Torin and Hassan. "Please clasp forearms, linking your arms so your pulses beat as one."

Once the men had arranged themselves, StarLeaf wound its root around their locked arms several times.

"Torin and Hassan, do you promise to share with one another—be it food, water, shelter, grief, or joy? Do you promise to give energy when the other is low or sick, to protect and to nurture one another as long as your two hearts beat?"

"We do," they said in unison. I put my hands up to clap but Tai grabbed them gently—it wasn't the time. In fact nobody else was moving, let alone cheering. Anxiety drifted over me like a morning fog. What was everyone waiting for? There was a rustle in the night and then more roots shot over the deck edge like grappling hooks. Faster than darting cobras, they wound themselves around the two men, over and over until the pair was ensconced in a wicker cocoon. The structure began to vibrate and pulse as if the roots were taking huge gulping breaths. Joyful barks and squeaks came from the ocean; the whales were singing again, but louder this time. The cocoon withdrew as fast as it had come and Torin and Hassan embraced while the rest of us erupted in cheers.

Adrian whispered to me, "StarLeaf accepted them—they're bound for life."

Zo and Kes put their hands up, and the crowd quieted. Kes said, "Before the debauchery begins, a final step."

Zo continued, "Just as no two trees stand by themselves in a forest, Torin and Hassan will not be alone in their promise. As a community, we too will share with them what we can. We will nurture, nourish, and protect. If you're able, please join hands with the folks around you."

Tai grasped my left hand and Adrian my right. Something rough brushed against my arm. A root was threading itself around us, looping between stomachs and backs, braiding us together.

I asked, "But what do I have to do? Say?"

"You just have to raise your arms when everyone else does, relax," Tai soothed.

"OK, fam, let's send some of that love we're all feeling to our new rootbound kin," Kes called, smiling widely.

People screamed and stomped their feet. The root pulled me closer to Adrian and Tai, vibrating once more. I felt it all— the energy of the crowd, the energy of the forest. When we were little Aspen and I had been obsessed with creating miniature whirlpools whenever we went swimming in a pool. We would slosh and slosh through the water, moving as fast as we could in the same direction until we'd created a vortex that caught us up in its power while we shrieked in delight. Whatever was happening in the circle, it felt like that. Energy was flowing through me, around and around, faster and faster as more people and trees fed into the momentum. What were we building towards? I needed to be part of it, to help us reach the crescendo. I tried to remember how I'd freed my energy before, at the protest, but couldn't summon the fear.

Kes caught my eye and I smiled back at them. Something exploded out of me, like a newborn star. And then a horrible sound ripped through the song of the whales and the stomping and the celebration. It was a scream, a scream of such raw agony that I pulled my hands away and clamped them over my ears.

With bone deep certainty, I realized the screamer was Aspen. I could feel her energy everywhere, clinging to me like oil.

"Aspen!" I yelled. "Aspen, where are you?" I tried to sprint towards the sound but was still held fast by the root. I struggled against the wood but it only seemed to tighten. "Help me, help me." I swung my head between Tai and Adrian but they were looking at me in horror. I glanced down; my hands were bleeding freely, skin hanging from my palms from scraping against the root.

Something stung the back of my neck, and I swung around to see Ramaya. I sagged in her arms, suddenly too tired to stand, and had a moment to wonder what kind of poison she'd given me before my world went black.

EIGHT

The pretty nurse pointed a needle the size of a steak knife at my heart and advanced towards me, face emotionless, while I struggled and screamed against my bindings. Over and over she came for me, the tip of the needle getting closer and closer to my skin. She started whispering words I didn't understand. Something about "binding" and "my sister" and "promises." I strained to catch her eye, to plead for mercy.

When I finally did, I screamed, and the bile rose in my throat.

Where the nurse's face had been was now Aspen's. Her eyes lit with baleful determination, she pulled the bindings at my wrists tighter and tighter, drawing blood and whispering the same jumbled incantation without end. "Binding," "my sister," and "promises." I heard something that sounded like "Bonnie," just before Aspen jabbed a needle into my heart.

Someone shook me and my mind rose towards consciousness, but it felt like swimming from the bottom of the ocean. I could see the sunlight but it was so far away. The shake came again; it was not a gentle touch. I blinked as my senses came back to me. My arms and legs were bound, this time by the same vine I'd seen the enemy soldiers hog-tied with. I was lying in a ball on my side in the cargo hold of a van, my face towards the windshield. I could make out Ramaya in the driver's seat talking quietly to someone else.

"Where is my sister?" I said, trying and failing to sound threatening. Kes's face swam into view and I trembled at their betrayal. "You lied to me—you ARE the bad guys. Where is Aspen? What have you done to her? Whatever you plan to do to me, just let me see Aspen one more time. Please. *Please*."

Kes sighed and rubbed their eyes. "Nobody's trying to hurt you, Mira, I promise."

"You're leeching me—I can feel it."

"I'm trying to calm you down—you practically had a heart attack at the rootbinding."

"Which you ruined, by the way." Ramaya caught my eye in the rear view mirror. "Can't say I'm not pissed about that."

"It's not her fault," Kes said. "She can't control her connection to the Rhiza."

"I should be at the best party in the world right now," Ramaya grumbled. "Not driving around in circles for hours."

"Why have you tied me up like this?" I demanded. "Where are we going in the middle of the night?"

"The vines are for your protection," Kes soothed. "We put them on you because you were thrashing so hard you hurt yourself. Just ask them to release and they will."

At their words, the vine binding my arms slithered out of its complicated knots and fell to the car floor. But something was off.

"You're lying," I said. "I felt Aspen there at the rootbinding. Like she was there with me, alive."

Ramaya swore and then sighed. "We should have known this might happen."

"Known what might happen?" I knew what Ramaya was going to say. It was the same thing my parents had said. My friends. My counsellor. The loss of Aspen had broken something in me. I was obsessed, consumed, imagining things that weren't real.

"It wasn't your sister," Kes said sadly. "Well, it was, in a way. The rootbinding is one of the most potent connections humans can have with each other. If a person has experienced a great loss, like the loss of a loved one—"

"No. Don't say it. Don't." I covered my ears with my hands.

"It's understandable," Ramaya said. "Seeing Torin and Hassan, Adrian and Tai, grieving your own lost bond with a sibling..."

"It wasn't like that!" I yelled. "I'm not imagining things! I'm *not* broken!" Heat billowed through my body like my gut had become a steam engine being shoveled full of coal—faster and faster. Hotter and hotter. I couldn't breathe. I closed my eyes trying not to panic as the heat and the pain and the fear overwhelmed my nervous system. My consciousness swam and blackness interrupted my vision.

Someone was touching me, lifting. I tried to kick at them but could barely move my limbs. I felt myself rising and then I bucked wildly and fell hard into soft dirt.

"Ramaya!" Kes yelled. "Be careful."

"She's burning up." Ramaya's face loomed over mine and I shivered. She ran cool hands across my temple, down my jaw to my collarbone. She repeated the soothing motion up and down my arms and legs, leaving a whisper of ice in her wake, dousing the furnace in my core. The fever and delirium passed. I felt lucid...ish.

"Better?" Ramaya asked gently.

I pushed myself up and examined my hands, which now smelled of peppermint, cloves and other plants I couldn't identify. "Thank you. I can't always...it's hard to think straight when I'm..."

"In pain?" Ramaya finished for me, nodding. "No wonder; what your nervous system is doing to you definitely qualifies as cruel and unusual punishment."

No, that's just the grief. "Yeah, docs say I have complex regional pain syndrome."

"The pain's trapped on a loop in your body," Ramaya said with a nod.

"You know it?" I asked.

"Rama knows everything," Kes said, beaming at their friend.

"I am—I *was* pre-med at Harvard before the Seven called me back."

"Oh. *Wow.*"

"Kes, can you toss me the emergency pack?" Ramaya asked.

"What for?" They hesitated next to the car.

"Just do it." Ramaya hauled me off the ground, dusting dirt from my back and shoulders. Kes appeared with a black duffle bag, which Ramaya proceeded to heft onto my back.

"Ramaya, seriously, what are you doing?" Kes asked again.

Ramaya ignored them, turning to me. "The U.S.–Canada border is due south from here, about ninety minutes of hard walking—"

"Are we crossing the border?" I sagged under the weight of the backpack.

"There is no 'we.' You want out, right? Cause we're the bad guys. Even though you begged to join us, more than once. You think we'd kidnap your sister? That we could show you our home and lie to your face?"

"That's not fair," Kes said. "She didn't know what was going on."

"This is your chance to leave. We won't stop you. In fact we'll follow at a distance and make sure you get back home safely."

Let's go, Aspen said suddenly. *Back home. Back to Seattle. Back to Mom and Dad.*

The only way I'm going back home is if you're with me, Asp. I dropped the heavy duffel. "I'm staying."

"You sure about that? Because you don't seem like you're all in." Ramaya added more gently, "And it's OK if you're not ready."

Kes looked from their friend to me. "Rama, as usual, you're being blunt as nails. But, Mira, she has a point. This whole thing feels like way too much for someone in such fresh pain. You're not in deep yet, you can still go home. Tonight is the perfect chance. We'd barely have to leech your memories. And I could...I could take the edge off your grief about Aspen, if you wanted?"

I held in the HOW DARE YOU that burned like lava in my throat and locked eyes with Kes. I could see it now, how serious they were. Ramaya was getting ready to cut me loose, and Kes wasn't going to stop her. They wanted to protect me from the pain and violence of their world, but it wasn't their right to choose for me. If I didn't do or say exactly the right thing next I was going to lose my place amongst the rootbound. Maybe even lose my memories that the rootbound existed, that my sister ever existed. Ramaya protected the vulnerable with her life, but she respected the strong and the brave. I needed to be brave. "What would it take to convince you I want to stay?"

"I need you to make a vow, and I need the trees to vouch for you."

"I'll do that on one condition. You tell me exactly who the Huntsmen are and how they're connected to the disappearing climate strikers."

Ramaya laughed. "Making conditions when you have zero leverage, Blue Hair. See what did I say? Guts of steel. I hope the trees hear the truth in your words—we need you."

She stuck her hand out to shake mine. I shot a pleading look at Kes and then stepped towards Ramaya, holding down my panic as silvery webbing spun out of the ground, up our trunks, and finally encased our joined hands. I felt nothing from the trees, no sense of warmth or welcome. But I soldiered on, meeting Ramaya's eyes and pouring the force of my desperation into my words. *"I want to stay. I want to be rootbound."*

Nothing happened.

A long moment later Ramaya's brow furrowed and she shot me an apologetic look. Then came a cacophony of cracks and snaps. All around us the tree limbs bent, arching towards us and pulsing their approval.

Ramaya exhaled audibly. "That was close, but the trees got there in the end—you're still in, Mira. I'm glad you're going to stay. But you need to hear me as I say this. We've *all* been through a lot. I'm sorry about Aspen, I truly am, but nobody in the Seven is a stranger to loss. Not a single one of us." Ramaya's voice trembled as she said the last bit and I would have blushed if I was not already burning up. "If you stay with us, remember—you're not the victim you think you are. You *chose* to follow us back to Salish Sea Hub. You *chose* to join our ranks. You *chose* to go to the rootbinding ceremony. You've got to start owning those choices."

I nodded, knowing deep down that Ramaya was right.

"Hey Rama," said Kes, "I'm picking up on some owl chatter about a possible tail. Do you want to check it out before we head back?"

"As if anyone could tail me. Owls and their utter paranoia." Ramaya rolled her eyes, but tromped off into the woods, leaving Kes and me alone.

As soon as she was gone, I whispered, "You helped me didn't you? Why?" I remembered the way I'd looked at them, the ferocity of my stare. "Please tell me I didn't make you? Did I leech you?"

"No...I wanted to. I don't understand. I shouldn't have, like *really* shouldn't have. I've never betrayed the order, or Ramaya. I'm not sure which one feels worse."

"I'm sorry. I don't want to make things harder for you, I see how much you carry already." I thought about Harriet asking Kes to plead her case to the Council.

"Are you saying I look tired?"

"A little—"

"Ouch. And here I was thinking I looked all cool and mysterious. But I just look tired."

"Oh no. You're definitely pulling off hot and mysterious." I turned flamingo-pink. "I mean, cool and mysterious."

"What'd you do to poor Blue Hair?" Ramaya launched herself out of the trees. "She looks like she's burning up again."

I was so embarrassed it took me until we were back in the bunker to realize Kes had never answered my question. Why were they betraying everything they held dear to help a girl they barely knew?

A crow—no, bigger—a raven perched on a low branch in a gnarled tree. Moss hung like decaying green streamers in great waves from the tree's limbs. The raven cawed and the caw was joined by more caws of more ravens, hundreds, thousands of them overhead. The caws were met with chirps and hoots—

pigeons and robins and owls joining the chorus, all merging into a single melody. I was sure I'd heard it before. I stepped towards the raven, mesmerized by the sound, and reached out a hand to stroke it without thinking. The bird turned and slashed its beak at my wrist and I screamed, but not from the pain.

Where the raven's eyes should have been were two glimmering red jewels. I gaped, frozen, as it began to lick at the blood now trickling down my arm from where it had bitten me. Another bird landed to feast on my flesh, and another. They snatched me into the sky as I struggled against their claws, blood staining the clouds below me. On and on we flew, across land and sea. We dodged a tower of steel knifing into the sky, and I jerked to attention. The space needle. We were in Seattle. I caught glimpses of other landmarks from my neighborhood—the brick smokestack jutting up from my middle school. The creek smothered in a riotous patchwork of wildflowers. The spires of the wooden playground around the corner from my house. My house. The familiar green paint with pink trim – the wee lil watermelon as Aspen and I had called it.

The ravens swooped into the open window of Aspen's room, dragging me through as my belly scratched against the rough wood of the sill. My breath caught at the familiar sight of vines from dozens of ceramic pots tangling around books and bed like some kind of leafy octopus. My breath caught again as something knocked into the space between my shoulder blades, propelling me onto the bed. I flipped around to face my attacker only to see the branches of a tree windmilling into me. The branches had come right through the same window as the ravens, who were now shrieking in approval at my tree-attacker.

"Bonnie," I whispered, realizing it must be our old cherry tree. "It's me."

The branches paid me no mind. More jammed through the window as if the whole tree could wedge its way into the room and pinned me roughly to the bed. I felt pressure at my wrists and ankles as the tree bound me just as the fake nurse had. Bound, always bound in this new life, post-Aspen. By grief. By fear. By physical restraint. I screamed in frustration and terror and suddenly there was the feeling of warm water rushing down my back, the smell of oak and lavender.

"Mira, you're safe," a familiar voice above me said.

"It's just a dream, just a dream, and we're here now." Another voice, full of warmth.

Kes. Ramaya. I was safe. Far from the horror of my dream. I opened my eyes to see the rootbound warriors staring down at me in concern. My whole body was damp with sweat and I still felt cocooned by the fear of the dream.

"You're safe," Kes repeated, running a gentle hand down my arm.

"And we brought you breakfast," Ramaya added. "Eat up, it'll help." She set a tray on my lap loaded with tofu eggs, fluffy white rice, pickled broccoli, orange juice, and coffee. Too exhausted to speak, I did as I was told. With each bite I felt a little better, a little more present in this world and removed from the nightmare version of my house, where my own beloved tree had held me in a chokehold while zombie-birds feasted on my flesh.

"Do you want to talk about it?" Kes asked.

"No talking. Just eating," Ramaya commanded. "We've got to get some more color in those cheeks."

Finally, after a few minutes, I croaked out, "What...what are you two doing here? Not that I'm not happy to see you."

"We're here to hold up our end of the bargain," Ramaya

answered. "I made a vow, and I never break my vows. But maybe we should re—"

"No!" I shouted, choking on the sip of orange juice I'd just taken. "Tell me. Tell me about the Huntsmen. How they're connected to the missing climate leaders."

Ramaya and Kes traded a questioning look. "OK," Kes said. "But you know what I'm going to say next. You have to let us know if any of this is too much."

"It's all too much," I muttered. "Every single part of my life right now is too much. But what else can I do but...keep going?"

"Here, here," Ramaya said heartily. "The only way out is *through*."

I repeated the words, enjoying the way they felt on my tongue. "So let's go, *through* this godforsaken bunker and *out* to wherever you two are waiting to take me."

"Hmmm...this is more of a down and deeper situation. But metaphorically speaking, we're still moving through."

"Great, deeper into the dark with all the friendly roots." I thought about my nightmare, the way Bonnie had held me down, scraping rough bark across my wrists.

After a characteristically lightspeed golf cart ride, several elevators, always down, and zero redhead ambushes, we arrived in a section of the bunker with raw rock walls and arching steel beams. Harsh yellow lights set in the low ceiling stretched on down straight tunnels like highway lines on a pitch-black road. Occasionally we passed fresh tunnels dug in the rock, or in the processes of being dug by armies of white-capped roots, obvious additions by the Seven. The place was both eerie, and oddly comfortable.

Ramaya parked in front of one of these fresh holes, though how she could tell them apart I had no idea. She led us inside into what was essentially a dirt cellar, awash in a sweet, tangy smell of mulch. The domed ceiling emitted a greenish glow and seemed to move. Looking at a neon green spot on the wall I saw swarms of bioluminescent pill bugs.

On the far side, a body hung suspended against the wall of dirt, entirely covered by a feathery web of faintly glowing threads. But I was used to bodies stuck in the dirt at this point.

"This is Sarah," Ramaya said. "The girl we rescued from the plane."

"And these are mycelium," Kes explained, taking one of the glowing filaments in their hand. "The threads of fungi that work symbiotically with tree roots to send chemical signals, break down minerals, and even transfer nutrients between different species. We can use them to connect people to the Rhiza to rest and heal."

I moved closer to Sarah, checking her neck for that nightmarish metallic tick. But it was gone, replaced by two deep puncture wounds. "That horrible thing was feeding on Sarah somehow, wasn't it?"

Kes came up behind me, putting a comforting arm around my shoulder. "Yes but she's free now. Thanks in part to you."

"What did these Huntsmen want with her? A little girl? Who are these ghouls?"

Ramaya answered "During the rootbinding, do you remember Teddy talking about William the Conqueror?"

I nodded. "Yeah, and I had to learn about him in AP Euro. Some dude from Normandy who invaded and conquered England in 1066."

"Exactly. Well, after the conquest, William made his closest dude bros into feudal lords, parcelling out huge estates to them, and creating a new peasant class they could rule over. Just like that—a snap of the fingers to dispossess a world. Most of those families still own that land a thousand years later."

Kes chanted, "'*Since William rose and Edward fell, Huntsmen have roamed the del.*'"

Ramaya continued, "William and his baron bros were obsessed with hunting. After they stole the land from the Anglo-Saxons, they invented forest law, essentially banning anyone but them from hunting on the king's land. Only problem? Those peasants they'd dispossessed were starving. Some of them snuck onto the king's land for food and were punished with blinding or worse. This fun little sadistic crew swore oaths to one another to protect their families, and, more importantly, their property."

"And that," Kes added, "was the very beginning of the Huntsmen."

"Yes," said Ramaya. "These families have kept their oaths to each other, raising private armies, pushing England's genocidal imperialism, funding arms' races, staging coups—all in the service of maintaining and expanding their private empires."

"But," I asked, "how can they possibly stand up to the rootbound's magical connection with the trees?"

"They have 'magic' too," Ramaya answered. "The boring kind. Propaganda. Property law. Tax shelters. Writing loopholes into regulation."

"I don't get it though," I said. "They already have everything. What do they even want?"

After a long moment, Ramaya murmured, "*More.*"

"More...money? Power?"

"Yes, in a way. Just more, always more." She gestured at the surroundings.

I didn't quite understand but I could *feel* that endless need. Here, in this lavish underground city built for a family of five.

The longing felt grotesque.

I opened my mouth to ask another question, but my attention was drawn to something glinting in an alcove of the dirt wall. I stepped towards it without thinking. A wave of energy pulsed through me, lifting the hairs on my arms. I took another step, felt another pulse of energy. I beamed; I felt *good*. Like I had at the rootbinding ceremony. The fiery nerve pain that was so part of my day-to-day existence it was barely worth mentioning faded. Was this how other people felt every day?

"It's really affecting her," Kes said and it took me a moment to realize they weren't speaking to me, but about me.

Ramaya snorted. "Of course it is. Mira is a mystery wrapped in an enigma wrapped in a burrito. Earth to Mira—come back to us."

I started and realized I was standing mere inches from a marble-sized ruby lodged in the wall. It looked wet somehow, slick with blood. I shivered. "That's the thing from Sarah's neck."

The jewel was pinned to the wall by the same feathery thread holding the teen. Why? Was the gem plugged into the same system? I squinted at the delicate metal tag hanging from the ruby: Sarah Churn, birthday, May 24, 2011. Pain flared in my limbs and the warm *good* feeling vanished. A horrible suspicion grew in my mind.

The walls shook faintly, and more alcoves opened as roots shifted the dirt. More sparkles. More gems. Dozens of them. Hundreds. I moved along the wall, looking up and down, reading the tags.

Drew Vintner, birthday, April 7, 2010. A diamond. Manpreet Chadha, birthday, February 10, 2009. An emerald.

"The gems..." I said. "They feed off people somehow and store the energy. The Huntsmen are kidnapping climate strikers and...stealing their energy."

Ramaya spoke, "The Huntsmen call them siphons."

"That's what they were doing to Sarah when we interrupted them," Kes said.

"But why climate strikers?"

"Two birds one stone. Or so we think." Ramaya shook her head. "The owls, our intelligence unit, have been so overwhelmed by all the kidnappings that they haven't figured out the bigger picture. The kidnappings, the whispers about this mysterious Confessor, the song, they all started around the same time. Something's happening. Something big, something terrible—"

Kes put a hand on their friend's shoulder, gently cutting her off, "There's a lot we *do* know. Climate strikers have some of the strongest, most powerful wills, so it makes sense Huntsmen would want to steal their energy and amplify it through their siphons. And if they kidnap the most powerful youth protesters, they can neutralize them before they Awaken and join the rootbound."

I pictured Sarah alive, seemingly awake but trapped by the Huntsmen's siphon. How long would she have lived like that, stuck in an eternal scream, her life force slowly bled to fuel the Huntsmen's carnage?

"Stay with me, Mira. I know your mind is going to Aspen. But don't let the 'what-ifs' take you." Kes's voice was gentle yet firm. An anchor holding me to the present like the meditation tapes my counsellor had given me. "Breathe. I understand your pain, but the best way to help Aspen is to stay in the present. To stay in your body."

Ramaya's words came back to me—*nobody in the Seven is a stranger to loss.* Kes wasn't giving me empty platitudes. They were showing me how they moved through their own grief. The fireworks of pain continued exploding but I pulled my attention elsewhere, to Kes, to their kind, calm face, and forced myself to exhale.

"We're not going to lie to you, Mira," Ramaya said. "There's a chance the Huntsmen have bound Aspen's will to a siphon. We thought it would be better if you heard it from us rather than piecing it together yourself over the coming weeks. But Kes and I swore a vow to save as many kidnapped teens as possible—it's why I left Harvard."

"*Thank you.*" I wasn't the only one shouldering an impossible weight.

"Zo should be here any second." Ramaya held up her watch, which had no numbers but symbols for waxing and waning moons, rising and setting suns, and seeds sprouting into trees. The many hands spun around in different directions and then all pointed at a symbol of a full moon. "Ah, here they come now."

The earth trembled slightly and another alcove opened in the dirt, widening into the size of a doorway, buttressed with thick grey roots. Zo stepped out, brushing the dirt off their shoulders. They looked around and nodded in approval. "Good, you've begun telling Mira about siphons. Thank you, Mira, you have done us a great service."

Kes too had thanked me a moment ago. "I don't understand. What did I do? Didn't I ruin the rootbinding?"

"Let's gather around Sarah while we explain. She should be stirring soon and our presence will help ease her transition."

We followed Zo to stand in a close semi-circle around the teen. Ramaya spoke, "From the very start, the Huntsmen had an immense advantage over the Seven Sisters—money, power, empire. But we were rootbound, tied to the trees and one another. We had treetalkers and willbinders when the Huntsmen had none. They would've been no match for us, even with their armies and castles, not if we could sway them with leeching."

"Exactly," Kes added. "Which is why they figured out how to steal our power. At first, they tried to treetalk."

Ramaya snorted. "Lots of early Huntsmen died trying to plug into the Rhiza. Like I said, the trees are way more violent then we are, and not bound by our oath."

"So they turned to leeching," Kes said. "And they beat us at our own game."

"*Destroyed* us at our own game," said Ramaya.

"Because willbinding is based on the inherent connections between people," Zo said, "it doesn't require communion with the Rhiza or any other aspect of plant life. And so the Huntsmen focused all their considerable resources on willbinding. They discovered things we could never have dreamed of."

"Because no one in the Seven would be diabolical enough to try," Ramaya said darkly.

"And we certainly wouldn't lock up dungeons full of people for our experiments," Kes added.

"The early Huntsmen discovered how to leech human energy and store it in special jewels," Zo said. "Which then bestow that energy to the wearer."

"Most Huntsmen can't willbind on their own," Kes said. "But using the jewels they can be as powerful as any willbinder in the Seven."

"Like so many other things, they outsource the dirty work. They have their mercenaries, their lawyers, their accountants, and their leeches," Ramaya said.

My head swam. "Wait a second, I want to get this right—you keep jumping back and forth between leeching and willbinding. The only difference is that leeching is willbinding without consent?"

"Exactly," answered Kes.

"And the Huntsmen only ever leech," Ramaya said. "No one consents to the things they force people to do."

"The Huntsmen have other means of strengthening their willbinding," Kes said. "They control much of the media. They cultivate influence over political parties, newspapers, radio stations, TV, internet providers, and more. They use this to enforce their narrative, to shrink the box of what the world population thinks and believes, so that people are only ever exposed to ideas approved by the Huntsmen. And because so many people already believe Huntsmen propaganda, they are easily controlled by leeching."

"She's stirring," Ramaya said excitedly.

Sarah shifted in the netting. Zo placed a hand on the teen's forehead. The mycelium knitted itself up their arm.

Ramaya shook her head. "I'll never get over how much the Rhiza responds to you."

"Some of these trees are hundreds of years old." Zo gently tugged their arm free of the netting. "They've known my parents and my parents' parents and so on."

Sarah's eyelids fluttered and we held our breath for a long moment but her eyes didn't open.

"I wanted you to be here when Sarah woke, Mira," Zo said. "We could not have freed her from the Huntsmen's siphon without you. When you joined hands with the others at the rootbinding, your energy crashed into the Rhiza like a boiling tsunami—it was so powerful that some rootbound who felt it are still in bed recovering. We're not quite sure why, but that surge of energy appears to have overridden the siphon, like blowing a fuse."

"That was the scream we heard last night? Sarah yelling as the siphon released?"

Ramaya nodded. "It's getting harder and harder to free

kidnapped teens from the siphons. If you could control your power…" She gestured around the room, at the hundreds of gems in the alcoves, and her meaning was clear. If I could control my power, I could save teens just like these, just like Sarah.

"Of course. I'll do anything to try and help," I said quickly, intent on keeping myself in the order after the disaster of the night before. But a moment later, I realized I meant it. The gems around me represented hundreds of young people trapped in an unending nightmare. If I could help free them…

Zo nodded solemnly. "Thank you."

Sarah's eyelids fluttered again and she opened her eyes, a beatific smile coming to her face. She looked angelic, suspended in the air, criss-crossed in glowing thread.

"Sarah, welcome—" Zo started.

"The rich man in his castle," the girl began singing sweetly. "The poor man at his gate. God made them, high or lowly, and ordered their estate."

"No!" Zo looked stricken.

Stepping past Zo, Kes put a hand on Sarah's wrist. "Sarah, how are you? Do you need food, water? You're safe and sound —we'll bring you to your family very soon."

The suspended teen turned shining eyes on Kes and sang again, "The rich forest, verdant and pure; untainted by human greed and gore."

I tripped and realized I'd been backing away from the rescued teen. Zo closed their eyes and took a deep breath, putting a hand against the dirt wall. The webbing threaded around their hand, forming a glowing glove. When they spoke again, they had regained their former calm, "Take Mira away from here please. The trees and I will deal with this."

I opened my mouth to protest, but was horrified to find myself humming along with Sarah instead.

"Get Mira out of here, *now*!" Zo hissed and Ramaya and Kes looped hands under my elbows. They half-carried me away as Sarah continued singing, "Protected for a thousand years and more; By the Huntsmen who through it all endure."

I ground my teeth together, drawing blood from my lip as I fought the compulsion to join her.

NINE

Kes and Ramaya didn't speak as they tugged me through the maze of bunker tunnels. I clamped my jaw so tight my cheek muscles began to cramp but could still feel the vibration in my throat as my body tried to hum along to the song.

"Breathe, Mira," Kes murmured. They ran their hands up and down my arms. "Do you still feel the compulsion to sing?"

I nodded, my cheeks red from shame and lack of air.

"Breathe. Just *breathe*," they whispered, and I shivered at the invitation in their voice, the way their hands slowed on my skin. At the sensation of warm water streaming down my back, I unclenched my jaw, drawing a deep breath. I turned my face up to that same steady gaze, as if turning towards the sun.

They're leeching you, Aspen warned.

My lips were still moving with words that were not my own and now I could feel Kes probing my mind. I pushed them away, erupting, "How dare you! You're leeching me? Get out of my head, GET OUT!"

Kes backed away from me, putting their hands up. I felt

suddenly freezing, like I'd stepped out of the bath on a winter's day, and terribly alone.

"Sorry," Kes said. "I was trying to help."

"No...I'm sorry. I just...what was that?"

"I wish we knew," Ramaya growled. "The Huntsmen have always kidnapped people to fill their jewels. But something's changed. They're kidnapping more and more teens, getting sloppy. When we intercept their chatter all they're talking about is The Confessor. We don't even know if he's a real person or code for some project. But whenever we get a chance to interrogate any of their goons, they just sing that same song. Now even the teens we rescue are singing it...even you." Ramaya's eyes flashed. "I need to interview you, while the experience is fresh."

"Good idea," Kes said. "But let's go somewhere more private."

They led me up several floors to a room that I instantly recognized even though I had never been there before—Kes's. Compared to my luxury suite it was small and plain, but much homier and cozier. The fake window screens showed rolling waves crashing against dramatic forested beaches. Pictures of grinning friends and family covered the dresser. An easel next to the mattress that served as a bed (unmade) showed a half-finished painting of a crow perched in a gnarled tree. It smelled of oak and lavender. I could smell that smell forever.

"I'll be right back," Ramaya said, darting out the door.

Kes sat me down next to them on their bed and felt my forehead. "How's your body?"

"Fine." Tossing out the casual lie to Kes felt wrong. "No, it's not fine. Sometimes I feel like a quilt fraying at the edges, and one day I'll just tear right open."

"I'm sorry you've had to go through so much pain." They inched closer to me, their voice dropping, their eyes so full of empathy I flinched. I could feel how much they meant it. They put a hand on my knee, and my whole body relaxed.

"Thank you," I whispered.

"For what?" Kes asked.

"For reminding my body it can feel more than pain." Without thinking, I traced a finger over Kes's hand.

They breathed in sharply. "Mira—"

"Back!" Ramaya barged through the door balancing three steaming mugs of hot chocolate. Oblivious to the moment, she shoved a mug at each of us and plopped into a bean bag chair.

"Drink that," she ordered, and then took a deep gulp. Kes did the same, leaving a whipped-cream mustache on their upper lip. "We need to be nourished to resist." When I hesitated, she repeated, "Seriously, drink. We have to give ourselves the things we need. And right now you *need* some hot chocolate."

I sipped the hot chocolate. To my surprise I did feel better.

Ramaya took out her phone. "I hope you don't mind if I record this."

"No. That's fine."

"Great." Ramaya tapped the screen. "Interview with Mira Bracken. Date: June 3, 2025, 2:46 PM. Keywords: Kidnapped Climate Striker, Confessor, Sarah Churn.

"The refrain Sarah and the Huntsmen lackey were singing is modified from a nineteenth century hymn. The larks have known about the song since it was written—it's classic Huntsmen propaganda—and they've been trying to stamp it out for more than a century. But this is something else entirely. It's like the song is *alive*."

Ramaya reached towards me. "Give me your hand, Mira?" I put my own hand up and mycelium seemed to shoot from Ramaya's pointer finger like she was Spiderman slinging webs. The fungal threads spun around and around our joined limbs and I felt...nothing. The absence of pain, of fear, of noise, of ideas exploding in my head.

"You feel it?" Ramaya asked. I nodded, afraid to break the spell. To let the world rush back in.

Ramaya sang, her voice rich and true. I felt a gentle pressure like I was in a plane cabin at takeoff, and clenched my jaw against the force of the song, but nothing happened.

The rich forest, verdant and pure,
Untainted by human greed and gore,
Protected for a thousand years and more,
By the Huntsmen who through it all endure.

The Huntsmen stand proud and free,
Courage, strength, power—they embody the three,
Guardians of all the eye can see,
They know not how to bend the knee.

To be a Huntsman is to choose your own fate,
Bowing to no man, no beast, nor state,
The choice is yours—do not wait,
The die is cast, the hour's late.

"Ominous," I said, before Ramaya had even closed her mouth, too eager to show how unaffected I was by the song.

Ramaya gave me a small smile, as if she knew exactly what I was trying to do. The threads dissolved back from where they came and she continued, "From my interviews, I can place the earliest instance of the song's reappearance during a flower of truth ritual fourteen months ago. In the last six months, there has been an exponential rise in the song's use, coinciding with the growing wave of kidnapping attempts on youth climate strikers." Ramaya took a sip of hot chocolate. "I've consulted with the Seven's linguists and semioticians and there's no underlying meaning or code to the language."

"Yeah, I'd say it's pretty on the nose for the Huntsmen," Kes said. "Rich people have a divine right to rule and conquer. And to build elaborate underground cities complete with Michelin star restaurants while speeding the apocalypse for the rest of us."

"Preacher, meet choir." Ramaya gestured towards herself and me. "But this is not just some summer anthem to make rich people feel better about hoarding an obscene amount of the world's resources. It's a terrible and brilliant evolution of binding, a kind of mass leeching that the Seven haven't even truly acknowledged, let alone understood."

"A mass leeching?" I shivered, picturing an army of people bound to do the bidding of the Huntsmen.

Ramaya explained, "The way the song binds is more important than its message. It seems to be viral, infectious. My initial theory, which I shared with the owls, was that the hymn was a clever way to evade giving up information when Huntsmen were interviewed with the flower of truth. I guessed that through powerful and consistent leeching of a single story, or song, Huntsmen could embed that story so far into their deepest subconscious that they'd believe the story with every fiber of their being. This unshakeable belief would in turn allow them to evade the compulsion of the flower of truth, which is, as I have tested on myself, essentially impossible to subvert."

"Of course you tested it on yourself," I said.

"I test everything on myself. But tonight proved my theory wrong. Sarah was with the Huntsmen for less than twelve hours. And you, Mira Bracken,"—Ramaya added for the benefit of the recording—"felt the compulsion to sing from just *hearing* Sarah sing."

I blushed and took a long sip of hot chocolate.

"Sorry, Mira, that was an observation, not an accusation."

"Don't worry. There's nothing you could accuse me of that I haven't already accused myself of."

"Are you ok to talk about it? What it felt like when you started humming?"

I stared blankly at Ramaya. What did it feel like? What did my body ever feel like besides heat and fear and grief?

She prodded gently, "Did the tune feel psychologically addictive somehow? Did it feel like some kind of second-hand leeching?"

I forced myself to think through the last hour, fighting the rising tide of pain and grief to wade back into my body's memory. I saw Kes, Ramaya, and Zo standing in a semi-circle, saw myself backing away from the suspended teen. I felt the hairs on my arms and neck raise on end. But why? From fear for Aspen? From unease at the fervor in Sarah's eyes? No, from *recognition*. Forgetting about the mug in my hand, I raised my arms in triumph, and spilled hot chocolate all over my t-shirt.

"What? What?" Ramaya leaned in, waving her phone in my face excitedly.

"It felt like *remembering*. Like I'd heard the words before."

Ramaya squeezed my hand and I felt her thanks flooding through me. "How long before? Months, years?"

I closed my eyes in concentration, trying to dredge up a trace of the memory. It didn't seem fresh. "Years."

"It's worse than I thought." Ramaya stood abruptly. "The Huntsmen are building towards something—we can all feel it. And if Mira heard the song *years* before, that means whatever is going on with the song, and the kidnapped teens, and this Confessor figure was put in motion a long time ago."

A crow shrieked as if to echo Ramaya's point. My head swiveled automatically to the "window" in Kes's room but it held only the same lonely beach scene as before. I squinted, looking for the telltale blur of flapping wings in the pixelated sky and felt a sudden, overwhelming sense of suffocation at being underground in this fake world.

"Rama, you've reported your suspicions to the owls—let them handle it. You have enough on your plate." Kes's words had the rhythm of an oft-repeated argument.

"I know you brought it to Zo and the other Hub leaders. But maybe...maybe it's time for you to go directly to the Council? They might listen if you speak," Ramaya said.

Right, Hot Kes is some kind of god in the Seven, Aspen whispered.

Kes ran a hand through their undercut, obviously uncomfortable. "It's just...hectic at the moment."

"Exactly. Somebody's trying to make it hectic. To distract us. To keep us from putting the pieces together." Ramaya added, "I know you hate drawing on your family name, I *know* that, and you know how much I hate asking you to. But I'm doing it anyway; it's that important. *Please*, Kes."

I'd known Ramaya long enough to know it wasn't easy for her to ask for help. Kes obviously knew the same. They turned their steady gaze on their friend, suddenly solemn. "Of course, Rama. Let's go now. We can send word to the Council together."

Ramaya put a hand on Kes's arm, giving them a squeeze. "Thank you."

"That was beautif—" I trailed off, swallowing my words in a giant yawn. Kes and Ramaya looked at me, brows knitted with concern. "Don't mind me. You're very important people doing very important people things..."

"And you're a very important person who needs to do the very important person thing of resting," Ramaya said. Kes snorted at the obvious hypocrisy. They pulled me to standing and settled me in the hallway outside of Kes's room. "Sorry to cut and run. The bunker tram will be here any minute to make sure you get back to your room and we'll find you for your first treetalking lesson as soon as you've slept. The stronger your connection to the Rhiza, the more protected you'll be from the song."

I shooed them away, assuring them I was fine. As soon as they'd turned the corner out of sight, I slid down the wall, collapsing like a deflated balloon. A few minutes later I startled back awake to a high-pitched beeping sound. What must've once been the bunker's tram zoomed into view. Every square inch of it was wrapped in rainbow LED lights and the seats had been ripped out and replaced by a row of eye-popping silk hammocks, which swung wildly as the tram swerved to a stop a split-second before running over my prone body. I recognized the redhead in the driver's seat. He'd tackled Ramaya in the elevator before the rootbinding. What was his name again?

Sheldon, Aspen whispered.

"Hop on!" called Sheldon without preamble.

I eyed the hammocks skeptically, shoving my limbs into a lime green silk with the grace of a newborn giraffe. A few minutes later, my skepticism vanished. We zoomed through tunnel after tunnel, the hammock swinging in wide arcs every time we took a corner. With the rhythmic rocking making me feel like I was back in the womb, a purring rescue kitten curled on my chest, and the sound of laughter echoing through the vaulted ceilings of the bunker, I drifted off with a smile on my lips.

Kes fled down the corridor and I gave chase. They wound me deeper and deeper underground. Roots reached out from the wall like hands, encircling my wrists, my ankles, even my neck, growing more and more resistant with every step. The roots didn't want me to reach Kes, the golden child of the order, the descendant of the Seven. I charged forward against the bindings. They held fast. As I struggled, the roots around my ankles began to pull me into the earth. I fell to my knees, nails digging uselessly at the root at my throat, trying to call out but having no power. They could choke me and drag me deep into the earth like an alligator in a swimming hole and nobody would know the difference. I tried to scream again.

And then suddenly the roots slithered away back into the wall. I looked up to catch a figure disappearing around another curve in the tunnel. They moved with a curious skip to their step, as if dancing while they ran. I knew only one person in the world who moved like that.

"Aspen," I screamed hoarsely, stumbling to my feet to give

chase to the figure. "Aspen, it's me!" Every breath was agony against my bruised throat but I barely noticed. My world had narrowed to one goal. I skidded around a corner, half-falling, and realized I'd reached a dead-end with a row of doors. Aspen was here in one of these rooms. One of the doors was ever so slightly ajar. I pushed through it with a surge of hope and immediately felt a sense of wrongness. The room was bathed in blood-red light and somebody was humming softly in the distance. The sound was cloying, over-sweet. Just as I turned to run, a voice commanded, "Wake up, Mira Bracken."

I pushed myself towards consciousness to escape the sense of wrongness. My nose filled with the scent of spice and decay. I opened my eyes and saw Sarah hanging before me in the dark cellar, her face lit by glowing thread and the same blood-red light of the gems. While chasing Aspen in my dream I had sleepwalked deep into the belly of the bunker to this terrible place. The suspended teen was singing a verse I hadn't heard before, "Edward fell and William rose, but evil waited not in repose..."

I ground my teeth against it, but a whisper of sound escaped my lips as I finished, "Sins and secrets untold, The Confessor knows. He'll bring this poisonous chapter of man to a close."

"You remember, Mira Bracken. You remember," Sarah said, her eyes fixed on me. "The Confessor wants to speak to you."

I stood frozen, as if bound once more by the roots, enthralled by the jewel and the song. A memory of Kes and Ramaya dragging me away from this same spot earlier drilled into my mind and I came back to myself. With a whimper, I forced my pain-filled body to turn and run.

"The Confessor will find you," Sarah called after me.

I hurled myself through the door. Before I made it three feet a mass of roots shot from the wall and wrapped around me. The roots pulled me so tight into a cocoon of mycelium that I couldn't see anything besides their silvery threads. But I could feel my body hurtling through space, up or down, side to side, I had no idea. Without warning, the mycelium pod unravelled mid-air and I fell through pitch black to land roughly on my hands and knees.

Where was I? Were the roots friend or foe? "You're root-bound, you *love* the dark," I whispered to myself, trying to hype myself up to move. "You love the dirt. And the bugs, so many bugs. And the stale air. And the smell of death..." I started crawling forward and was surprised to find the feel of something soft and luxurious under my hands. Could it be moss?

Something skittered across my hand, and I started screaming. Once I started, I couldn't stop. The earth rumbled, vibrating from somewhere deep underground. And—

The lights came on.

I blinked, still screaming and tried to stand as a woman emerged from the corner. I recognized her pale eyes and solemn face from the rootbinding ceremony. Standing in front of me was none other than Naomi Squall, First Magpie.

"Hush!" The woman commanded, holding a finger to her lips like some kind of goth librarian. "You'll bring the whole bunker down on our heads if you keep that up."

"Where are we? What's going on?" I rasped. Speaking felt like swallowing staples. I traced a hand over my neck, feeling the angry, raised line where a root had almost garroted me. The attack hadn't just been a dream.

"Calm yourself, Mira. The Rhiza responds to your distress in extraordinary fashion." The woman glanced at something and I followed her gaze to see a me-sized hole in the brick accent wall. The earth rumbled again and a cloud of silt billowed through the hole.

"*I'm* causing that earthquake?"

"Little old me?" Naomi said, mimicking my tone and inflection so perfectly that I looked around to see if the words had somehow come from a recorder, or a parrot.

"You think the best way to help me calm down is to mock me?"

Naomi waved a hand as if swatting away a troublesome fly. "It's boring. The false modesty."

"It's not false—" I spluttered. "You know what? I don't need this. I've been hopping from one nightmare to another—in the last twenty-four hours alone I've nearly been decapitated and suffocated, not to mention launched head first through a brick wall into this...this *tomb*."

"Not a tomb," Naomi clucked. "Look more closely."

I'd thought it was a tomb because of the dozens of works of art ringing the wall, each clearly depicting the same woman—dark-haired, dark-eyed, fierce and beautiful. My eyes were drawn to a silk tapestry of the woman's profile, mouth parted as if to whistle. Out of her lips spun a tornado of winged creatures. I looked at another—an oil painting of the woman with a hawk perched on each shoulder like some kind of fabulously tall winged shoulder pads. Another water color showed a form that was half eagle, half woman. "Are we in some kind of shrine to Godda?"

"Godda?" Naomi snorted. "Salish Sea Hub has taught you nothing, as usual. Another instance of Kes breaking protocol, as if the rules do not apply to them. This woman is Edeva."

"Oh...she saved Godda from the Huntsmen a thousand years ago?"

"Is that all you know of her?" Naomi's eyes searched mine, probing as if she could read my mind.

I struggled to think of anything else, not wanting to give the First Magpie any more ammunition against my friends, but couldn't unearth anything. I shook my head.

"You know the rootbound have an oath not to kill, I presume?"

"Of course," I said, my voice ringing with a confidence I didn't feel. I could see now that Naomi would prey on any weakness I showed.

"That was not always so. Indeed, while we no longer advertise it, our origins were more than a little bloody. Edeva thought the only way to stop the gangrene of the Huntsmen was to...cut it out entirely." Naomi's face remained impassive. "From the very moment of our founding there has been tension between violence and pacifism. Godda believed that violence could only ever beget more violence. Edeva believed that some humans were so evil they deserved the violence that came for them. Legend has it that she saw terrible things before running away to the rootbound."

"They fought?"

"Yes and no. They were very close." Naomi's eyes looked glassy, faraway. "While our order has chosen to walk Godda's path for many centuries now, there is still a shadow contingent within the rootbound pushing for us to take up the mantle of Edeva and carve out the gangrene of the Huntsmen."

"I take it you're part of that contingent?"

"*How dare you.*"

Something clipped me in the back of the head, like a basketball slamming into my skull. I covered my head with my hands instinctively, as bats began to flood out of the hole in the wall, circling above me and shrieking angrily. I felt more awe than fear, remembering how the ravens had responded to Aspen's emotions in similar fashion.

"It's OK," Naomi said gently, and I was struck by how vulnerable the goth librarian suddenly looked.

"Thank you." I realized too late she was talking to the bats and blushed, feeling like the little kid in the cafeteria caught waving to somebody who wasn't waving to me. "Right, you're an animimicker."

Whether Naomi heard me or not, she didn't answer. Instead she cooed at one of the smaller bats, who purred back and curled up in her neck. "I...apologize. My friends are very protective of me." The little bat draped around Naomi's neck showed me its fangs. "You're obviously new here. For one rootbound to accuse another of following the path of Edeva is a most grievous insult. One that could have serious consequences for accuser and accused."

"That's giving serious Salem Witch Hunt vibes."

"You have no idea." Naomi shook her head. "I already inspire some distrust within the order, as the first and only animimicker in many centuries. One of the last, and certainly most powerful animimickers our order has ever known was Edeva herself."

"Oh, gotcha." I blushed. I'd just accidentally compared the woman in front of me to the Darth Vader of the rootbound. I looked around at the paintings, rushing for something to say, "And Edeva had some kind of special relationship with the birds?"

"Some say she could join her mind with theirs, even use birdsong to leech her enemies. Together, she and the birds came up with some extremely creative and *gruesome* ways of terrorizing the Huntsmen." Naomi nodded at a piece of needlework hung farther along the wall. Two men on horseback, one wearing a conspicuous golden crown, were being attacked by a flock of birds. Embroidered red rivulets flowed from dozens of cuts on their bodies and one of the birds was holding a human eyeball in its talons. The embroiderer had used great skill to detail the veins still hanging from the plucked eyeball. I shivered and one of the bats made a hacking noise that sounded suspiciously like laughter. "I can read the question shining in your eyes like your face is a Times Square billboard. Another thing we'll have to work on—being less emotive. Go ahead, ask it."

I had an urge to shove the woman in front of me, *hard*. But something told me she would shove back. "If Edeva is so hated why is there a literal shrine to her in Salish Sea Hub?"

"Edeva was always more *aggressive* than the other Sisters, but according to our archivists, something changed and she became violent. Extremely violent. Now we know to call it OS, or oversaturated, when the horrors of the Huntsmen become too much—the torture, maiming, murder, arson—and we ourselves succumb to their inhumane methods. It was once mandated that every rootbound hub in the world maintain a Recollection Room, lest we forget the dangers of going OS and become tempted by the violence of Edeva." She ran a finger over the nearest painting, holding it up to show years' worth of dust. "But as you can see, the Recollection Rooms have fallen out of favor. Our current leadership would prefer to gloss over this ugly stain on our history, erase it for the newest generation. And yet the roots took you here, of all places. I'd heard that Salish Sea Hub had encountered a treetalker who caused the Rhiza to behave in unexpected ways. But this is *quite* unexpected. Who are you, Mira Bracken? And, more pressingly, why is your neck bleeding?"

I'd practically forgotten the trauma of the night under the force of Naomi's presence. "I'm not quite sure. It was like this when I woke up." It was the truth, sort of.

"The Confessor. Does the name sound familiar to you?"

"No. Or, only vaguely—I think someone mentioned it at the Hub."

Naomi smiled, but her eyes didn't change. "Interesting." The bats hissed, making it clear they didn't believe me. "Let's go then. It's time for your lesson."

"My lesson?"

"Yes. Your education here has been entirely unsatisfactory. And the order can only spare me a few days. If you are to be of use to the Seven, we must begin practical training at once. Come." A wide entrance opened in the dirt wall, revealing a swarm of roots. Naomi stepped into it and gestured for me to follow.

I hesitated. I really didn't want to go with her, but I wasn't sure what authority she had or what she could do if I refused. And the way the Rhiza responded to her, she was obviously very powerful. Gritting my teeth I stepped into the hole. I was more prepared this time as the swarming roots wrapped me tight and pulled me through the dirt at incredible speed. A lightness appeared in the knit of roots and then I burst from the earth in a miniature geyser and tumbled to my knees.

I spat dirt from my mouth and brushed it off my clothes and rubbed it from my eyes. We were in the lawn meadow behind the mansion, close to the treeline. Naomi stood a short distance away, not a speck of dirt on her.

"I am told you can only access your powers when under duress," Naomi said.

"Who told you that?"

"The Rhiza. I find it strange the Rhiza doesn't speak to you, despite your apparent power. In fact, the Rhiza is rather reluctant to even speak *of* you."

The comment stung. "I've only been doing this like a week."

"Also strange. You have no hints or indications of your power your whole life, and then suddenly ancient maples are throwing themselves in harm's way to protect you...and you're bumping into Kestrel, Descendant of the Seven."

The First Magpie suspected us, I was sure. Did she know what I'd done? What secrets Kes was keeping for me? I shrugged and tried to play it off. "Nobody tried to hit me with a car before then."

"One theory is you're blocked. Anxiety, overwhelm, unprocessed trauma—they undermine our connections to our fellow humans and the Rhiza. It's one of the many reasons Huntsmen seed propaganda intended to immiserate people."

Immiserate? Aspen hissed. *Did she swallow a textbook? Just say they seed propaganda to make people sad and miserable.*

"And your sister is missing. That could generate a great deal of grief. Enough to block your powers, so that they cannot come out in controlled instances, but only in great bursts when your life is threatened and you panic. You stink of grief, of fear, like a dog that rubbed in something dead."

"If you're trying to make me angry, it's working."

"Anger may cause a dramatic spurt of power, but it can't sustain you. The only way to truly master binding is to cultivate trust. You must learn to trust that the universe, although cruel, can also be kind. Trust your fellow rootbound. Trust that you are safe. Trust yourself. You could begin by trusting me."

"Gotta say, you're not making it easy."

Naomi smiled that anti-smile. "Well, then we have no choice but to do this the hard way. The only way you seem to know how to use your powers."

Naomi made an upward stabbing gesture and a root shot out of the ground like a spear right in the space between my cheek and neck.

"What are you doing?"

"Helping you summon your powers." Naomi repeated the gesture with both hands and two more spear-like roots shot up, narrowly missing my eyes and throat. "Hrm. Nothing? Oh well." She spun gracefully on her heel casting out her arms as though dancing. The ground rumbled and roots shot up all around me, forcing me to run and stumble and dodge. One of them nicked my cheek and I felt the wet warmth of blood trickle from my skin.

Oh no she didn't, Aspen said.

"Cut it out!" I yelled and dropped down, slamming both hands into the grass.

Radiating from my spread fingers, tiny shoots unfurled and grew and spread, so the entire lawn transformed into a meadow of wildflowers. From the multicolored petals streamed clouds of pollen, filling the air, obscuring it in a dense, heavy yellow fog. It was so thick I could barely see Naomi, but I could hear her inhale sharply.

"Extraordinary."

Almost as fast as they came the flowers withered and died. The pollen blew into the forest or drifted back into the grass. I noticed it had landed everywhere but Naomi, as if it too was afraid of the woman in black.

"It takes winterseeds years to prepare an event like that," Naomi said. "If you could execute that on purpose, you could weaponize the pollen, maybe even change the chemical compounds to deliver a paralytic or soporific. You could take out an entire Huntsmen base." She walked over and offered me a hand. After a moment, I took it. She hefted me easily to my feet and put a surprisingly gentle hand on my shoulder.

"Breakfast?" she asked.

"Breakfast," I agreed.

CHAPTER

ELEVEN

Naomi led me underground past a sauna and the bowling-alley-turned-nursery to the main dining room, which had the high ceilings of a church. We joined the short queue moving through the industrial kitchen to make their own burritos. To my surprise I saw Zo at the sink washing and drying a huge stack of dishes, with the help of a towel-wielding root.

"The Seven are an egalitarian society," Naomi commented, noticing my stare. "Our leaders don't ask anyone to perform a task they themselves wouldn't do. I know you think I was harsh with you, but if I were in your place I would want someone to push me."

I'll push you, Aspen said. *Right off a cliff.*

One of the cooks, who wouldn't quite meet my eyes, pulled Naomi off for a hushed conversation. Knowing how to take a hint, I grabbed a burrito and drifted past them towards the dozen or so mis-matched antique tables that had been assembled into a makeshift communal dining space. Spotting Tai and Adrian amidst a group at one of the tables, I made a beeline for them.

Tentatively I pulled a chair out to sit, and when nobody stopped me, collapsed into it.

"Watch out, Mira 'Troublemaker' Bracken's back in the building," Adrian teased.

"Back in the *weirdest* building. Are we in a ballroom?" I took in the shiny wood parquet floors.

"Apparently the Athleisure King who built this obscene bunker has a daughter obsessed with ballet."

I shook my head. "It's like they're trying to find ways to waste money. Hey, sorry about what happened at the root-binding."

"It's no big deal," Tai said. "We're used to things going bonkers. Lots of rootbound struggle with their powers. You wouldn't be the first to cause a commotion. Just last month someone accidentally turned the pool into a lily pond and we had to rehome about a million frogs."

"What have you been up to?" Adrian asked, eyes gleaming. "Since Kes and Ramaya threw you into a van like a carpet and drove you into the night?"

I tried to make my face look as bored and boring as possible. "Just playing catch up with the rest of you—there's a lot to learn. Rhiza. Tree gossip. Leeching. Magical evil rich people."

"Don't be a tease," Adrian said. "Give us the juicy details."

A girl with a turquoise septum-piercing leaned in to join our conversation. "Somebody said they saw you come in with Naomi Squall. Are you working with her?"

I took in the expectant faces around me. "Why? Is that unusual?" I fished, dumping hot sauce on my burrito.

"Godda preserve us, it's like you've stumbled into the Zendaya of the Seven and you don't have a clue," said Adrian.

"Her Awakening might even beat yours," Tai said. "No offense."

"Oh. My. God. She's coming over here," Adrian whispered.

"Hey," I said, waving to Naomi. "These two were just about to tell me about your Awakening. Care to share?"

"Traitor," Adrian hissed in my ear.

"Naomi Squall." Ramaya emerged from the crowd, setting down her plate with a clatter. "Don't tell me you're bragging about your Awakening again."

"Ramaya Astre," Naomi replied, curling her lips into a smile. "No, I leave the bragging to you. You certainly do enough for the both of us."

The crowd moved back as the two of them adopted fighting stances and circled one another. They charged at the same time, grappling—and then laughed as they wrapped each other into rib-cracking bear hugs. For the first time, Naomi looked genuinely happy.

"Alright, let's hear it." Ramaya slapped Naomi's back. "The epic saga of Naomi Squall's Awakening."

"Hold on one second, let me grab some dessert," Adrian said.

"Ignore him," Tai said.

"But it's vegan strawberry rhubarb ripple ice cream," Adrian stage-whispered with a dramatic sigh.

"No, please, tell us," a chorus of voices came from around the table. Several more people drew up chairs to listen.

"Very well. I'll give you the short version. It could be... educational." Naomi gave me a calculating look. "I grew up in the water. My mom taught me how to surf before I could even walk. Every day we swam far out into the sea together, so far out we could barely see the land."

"Weren't you afraid of sharks?" Adrian exclaimed.

"My mom taught me to respect the sharks, but never to

fear them. By the time I was fourteen I could hold my breath even longer than my mom—four minutes."

I'm holding my breath waiting for this to get good, Aspen said. She really didn't like Naomi.

"One day, I was out for a paddle in my kayak, something I'd done a million times before, and suddenly I was having a panic attack. The kind that feels like you're gonna die—like you're drowning, but above water. I'd gotten panic attacks before, but never, ever near the water—that's where I feel safest. I couldn't get enough air. Dizzy and disoriented, I leapt overboard into the waves, hoping the ocean would shock me out of it."

Naomi paused to sip her tea. Nobody at the table moved. She continued, "As soon as I felt the ocean's embrace I calmed. As my breathing stilled and my senses returned I realized—the panic wasn't *my* panic. Something was struggling for its life below me. And whatever or whoever it was, it was running out of time.

"I took several deep breaths and dove beneath the water. The panic returned and I swam in the direction that made it stronger until my limbs were buzzing with fear. Fear and panic suck up your oxygen real quick." When she said this she looked directly at me. "They can also draw predators. And there were a lot of predators in the water that day—tiger sharks everywhere. I soon saw why. As the panic reached a crescendo I came upon a humpback whale exhausted, thrashing, tangled in discarded fishing gear.

"It was *her* panic that had overcome me back in the boat. I sped towards her, assessing the situation, and tried to think of how to free her before I would need to resurface for air. The only semi-sharp thing I had was my house key tied around my wrist. I began sawing and hacking at the gear but it was slow work and I was running out of air. I could see how tired the whale was, how the sharks circled, and I swam until I was looking her straight in the eye. I put a hand out and made a silent promise to rescue her or die trying.

"And so I surfaced and swam down, over and over again, hacking at the synthetic nets, biting, cursing the commercial operations that had left their murderous trash behind. We must have looked like easy targets by the end, girl and whale, because a tiger shark swam especially close. I hulked my shoulders and glared at the shark, instinctively letting out an underwater roar. The shark backed off and so did the others. Finally when I thought I might collapse from the effort, I freed the whale enough for her to surface. She pulled me back up with her, breaching. Joy and relief overwhelmed me—hers and mine—sweeter than any feeling I'd felt before. Or since. I collapsed in my kayak, trying to stay conscious long enough to make it home. It jerked forwards and I realized the whale was tugging me back to shore. Right before she dropped me off, she threw herself out of the water, turning that body the size of a bus a full three-hundred-and-sixty degrees. Everyone at the marina saw, and the photo of the thank you jump made the front page of the paper. The image was quickly spotted by larks and a few days later I was contacted by a Seven liaison charged with introducing new members. The rest is history."

After a second of total silence Adrian started clapping and whooping, and the rest of the crowd joined in.

"We are not worthy," the girl with the septum piercing said.

"What even? And you were only fourteen?" asked a teen with Princess Leia buns.

I chimed in, "But how is that an Awakening? I thought you had to connect to the Rhiza or the trees somehow?"

Tai answered, "That's true for most of us, but obviously

animals are deeply embedded in the web. That whale has eaten literal tons of plant matter in its life."

"She's a mystery!" Adrian called.

Just like me, I thought, and warmed a little more towards the imposing woman.

"Just like The Confessor," someone else said.

The crowd grew quiet, except for a peal of nervous laughter.

"The Confessor isn't real," Princess Leia Buns said. People looked around, glancing at Naomi to see if she would confirm or contradict the statement. But she didn't answer; she was studying me again.

"Who wants ice cream?" Adrian piped up in a false cheery tone. "I'm buying."

Ramaya looked around at the drawn faces and lifted her mug of kombucha as if it was a chalice. "Confessors, Huntsmen, what does it matter? We'll take them all on! We are *rootbound*. We are sworn to share our power, our grief, our joys, and our burdens as if our many hearts beat as one. Together, we rise."

"Together we rise!" the crowd echoed, raising their glasses.

"We rise," I said a second too late, missing the beat. I felt ridiculous holding up my water glass alone, joining a toast I didn't know. After a moment, the glass felt weirdly heavy. The water was sloshing like waves. My arm was shaking. My whole body was shaking. My head ached and I felt faint.

Ramaya looped an arm around my waist and pulled me upright as I tottered backwards. "Mira, are you OK?"

"So tired," I mumbled. "Thank you."

Naomi helped support my body weight and the two of them guided me out of the dining room.

"She's on the brink of passing out," Ramaya hissed. "What did you do to her, Naomi?"

"Me? What has Salish Sea Hub been doing to her? A root-binding right after an Awakening? She must've been running on pure adrenaline."

They argued all the way back to my room, getting more and more animated. My tired brain struggled to match their flushed cheeks with their verbal warfare. Did they hate each other? Were they flirting? Once in my room, Ramaya tried to help me into my bed but I pulled away, crossing my arms.

"No, please. Keep me awake. Don't you have anything for that? A stimulant?" I looked at Ramaya.

"She's sleepwalking," Naomi said. "She walked all the way to the gem safe. The teen held in regenerative stasis somehow woke up and addressed her directly. She said The Confessor wanted to meet her."

"You knew?" I said, the words fuzzy in my mouth. "You knew what I'd been through last night?"

"And you didn't think to tell anyone?" Ramaya added. "To get Mira medical attention?"

"I left it to the trees of Salish Sea Hub. If they had wanted you to know, the Rhiza would have told you."

Ramaya scowled. "The Rhiza...it doesn't like to talk about Mira, which you obviously know."

"It was the first thing I noticed," Naomi said. "It told me nothing. Not even where she was. But somehow this teen in the gem safe knows she's here and The Confessor wants to speak to her? And that's not the only mystery. The Rhiza took her to Edeva's Recollection Room."

Ramaya's eyebrows shot up. "That still exists?"

Naomi ignored Ramaya, her pale irises catching me like the flash of a camera at night. "I ask again, who are you, Mira Bracken? And why does everybody want a piece of you?"

"Not now, Naomi." Ramaya stepped between us. She took a

seed from her pocket and blew on it. It blossomed into a stem with a white flower. "Open your mouth, Mira."

I complied. She held the flower over my mouth and squeezed it gently. A single clear drop fell from the pistil onto my tongue.

"That's a valerian flower I've bound to produce a hyper concentrated dose of the sleeping compound. It will put you into a dreamless sleep." Ramaya turned squarely to Naomi. "You may be the Squall of the North, but Mira is my friend. You be gentle with her, or I *will* do something about it."

"It's not a kindness to coddle her," Naomi said.

"No one is being coddled here," Ramaya shot back.

The air held that same static feel of a brewing thunderstorm. I wanted to see where this conversation was going, especially because it was about me, but whatever Ramaya had created really worked. My eyelids slid down like garage doors and I entered a space of infinite nothing.

CHAPTER

TWELVE

The next morning I sat mesmerized as I watched a teen fill what looked like a toy bucket with six different kinds of soda from the soda fountain next to the breakfast buffet. The ballroom that served as a dining hall was full of new faces but all I could do was stare goggle-eyed at the parade of teens drinking their weight in neon liquid before the sun came up. I'd no idea the rootbound bunker was such a lawless place.

Naomi came over holding two steaming thermoses. She followed my line of sight and sighed, watching as another teen filled a golden goblet with whipped cream. "Newly Awakened teens. They're coming so frequently we don't know what to do with them. We're just warehousing them at this point, trying to keep them out of danger."

I nodded, my tongue too heavy to speak.

"Ramaya's potion worked a little too well, huh?"

I blinked, realizing Naomi expected me to answer. I'd been dead asleep for almost a whole day and my throat was still sore from being strangled by the root the other night. "Yarghs," I managed.

Whether it was threats, logical arguments, or their confrontation ending in a night of hand-to-hand combat—whatever Ramaya had done with Naomi also seemed to have worked. The First Magpie sitting across from me wasn't steely eyed and studying me like a microscope slide. She was softer, kinder.

"Ramaya really is something else," Naomi said, almost dreamily. "You should check out her lab when you have a chance."

"Okarmph!" I tried again.

Naomi smiled. "Got it. No more talking. Just eating."

While I forced myself to eat a bowl of granola and oat milk, people kept coming over to say shy hellos to Naomi. She really was a celebrity of the Seven. And she was interested in me.

"You ready?" Naomi clapped a hand on my shoulder.

"Bligarfgh," I said. "Blurgle."

Naomi snorted. "That's the spirit."

We exited the ballroom and rode an elevator up to the surface mansion. Halfway down the garden path, Naomi stopped.

"Godda's curse," she muttered. "I forgot the spoons."

"Shpoons?" I asked.

"Yeah, let's see if we can get you out of your head for a moment."

Naomi kicked off her combat boot and plunged her foot into the dirt, narrowing her eyes in concentration. "Hopefully Dawn's still in the kitchen."

A minute later a root emerged from the ground, two dirty forks braided through its tip. I let out a burst of laughter and to my surprise Naomi joined in. "OK, Dawn, I see how it is." A few seconds later, the root emerged clutching similarly soiled spoons.

"Follow me." Naomi held the spoons in front of her like she was striding into battle.

I tried to quiet the question that had been bubbling in my chest for the last hour but could hold it in no longer. "Why are you so interested in me?" Do you know my secrets? I added in my head.

"You know the answer to that question."

"I don—" I started and then trailed off. "I'm powerful. Really powerful. And a weirdo mystery."

"Welcome to the club, Mira. Over the years, the owls have noticed an unfortunate pattern. It tends to be the most powerful rootbound who share Edeva's vision. Maybe the power goes to their heads. And every once in a while one of them leaves the order and decides to take matters into their own hands. They usually end up inside a Huntsmen siphon, being endlessly tortured while giving their immense power to the enemy."

"*That's* why you're so interested in me? You think I'm going to go rogue?"

"Maybe. You're looking for your sister. You might learn just enough from us to access your powers and then go off on a side quest." Strange. Naomi's voice sounded more like a suggestion than a warning. "But I don't think so," she added. "Kes trusts you. Even more than that, Ramaya trusts you. So I trust you."

You shouldn't, I whispered to Aspen. I *would* go rogue if I thought it would help you, Asp. I would do literally anything.

I'd been going rogue from day one, lying about who I was and what I could do since the moment I joined the rootbound. I didn't say anything back to Naomi, too afraid the woman would sniff out my guilt, see through the lies Kes and I had told, and we lapsed into silence. We reached the forest edge at the far end of the grounds and plunged into the canopy. There was no path but Naomi seemed to know where she was going. She hardly slowed when we entered the densely packed trees, but I on the other hand had to weave around trunks and climb under fallen logs. At no place in particular Naomi stopped and waited for me to catch up.

"Alright," she said. "Time for your next lesson. As gentle as it gets, courtesy of Ramaya." Naomi inhaled deeply. "Focus all of your senses on the forest—feel the spongey softness below your feet, the moistness of the air; smell the spicy, nutty scent of the plant matter and hear the chitter of forest creatures."

I closed my eyes, took a deep breath, and then lost my balance and fell into a heap of half-decomposed leaves. I waited for Naomi's reprimand, but she just helped me off the ground.

"What do you know about the root systems of forests?" she asked.

"Erm." I squirmed. This was my pop quiz nightmare. I racked my brain, mentally flipping through my grade ten biology textbook and the things Kes and Ramaya said. "I know they have some kind of symbiotic relationship with fungi, so that each can get the nutrients they need. The mycorrhizal system. Which is where you get the word Rhiza, I guess."

"Yes. Rhiza is the Greek word for root. That's what we're hunting with our spoons." Naomi knelt next to a tree. "This is a western red cedar, about two hundred years old. Pick a root, any root." She demonstrated, running her hand down the base of the trunk to one of the large roots unspooling into the forest. I picked one right next to hers. "Now you're going to follow that root as far as you can." Again, she went first, tracing the path of the root through the pungent debris of the forest floor until it disappeared into the ground. With obvious reverence, she shifted the topsoil away with her spoon. "Your turn."

Naomi handed the other spoon to me. I knelt next to my own root, trying to ignore the scent, like my parent's compost on the hottest day of the year. I tried to touch the root as little as possible, jabbing my spoon through the wet leaves covering it. I jabbed again and a centipede skittered up the spoon and onto my hand. I just managed to hold in a scream, shaking the bug off back where it came from. I blushed, hoping against hope Naomi wasn't watching and judging. Aspen had been the one who loved playing in the dirt, making friends with the worms and the slugs and the bees. All I could think about was the way the dirt made my palms itch and the feeling of imaginary bugs crawling over my limbs.

"How you doing over there?" Naomi asked, now about ten feet away following the trace of her root.

"Good, good!" I plunged my spoon into the dirt.

"Gentle! Trust you to figure out how to wield a *spoon* with violence." Naomi sighed. "Here, come look at mine."

The First Magpie had created a channel in the ground about a meter long and a hand-span wide. At one end, closest to the tree, the root started out the thickness of a finger, quickly narrowing to the size of a string. As it got thinner it branched and knotted with neighboring roots, creating the illusion of fine lacework against the soil.

"You gotta get closer." Naomi stuck her nose in the channel. The woman had swum with—no, scared off—a swarm of tiger sharks. I could not and would not show her how scared I was to put my face near some dirt. Holding my breath, I leaned in as close as I dared.

"Do you see those thread-like bundles cocooning around the root?"

"Hm-hm," I managed, still holding my breath.

"Those are the fungi threading through the root system of the tree, connecting pretty much every tree in the forest in a gigantic web. In fact, they connect pretty much every square inch of this planet."

"And that's the network you tap into?"

"You too. You already have, in some of the most unusual ways we've ever seen."

There came a flutter of wings and with a sudden swoop a red-tailed hawk broke from the canopy and dropped onto Naomi's wrist. It nuzzled her nose with its beak and then let out a few soft screeches. Naomi screeched back, sounding almost identical, like she had when she'd mimicked me the other day.

"And you're *talking* to that hawk, right?"

"Yeah, just between you and me, I've always been more at ease talking to the animals than the trees, ever since my Awakening."

"What exactly are you saying?"

"Mostly I'm asking them—about their day. If they've noticed anything unusual in the forest. How the trees are faring in the new heat."

"Wow."

"Yeah. We usually use the trees as our eyes and ears, but birdsong is also a great way to give and receive information—it's like the fire alarm of the forest."

"When you say 'use the trees as our eyes and ears,' what exactly do you mean?"

"Trees are communicating all the time, through the web we just saw. More data than a super computer—air quality, weather conditions, disruptions in the forest—they're passing that info through the Rhiza constantly. When the trees sense intruders they release a cascade of chemical reactions through the network, warning other trees in the forest in just a few moments. And the birds take care of the other animals. The trees we rootbound ally with learn other chemical signals for sensing and communicating so they can speak to us in more detail. Mind-blowing, right?"

"Oh yeah. My mind is so blown I think I'm leaking brain matter out of my nose."

Naomi handed me a handkerchief with a sarcastic flourish. "Try to hold it together a little longer; we're almost there."

A few minutes later Naomi stopped in her tracks. I bumped into her back but managed not to fall. She grabbed my hand. "Our mother."

Goosebumps ran up my arms. Before us was a towering red-barked cedar set a little apart from the forest and bathed in golden light.

"This is a mother tree," Naomi said, the reverence back in her voice. "One of the oldest and most densely connected trees in the forest. Her root structure is ancient and strong and she pushes nutrients out through the web towards the other trees that need them, regardless of species. The mother is the one healing Sarah and the other teens through the web. She's like a thousand-year-old IV. Connect to her and you would pick up news from all over the world, trafficked through the web."

"All over the world?"

"With a really good treetalker and enough time, the mother could tell you the weather in Lisbon."

"No. *Through* the Atlantic Ocean?"

"It's not as robust, but the web stretches through the ocean, through a maze of marine fungi in places like coral reefs, and plant matter consumed by fish, sharks, and whales."

Seized by the sudden idea that the mother tree might know where Aspen was, I lurched forward to touch the gnarled red bark.

"No!" Naomi grabbed my wrist. "You might accidentally connect. You're not ready for that much information. It's dangerous without training." She tugged me a few steps backwards, away from the root and then gasped. She bent forward, clutching her knees as if she was going to be sick.

"Naomi?" I croaked. "What is it?"

Instead of answering, she crumpled into the loam of the forest floor. Threadlike roots spun around her like cotton candy. The threads wound around and around the woman, as if woven by an army of invisible spiders.

"What's going on? Can I help you? *Naomi.*"

A hand shot out of the cocoon of threads, grabbing mine, and pulling me closer. "It's too much," Naomi forced out, her voice hoarse. Something was making her very sick.

"What's too much?"

Naomi's fingers tightened around mine and something rushed through the connection of our joined hands. It was sour, corrosive. "The pain you're carrying over your sister."

I was accidentally poisoning Naomi with my grief.

I tried to pull my hand away but she clung to it. I had to stop the poisonous emotions. I heaved in a breath and exhaled so hard air whistled out of my nose. No, that was a caricature of breathing. I breathed in, pushing my ribs up and out like I was opening an umbrella and paused for a count of four. Then I exhaled, pushing air through my pursed lips like I was breathing through a straw. I repeated the steps over and over again, until my ribs stopped gnashing like stuck gears. I couldn't feel the roots but I could feel Naomi, all the thousands of threads of grief and fear wound around her—some from me, some already in her. I reached towards those threads, sending warmth and empathy through as many of the connections between us as I could.

"That's it, Mira," Naomi whispered. "Whatever you're doing, keep going. It's working."

I was binding, but not in the way she thought. Thankfully she seemed too ill to notice. I held us both in my breath, in my body, in the present, until the poisonous emotions dissipated. The roots next to me were rapidly unwinding, reversing their earlier course. Naomi unfurled from the cocoon like a ghostly butterfly, still pale but radiating calm power. She stood and pulled me into a tight hug. I pictured wings wrapping around us, enveloping us in the protection of the forest itself.

"That's it. Breathe, just *breathe*. Have you taken one deep breath since Aspen disappeared?"

Disappeared.

I squeezed my eyes shut against the onslaught triggered by the word. The sound of Aspen screaming, the whimper of her begging for her life. The endless ways I'd imagined her fate. Had I taken a deep breath since my sister had disappeared? Of course not.

"I'm sorry," I whispered into Naomi's shoulder.

Naomi shushed me. "You've been so brave, Mira. Just to survive, to keep going day by day, while carrying that much pain would be enough. And yet you've channeled it into action. Into finding your sister and fighting for a better world."

I trembled and sobbed and Naomi held me for a very long time.

THIRTEEN

Later that night, back in my room, I stared at my bed in hateful longing. Feeling sick with exhaustion, I lowered myself to the edge of the mattress tentatively. My eyes fluttered and my shoulders sagged with relief at the break from gravity.

Suddenly I saw Sarah's beaming face in the blood-red light, heard her whispered, *The Confessor is waiting.* I jumped, tumbling off the bed and hitting my head against soft carpet. They were waiting, waiting for me to fall asleep and find my way back to them. I was sure of it.

Not even sleep was safe anymore. I shuffled over to the toy fridge, grabbing an energy drink the size of my forearm from the shelf. I cracked the top, chanting to myself, "Just a little longer. Just hold on a little longer." I took a sip, wincing as the taste of acid-sweet pineapple bore into my teeth, and slid down the brick wall into a crouch. I tipped my head back to chug when I heard a grating sound from somewhere close, as if one of the bricks in the wall was moving. Without thinking, I threw the can I was holding towards the noise. It collided with something solid and ricocheted back at me, clipping the side of my shoulder.

I caught a darting movement out of the side of my eye and then a thick root wrapped around my hand. "Please don't, I'm on your side—" I cried out, but the root withdrew just as fast as it had come.

I looked down to see several vials containing sprouted valerian flowers—Ramaya's sleeping potion—and a folded piece of paper covered in dirt.

In case you can't sleep either.
-Naomi.

I uncorked a vial and squeezed the flower for a drop of nectar. I dragged myself into the giant bed and had a moment to wonder what was keeping Naomi awake before my brain fell into darkest night.

I woke from a deep, dreamless slumber to Adrian and Tai beaming in my face.

I groaned. "Can just anyone come into my room?"

"Yes," Tai said seriously. "Until you learn the great secret of the rootbound."

"How to use a lock," Adrian said.

"We're here on a mission." Tai sat on the edge of my bed. "We have strict orders to feast you, body, mind, and spirit."

"Translation: to show you around and make sure you rest up."

They marched me back to the ballroom and heaped my plate with toast and tofu scramble.

"Where is Naomi?" I craned my neck, scanning the clusters of people eating breakfast.

"Taking an over-stim day," Tai said. "You know how lots of us are neuro-spicy? Well, when we get overstimulated or dysregulated, we take the day off. Or we're supposed to."

"Rumor has it this is Naomi's first over-stim day in *six* years. The training must be intense."

I flushed and tried to shrug, as if I hadn't seen a living cotton ball wrap itself around Naomi to suck out the poisonous grief I'd accidentally injected her with. "You could say that." I caught sight of a tall, wiry figure out of the corner of my eye—*finally!* I was halfway out of my chair when I realized the figure at the buffet wasn't Kes.

"Looking for someone else?" Adrian wiggled his eyebrows.

Tai elbowed his twin. "Kes is off on a mission. Performing the primary duty of the magpies—'liberating' siphons from the Huntsmen."

"That's why they're called magpies—they love shiny things. Kes is probably seducing a socialite as we speak. They always prefers seduction to stealing." Adrian seemed to be speaking directly to me.

"Kes *seduces* the Huntsmen?" I asked, too loudly.

Tai elbowed his twin again. "*Flirts* with them. And it's not the actual Huntsmen. Many siphons are passed down through wealthy families for generations, ancient heirlooms and all that jazz. Some people today don't even realize the power of their jewels—only that way more people fawn over them when they're wearing them. And ignore Adrian; he's just jealous."

Adrian put his hands up in a you-got-me pose. "It's true. Kes hasn't been this excited about a new person in a *whole* week."

"They're...excited about me?" I asked.

Adrian rolled his eyes. "Of course that's the part you focus on. Hurry, we gotta show you the Lark's Nest. It's the coolest space in the Hub."

Adrian zoomed ahead. I looked at my half-eaten toast and grudgingly followed, walking at a slower pace with Tai. "Kes is excited about me?" I asked again, finding it easier to talk to Tai without the overwhelming presence of his rootbound twin.

"They *are*." Tai smiled. "You should see your face."

"Is it as purple as I think it is?"

Tai shrugged. "Purple suits you."

"You're so gentle," I blurted.

"Thank you."

"But Adrian is so…" I trailed off, picturing my school guidance counsellor begging me to stop talking.

"Adrian's been through a lot," Tai said simply and I turned a deeper shade of eggplant.

Adrian shot out of a door a few feet in front of us. "Finally!" He grabbed my hand and dragged me into a cavernous room shaped like a sphere. The walls were covered in hundreds of screens. My eyes darted from one image of despair to the next—fires, floods, hurricanes, tanks. One headline screamed, "HOTTEST DAY ON RECORD." I closed my eyes against the onslaught, feeling simultaneously overwhelmed and frozen.

"Plug her in. Hurry, Tai," Adrian urged.

"Right, of course. Mira, I'm going to touch your wrist if that's OK."

I tried to focus on what Tai was saying but my brain was pulling on all the other threads of despair in my life—glimpses of Aspen, of apocalyptic futures, of Sarah limp and bruised— weaving them together into a raging tornado of horror and fear. There was a gentle pressure on my wrist and then what felt like a giant warm hand scooping me up and yanking me out of the tornado. I opened my eyes to see the twins staring at me in concern.

"How did you do that?" I asked.

Adrian nodded towards my arm where a cuff of incredibly fine woven mesh was now looped around the skin of my wrist. I held it up to examine and felt the slightest tug of resistance. I looked closer and saw threads spinning out of the cuff towards the center of the room. I'd been so distracted by the screens I hadn't noticed the most striking feature of the space—a thick circular pillar of roots braided together like computer cables in the dead center.

"Is this a mycelium bracelet? Connected to...that thing?" I gestured at the pillar of roots, which was now shifting and churning.

"Carbon replicas," Tai answered. "The thinnest ever made. Apparently energy can flow through them from the Rhiza, at least over short distances. Ramaya rigged up the whole thing."

Adrian added, "Larks were dropping like flies trying to take in all of the news. More over-stim days than every other unit combined."

"But can't treetalkers just connect to the Rhiza?" I asked.

Tai didn't meet my eyes. "Well...yes. That's why I didn't plug you in right away."

"Oh, right, Naomi told me not to connect to the Rhiza outside of our lessons," I lied, hating myself as the twins nodded at me.

"How about a tour?" Adrian offered brightly. Before I could answer, he spoke, "So this wing of the Nest is lovingly nick-named Death Valley, cause it's where hope comes to die. Larks take turns monitoring the news and broader media for Huntsmen propaganda. We focus on news within Salish Sea Hub's jurisdiction—Oregon, Washington, and British Columbia."

"Obviously not all corporate propaganda is Huntsmen propaganda, but we try to keep an eye on all of it."

I took in the dozen or so people sitting or standing in front of the screens and tried to wrap my head around the enormity of their task. "Why?"

"Cause the two are mutually reinforcing. A constant drum beat of 'Don't care. Don't worry. Don't look. Don't change. Oh, and if you do look, and care, and worry, and want to change— we're the ones who will save you from the climate crisis.' Honestly their propaganda is more powerful than their leeching. The Confessor is probably the one who writes their children's books."

I noticed an older woman with purple hair who looked familiar reading a book with a big-eared dog on the cover. "They write children's books?"

"Oh yeah. Look up fossil fuel industry children's books, or gun lobby children's books, and you'll go down a very dark rabbit hole."

I felt the familiar river of overwhelm tug at my knees, trying to sweep me into its current. The woven cuff vibrated so hard it burned against my skin, and a rush of calming energy shot up my arm and through my body.

"Don't worry—we're almost out of Death Valley." Adrian motioned at me to hurry as we continued our way around the circular nest. The other half of the vaulted room could not have had a more different vibe. There was a pyramid of books twice my height stacked in rainbow order with a little hand-scrawled sign: *Mount Intersectional Sci-Fi, Elevation .01 KM*. I had the urge to scramble up the spines and tumble down again. Colorful protest art hung across every free surface. Instead of the hundreds of screens of Death Valley, this side of the Nest was dominated by a giant wall of greenery in gorgeous textures and hues, like the world's biggest patchwork quilt. After a moment I realized it was a living map with each continent represented by a different type of lichen and moss. Tiny blooms burst open across the continents, hundreds and hundreds more appearing with every breath.

"Every time a lark comes across a person or story embodying climate action, we feed it into the 'Rooting and Resisting Board.' Every Nest in every Hub in the world has one. A reminder of how many people are taking up their small piece of the work every second."

I watched hundreds more blooms burst open. "This is every climate action ever taken?"

Adrian laughed. "This is every climate action taken *today*. It'll reset at midnight."

I let out a low whistle and couldn't help but feel hope welling inside of me at my friend's words. "Just today? But I don't understand; why did the larks set the Nest up like this? It's literally like night and day. Heaven and hell."

"When new larks join they have to do the journey of the ten circles—" Adrian started.

Tai cut in, "Basically they just have to walk around the Nest ten times."

"Hey—cute and sardonic is *my* thing. You're supposed to be the earnest one."

Tai rolled his eyes. "It's supposed to be a sacred reminder that many people live only on one side of the Nest. For more and more young people—that's Death Valley."

"That's certainly where I've been living," I said.

"But both sides of the Nest are true and real," Tai said. "There is grief and there is hope, living side by side."

My arm yanked back and up and I yelped in surprise. The girl with the turquoise septum-piercing from lunch the other day stood a few feet away, fumbling with something I couldn't see. "Sorry," she said, edging past us, "I didn't realize anyone else was cuffed."

Adrian shook his head. "The big downside of the cuffs—they tangle easily."

"Usually you're supposed to take it off if you're moving," Tai said.

I pulled my cuff away from my friends without thinking—I didn't want to take it off.

A crew of youth sat around a table writing what looked like postcards. One girl was writing each word in a different color gel pen while another lark did cartoon doodles on his cards. He looked up and said, "Tai. Adrian. New girl. All hands on deck—you want to come help?"

"Actually, we probably should," Tai said. "They're writing postcards to youth in early voting states and they're trying to get 500,000 postcards sent."

I mumbled, "No thank you."

"Let me guess," Turquoise Septum Piercing chimed in. "Getting out the vote isn't 'cool' enough for the big, bad magpies."

"Not a magpie," I said, matching the challenge in her tone. "And not really a fan of electoral politics."

"You think we are?!"

Tai put a hand on Turquoise Septum Piercing's shoulder. "Hanna, I know it's frustrating, but Mira's new here and still learning how we do things."

"I'm just *so* tired of the magpies treating us like dirt because we try to keep actual fascists from controlling what remains of our public infrastructure—schools, hospitals, transit."

"Again, *not* a magpie," I answered. "And like every politician ever has failed us. Democrats. Republicans. Left. Right. They're all the same."

"That's literally Huntsmen propaganda."

"No that's how I think."

"That's how you *think* you think, but you've been exposed to hundreds of thousands of pieces of Huntsmen propaganda over your lifetime. And word on the street is you're pretty susceptible to things."

"What are you talking—"

"The rich man in his castle, the poor man at his gate—" Hanna mouthed the words so only I could hear.

I felt something in me stir at the song, dragging me away from the present moment, away from Salish Sea Hub.

"*Enough*," Naomi hissed, walking straight through the wall, a cloud of bats at her back. Every head in the Lark's Nest turned in her direction, eyes wide. The First Magpie was wearing her usual black, emphasizing how ghostly pale she looked after yesterday's adventure. "Lark," she said, capturing Hanna in her pale gaze, "what's your name?"

Hanna shrank in on herself. "She was repeating Huntsmen propaganda points, saying electoral politics are useless—"

"So you decided to publicly shame her in front of a group of people she doesn't know? What an *effective* way to convince her." Naomi's lip curled and I thanked every goddess I knew that I was not on the receiving end of her anger. "Your name. *Now*."

"Hanna. Hanna Brookman."

Naomi acknowledged the woman's answer with the barest nod and turned, clearly dismissing her. "Mira, there's somebody I'd like to introduce you to." She gestured for me to follow her.

As we walked back around the circular Nest towards Death Valley Adrian stage whispered, "Have fun peddling beef tallow on RikRok when they kick you out of the order, Hanna," and I felt a wild desire to throw my arms around my new friend.

Naomi led me to the purple-haired older woman reading the picture book. I realized where I'd seen her before—the rootbinding. She was the order's archivist.

Before Naomi or I could speak, the woman stood and pulled me into a warm hug. "Mira, is it?" the woman whispered as she held me tight. "I'm Teddy. So lovely to meet you." The longer the older woman held me, the more tension eased from my body. At Naomi's sigh of impatience we drew apart. "Pull up a chair, my dears."

I plopped myself down into the offered chair but Naomi stayed standing. "Ramaya threatened to unleash her zombie ants on me if I left the sick bay for more than an hour. I've got to get back."

"Of course, of course. Nothing more important than protecting yourself from oversaturation." Teddy looked suddenly solemn. "Take the whole week off, Naomi, please. We need you well."

Without speaking or changing her face, Naomi managed to convey a giant "yeah right" before disappearing back into the wall. One of her bats stayed behind to curl up in Teddy's hair and she stroked it absentmindedly.

I took in the plate of cookies and crumbs scattered across what looked like hundreds of books and pamphlets on the long wooden table. "Is that sheet music?"

Teddy nodded. "The first example of a fragment of The Confessor's song. From the nineteenth century. Jam tart? I made them fresh from wild berries this morning."

"Sure." While I worked my way through the cookie, I studied the book Teddy was holding. It had a small boy in blue overalls and a dog playing near an oil drum. "*The Adventures of Ollie Oil*. Is the song in that children's book?"

"Parts of it. Terrible I know, but sadly nothing new. The Huntsmen are always seeding their propaganda in popular media—TV, movies, influencers. The song has shown up here and there for more than a century, but now it's something much more dangerous."

"The song is a kind of leeching, isn't it? It takes over your mind?"

Teddy shot me a surprised look. "Exactly. But it shouldn't be possible. Viral leeching that can be passed from person to person completely divorced in time and space from whoever originally set it in motion." She gestured at the hundreds of books. "The mystery is consuming me. What has changed, Mira? *What has changed?*"

"Does Naomi think I can help? Because...because I'm more vulnerable to the song?"

"Naomi thinks you can help because you're smart and curious. And because you don't give a fig about rootbound protocol or history. The Huntsmen are clearly using fresh tactics; we need fresh eyes."

I blushed and tried to think of how to respond to the compliment. I was saved by Adrian's echoing shout through the Nest, "Rihanna, I need Rihanna! Play something with an actual beat and watch me write all 500,000 postcards myself. IN CURSIVE."

CHAPTER
FOURTEEN

In the week that followed, I found myself drawn back to the Lark's Nest and the warmth of the purple-haired archivist over and over again. Naomi was still recovering, and Kes and Ramaya were AWOL so I had nothing else to do with my time, and Teddy always welcomed me with open arms and a new flavor of jam tart. I felt a gnawing guilt that I was not more actively using my newfound connection with the rootbound to find Aspen. But I smothered the feeling by throwing myself into exploring my new home and joining the communal fun of mealtimes in the dining hall. Tai and Adrian introduced me to a stream of new people and caught me up on all the juicy gossip of Salish Sea Hub. I had to admit the rootbound and their chaotic joy were growing on me, especially as I got to spend time with people and away from the roots.

I hummed contentedly to myself as I wound my way towards the Nest through the underground bunker, the navigation of which I had nearly mastered. Just before the entrance to the Nest, Aspen's voice came sharply in my mind.

Watch out!

A stone-like hand closed over my mouth and dragged me backwards into a cramped, airless space. I tried to scream but all that came out was an *hhhrrmps*. My eyes adjusted to the dim light. I was in some kind of AV closet, where the wires and routers for the hundreds of TVs and computers were stored. The stony hand on my shoulder relaxed and I craned my neck to see Sheldon, the redhead who had driven the tram.

He's a lichenfist, he could really hurt you if he turns his hands to stone, Aspen hissed.

Sheldon turned a wild stare on me. "Please, no more. No more singing." Holding my jaw in one hand, he tore at the fabric of his shirt with the other. He was going to stuff the fabric in my mouth—I was sure of it. It was exactly how the fake nurse had fought me, clamping my jaw while preparing to jab me with a needle. The panic and the rage from that day in the hospital roared back to life. I jerked my head back, tearing myself loose from Sheldon's grip and kicked his shin as violently as I could muster. He let out a sharp yowl and backed away from me, eyes darting side to side.

"I'm not—"

"No singing!" he yelled and fled out the door.

I stumbled after him, into a crowd of confused larks. "He attacked me! He's getting away!"

"Mira?" came Naomi's voice and then a yelp. The crowd parted to reveal the First Magpie standing over Sheldon whimpering on the floor. She had his wrist caught in her hand and was twisting his arm in an impossible angle.

"What's going on?" Naomi demanded.

Sheldon pointed the finger of his free hand at me. "She was singing The Confessor's song, I heard her. Don't let her open her mouth. She'll infect us all."

"That's not true!" I yelled.

"Enough," Naomi commanded and Sheldon and I quieted.

She scanned the room slowly, and then released Sheldon's arm. "Tell me exactly what you saw?"

"I was on tech maintenance duty," Sheldon said. "And I heard her humming. I recognized the melody; it's the same song my cousin started singing after we rescued him from the Huntsmen. I knew it was dangerous so I grabbed her and pulled her into the server room."

Naomi's face softened. "Quick thinking, Sheldon, thank you."

"You're thanking him!" I exploded. "He assaulted me!"

"Sheldon, report to the infirmary. In fact, everyone here, after your shift, visit the infirmiry for a root scan. Mira, come with me."

Something in her tone forestalled any argument. I followed her out of the Lark's Nest and back to the surface mansion. The rage clawed against my ribcage, climbing into my throat. As soon as we were in the garden away from earshot, I growled, "You're *thanking* Sheldon? For essentially kidnapping me?" I dug my nails into my palms.

"Let it all out, Mira," Naomi replied.

"What?"

"The anger. At Sheldon. At me. At the world. Scream. Scream at the top of your lungs. I'll do it too." She threw her head back and howled. After a moment, I joined. The rage catapulted out of my throat, tearing at my vocal chords as I screamed louder than I ever had before.

There was a long silence. Free of the rage and the panic, I had a moment of clarity to reflect on the occurrence. An unwelcome thought slithered to the surface. "You think that I *was* singing the song."

"Can you be certain you weren't?" Naomi asked. "I don't see why Sheldon would make it up."

"I guess...maybe. But you said yourself the song was everywhere."

"When rootbound are together our collective bond to each other and the trees protects us from the song." Naomi gestured for me to follow her into the grounds. "We're only vulnerable after severe leeching, the kind of leeching that happens when the Huntsmen drain us with a siphon. You're the only rootbound I've seen with a connection to the Rhiza who is affected in this way. But this incident gives us an opportunity."

We reached the edge of the forest and plunged inside. After almost an hour of hard walking, we came upon the mother tree just as streaks of pink twilight appeared in the sky. The roots rose like serpents to meet us and we practically fell into their twining embrace.

"I want you to connect to the mother tree," Naomi said.

"Didn't you say it was dangerous? That I'm not ready?"

"It is and you're not. But for whatever reason, the song affects you differently than anyone else. It's possible that you are hearing the song in a way that other people aren't. That your exposure comes from a different place. It's a long shot, but if you connect to the mother tree, the Rhiza might be able to follow the path of the song back to the source. And if we find the source, we can stop it. Are you willing to try?"

A slender root lifted up and hovered before my forehead.

"OK," I said. "Let's do it."

The root slid forward and touched my forehead. I expected some kind of pain or shock after Naomi's warning, but instead it was...pleasant.

"What do you feel, Mira?"

"I can feel...Aspen. But it's nice somehow, like my body is reliving all of our best memories together. The smell of vegan banana bread. The press of our ribs together."

"It's natural Aspen would come to mind," Naomi said,

sounding far away. "See if you can move past it. Think of the song. Try and focus on the melody."

"I can't seem to focus on anything…"

Naomi didn't respond. In fact, I couldn't see her anymore, or even the mother tree or the forest. I was falling, slowly, down a tunnel of memories, pulled deeper and deeper into a current of sensation…

I was on a train, rushing by scene after joyful scene of my life. I pushed my face against the window, taking in a Christmas from when I was four or five. I'd felt drunk, dizzy with anticipation for the magic of Santa visiting our house. Aspen had snuck into my bed, cuddling me. I'd been scratching all over, itching with the overwhelm. She'd taken my hands, cuddling me close to her chest, coaching me to breathe until the excitement went from painful rush to a gentle shiver. Later, we'd heard the scrape of reindeer hooves against our roof. We'd clung to each other, shrieking and giggling, euphoric at knowing we were part of the magic, part of the story. Santa had come to *our* house! For years I'd tried to get Aspen to admit that she'd made the sound, secretly running her nails across my wooden headboard. But she never did. She wouldn't be the one who killed the magic.

Smells filled the train compartment as I hurtled on towards the memory of that Christmas morning and so many others. Fresh pine, cinnamon buns rising in the oven, the cherry tartness of hard candies, which our parents always tucked into our stockings and which we would eat a row at a time, stuffing our cheeks like squirrels. Mint. Mint in candy canes, in hot chocolate, in peppermint bark. The train went on and on, each memory infinite and yet passing in the blink of an eye. Finally the train rolled into pitch black and I was lost to my memories.

I crept into Aspen's room, desperate to tell her my news. Alex liked me back. *Alex liked me back!* We'd snuck a kiss at our crew's weekly 90s movie marathon. During the snack break between *Clueless* and *10 Things I Hate About You* we'd found each other in the pantry of our pal's enormous house.

My sister was sitting at her window, an outstretched hand full of seeds and berries, like some kind of Grecian deity. Ravens swooped down to feast and take off back into the branches of Bonnie, our cherry tree. Aspen didn't turn even though I knew she could hear me.

"Sis, guess, what?!" I called.

"Oh, a guessing game—my *favorite*. Did you make another boring friend? Ace a meaningless test? Find a new person to endlessly obsess over? Why do you keep choosing such a small, pointless life, Mira? Why do you insist on being like everyone else in this hellish suburbia?"

Tears sprung to my eyes. "Just because you don't have any friends doesn't mean it's pointless to have friends!"

"You think it's some kind of victory to be friends with Krish? Who hasn't looked up from his phone for more than ten minutes total since we've known him? With Jonnie? Whose only source of news seems to be memes of rich women fighting? With Alex—"

"No. STOP. You know how I feel about Alex."

"I know *how* you feel, the bigger mystery is *why*—"

"Aspen! I get that everything in the world feels terrible. Pointless. Stupid. But I'm here. I'm still here. What am I supposed to do? Give up on it all?"

No, no, no. I shook my head, not wanting to remember this version of my sister—how cynical, how controlling, how cruel she could be. I closed my eyes and jammed my hands over my ears until once again I was lost to the darkness. When I opened my eyes I was in a greenhouse. Aspen watered a row of seedlings, singing softly to herself. All the flowers in the space seemed to reach towards her, grasping. They had always done that hadn't they? Bloomed a little brighter when Aspen was in the room. I tried to focus in on Aspen's face but she wouldn't look up. She just kept singing. The hairs on the back of my neck raised as if somebody had brushed a cold hand down my spine.

"The rich man in his castle, the poor man at his gate..."

"Aspen," I whispered at the same time as a man's voice said my sister's name. She looked up, as if finally seeing me. But instead of joy she wore an expression like she'd seen a killer. "Get out of here. NOW!" she commanded.

I flung backwards, falling and falling and falling. I jolted awake to realize the mother tree had wrapped a root around my waist and was pulling me into the ground.

"No," Naomi shouted, pulling at the root. "No, mother, please. It's my fault, she wasn't ready. She's one of us."

Naomi shoved her elbows into the ground, whispering rapidly. Something was growing around me, cotton candy spinning to protect me. And then a tree branch swung into my side like a baseball bat.

CHAPTER

FIFTEEN

I woke to an alien landscape. The shine of the place made me wince—it was like an industrial kitchen crossed with a Lego set, with arms, scopes, and antennas poking out everywhere. "You're back," I croaked and tried to sit up. Oh great—I was in another hospital bed.

"Careful, Mira." Kes put a hand on my shoulder. "You've had a...rough time of it. Try not to talk or move too much."

"Where have you been? Wait, what happened to your cheek?" I moved to touch a fresh scar on their cheek but they grabbed my hand and guided it back to my side.

Kes groaned. "Mira, please. I'm worried about you. *We're* worried about you."

I opened my mouth to protest but was cut off by Adrian's shout of, "She's AWAKE!" He zoomed into the room, almost colliding with my bed. A moment later Tai followed.

"No fair," Adrian whined. "I want Kestrel, descendant of the Seven, as my personal nursemaid." He stared at Kes's hand still holding mine. I blushed and let go, but Kes held tighter.

"I guess I'll just have to get attacked by a mother tree,"

147

Adrian continued. "Not that I have even the slightest idea how to do that—"

"Adrian," Tai groaned. "Read the room."

"The mother tree...attacked me?" The moments before I'd blacked out rushed back to me. The full body sense of Aspen. Of rightness. Of aliveness. And then that horrible look. Those haunted eyes. "I have...I have to go," I managed, wrenching my hand from Kes's and rolling out of the bed before they could stop me. When my foot landed it felt like I'd stepped onto a scalpel and I teetered onto a metal robot arm. I could feel a deep cut in the arch of my foot—had the mother tree stabbed me?

Kes moved towards me but I put my hands up. "No, stay back! Stay back!"

"Why, Mira?" they whispered, their steady gaze holding mine.

I backed away from them, clanging into trays, scattering gauze and scissors across the room. I kept backing away until Tai grabbed me from behind, pulling me into a gentle hug. I leaned against his tall frame and let the sobs come.

"Can't they see I'm poison?" I whispered in Tai's ear. "There's something wrong with me. Everyone around me gets hurt."

"You're not poison." He kept repeating it, rocking me gently in the hug.

"You're not poison." Kes joined the hug.

"You're not poison," Adrian said, the front of his wheelchair nudging affectionately into my knees as he joined the hug. "Except for your breath. You need a tic-tac."

Adrian's stupid joke broke the tension and laughter flowed out of me like water from a burst dam. The others joined in; Kes clutching their belly, Tai leaning against the wall to support himself.

"Oof, I needed that." Kes wiped a tear from their eye. "Come on, let's get out of here."

"Adrian and I were thinking of taking Mira to see the mural today," Tai said. "Something fun and easy."

"What's the mural?" I asked.

"Hop on," Adrian said. "And we'll show you." He pressed a button on his chair and a second seat folded out of the back. "Ramaya rigged—."

"Ramaya rigged it up for you," I said at the same time, finishing a now-familiar phrase in Salish Sea Hub. "She does kind of hold the place up, doesn't she?"

"Oh yeah, without Ramaya," Kes started, "we'd be goners."

I made myself comfortable and we set off, winding our way through the tunnels in a small procession. After stopping for a herd of dogs and cats rescued from a kill shelter and taking a detour around a hall where someone had accidentally released a deadly poison from a clump of giant mushrooms, we arrived at an Olympic-sized swimming pool. But unlike other pools I'd been to, the tiled walls were completely covered in colorful graffiti.

"We've been running an unofficial art therapy thing in here," Tai said.

"Art anarchy," said Adrian.

Tai gestured at a life-sized image of Bezos, Musk, and Zuckerberg in a deep embrace on a rocket ship. The rocket ship could only be described as extremely phallic. "This is some of the lighter stuff. Real PG compared to the other corners."

Adrian picked a can of spray paint from a cluster on the floor and gave Bezos a villainous mustache. "Ah, I feel better already."

I climbed gingerly off of Adrian's chair and limped along the graffitied wall. It was beautiful, the mosaic of emotions spilling out in hundreds of colors and images. I stopped at a little girl swallowing a snake made of fire, next to a graveyard of stick figures. Somebody had stenciled a message beneath. *Here lie my dreams of future children. May they slumber peacefully and never meet this broken world.* "This is the lighter stuff?"

"Obviously we all have *a lot* of feelings about what's happening in the world." Tai admired a drawing of a teen trying to unscrew their own head with one hand and tear out their heart with the other. "Feelings that need to go somewhere so we can complete our stress response cycles, as Ramaya would say."

"What in Godda's name are you doing?" Naomi's voice echoed through the cavernous space. We froze like naughty schoolchildren. All of us except Kes. They strode forward with the walk of someone whose family had been around for a thousand years.

"Taking Mira for some art therapy," Kes said casually. "Want to join?" They grabbed a can of spray paint and tossed it to Naomi. She snatched it like it was a grenade about to explode.

"Welcome back," she said, in a way that suggested she was not pleased about the development.

"Thank you," Kes said. "I see you've taken it upon yourself to train Mira while I've been away."

They stood like alley cats—tensed, ready to pounce. Over me. I was the source of this tension.

"Indeed," Naomi said. "And to that end, I would like to take Mira on her first mission."

"That's ridiculous," Kes fumed. "Mira's a member of Salish Sea Hub. She's been in the order less than a month. She's just barely getting to know the Rhiza here."

"Mira has already proven she has the grit needed to face the Huntsmen, and she's connecting with the Huntsmen's new weapons in ways nobody else has managed," Naomi said. "I believe the sooner we get her into action the better. The Council agrees. I conferred with them this morning and after hearing my report, they approved her for fieldwork."

"I don't believe it."

"You're welcome to check."

"I will." Kes strode to the wall and punched their fist into a bare patch of earth.

"What's going on?" I asked, confused.

"The Council of the Seven are the highest governing body in the order," Tai whispered to me. "Usually the most powerful and respected rootbound. They don't meet like a typical council, instead supporting their own movements around the world. But because they're such powerful treetalkers they can vote and communicate from around the globe in close to real-time through the Rhiza."

Kes pulled their arm out of the dirt, looking stricken. "This is...what have you done, Naomi?"

"The right thing. Of course, Mira must consent." Naomi addressed me. "Listen, Mira, I was right—after you connected to the mother tree, the Rhiza was able to trace the song, kind of like tracing a phone call. The Rhiza has reported its renewed presence all over the world—every continent and growing exponentially. Hot spots include parts of Australia and Wales, Rhode Island, and..." Naomi trailed off.

"What?" Kes probed.

"Seattle," Naomi said.

"So I could've been exposed more and earlier than the others? That's why I'm so vulnerable?" I asked, ashamed at the hope that crept into my voice, hope that I wasn't just broken.

"It seems likely. I'm going to Rhode Island ASAP. The owls heard a rumor The Confessor might be at a party there and we have no time to waste with the song spreading so quickly and our defenses against it weakening for reasons unknown. Come with me?"

"Mira needs to rest," Kes insisted. "She needs more training."

"Do you want to know a secret?" Naomi said to me, ignoring Kes. "That whale that I saved with my Awakening, Bright Delve—we were rootbound. One of the few interspecies pairs in the history of the Seven. I could feel her feelings. Hear her thoughts, even at great distances. While I was carrying out missions for the order, I could feel her plunging the frigid depths of the ocean, and she gave me strength. But...she was... she is gone." Naomi's voice trembled. She paused. No one said anything. "I would do anything to bring Bright Delve back. She was my kin. But I don't have that option. You do. You have a chance to find your sister. To help hundreds, thousands more. But you're not going to do it putzing around Salish Sea Hub."

"Can I think about it?" I asked, although I already knew my answer. Naomi knew how to hook her prey.

"Yes, of course. We leave tomorrow at dawn."

"Why the rush?" Kes said. "What are you not telling us?"

Naomi looked at her watch. "I have to prep for the trip. I'm sorry for the short notice, Mira." Her eyes burned. "And remember, Kes, you can't protect everyone. The only way out is through. It's Mira's life."

Tai and Adrian clapped and whooped as Naomi departed.

"Good luck tomorrow," Adrian shouted.

"Wow, did you hear that?" Tai said. "So cool. And so sad."

"Really?" Kes said. "She's put Mira in danger. And there's something she's not telling us."

"Naomi's right," I said, quietly. "You can't protect me. I have to learn to protect myself."

"You're going with her tomorrow, aren't you?" Kes said.

I looked away, not meeting their eyes. "Are you mad?"

"For Godda's sake," Kes exclaimed. "No, I'm not mad at you. I'm sorry. It's an impossible choice. But I'm not going to let Naomi do everything her way. Can you two make sure Mira gets back safely?" Kes squeezed my arm and loped towards the door.

"Nobody loves a dramatic exit more than Kes." Adrian pretended to fan himself. "Wait, are you crying? They're hot, but not that hot."

I snorted through the tears and Adrian winked at me. I shot a glance at Tai, beginning to understand their bond. Adrian's seemingly out-of-touch exuberance was in part a much-needed break from the seriousness of the world.

"Why do I feel so sad to say goodbye?" I sniffled. "Is it trauma bonding?"

Adrian squeezed my arm. "Cause we're amazing, obviously. For the record, I'm just a little more amazing, right?"

"I feel like coming of age in this world is just trauma bonding," Tai said. "But we would've been friends in the real world too. I would've found you in honors psych."

"I need a distraction," I said, through a face full of tears and snot.

"To the darker ends of the pool?" Adrian asked, eyes glinting.

"I wouldn't," Tai said. "Seriously."

"Race ya?" Adrian plunged down a steep incline.

Tai rolled his eyes. "Give him five seconds and he'll remember you're injured. Five. Four. Three—"

Adrian hurtled back over the edge of the pool, like the first car on a roller coaster. "Sorry, sorry. I forgot, I'm the worst."

"What's that?" I asked, pointing at an image that had caught my eye. "Is that a baby Adrian?" The little boy had big blue eyes and freckles and seemed to wave us over with a mischievous smile.

"There's more of them." Tai wrapped an arm around me to take most of my weight.

"What a dumpling," Adrian cried at an image of the little boy sticking his hand into somebody's pocket and putting a finger to his lips.

"You've got a real Banksy in the order," I murmured. We moved along searching for the images among a sea of others.

"What's he holding in that one?"

"I can't quite tell." I squinted and we moved closer.

"Don't look," Tai said urgently. But I'd already seen. It was a bone—the little boy was holding what looked like a human arm bone. Clinging to Tai, I shuffled forward, scanning for the next image as if possessed.

"I never come back this far," Adrian whispered. "Who knew our wholesome rootbound kin could be so freaky? I'm both weirdly proud and seriously terrified."

There, at the very darkest corner of the pool, was an image of the little blond boy tossing another bone onto a pile of skeletons. Underneath was scrawled: *The Confessor is coming. Hide your sins.*

"New game!" Adrian yelled.

"Does that mean something to you two?" I asked. "What's going on? Why is this here?" I saw Sarah's feverish eyes again, telling me The Confessor wanted to talk to me.

"New game," Adrian pleaded.

"It's just a dumb joke," Tai said. "In really, really poor taste. Let's get out of here."

They ushered me away from the graffitied pool to a sauna that someone had also turned into a greenhouse for tropical plants. After a nice steam and gentle massage from a friendly palm tree, we wound up in the ballroom, which was now hosting a chaotic yoga session with the rootbound and the swarm of rescued cats and dogs. We helped ourselves to some vegan ice cream from the freezer and, after wading through an impromptu dance party, the twins delivered me back to my room.

As soon as I flopped into bed, a root unfurled from a nook in the wall and dropped a dirty piece of paper onto my lap. Carefully I brushed the paper off and read it:

Sorry for the quick exit—had to go see about getting reassigned. If you're going with Naomi tomorrow, I'm going too. I got you into this mess. Gotta at least stick around until you're out of it.
— Kes

I smiled and clutched the note to my chest. Then another root burst out after the first one with another piece of paper; it looked like a dirty napkin.

What? You and Kes are trying to sneak out on a mission without me? As if. I'll see you in the AM, suckers. Oh, and I'm driving—obviously.

It wasn't signed, but you didn't have to be a genius to know who it was from.

SIXTEEN

I woke to find Kes dozing next to me, clutching my hand like a lifeline. How had I never realized how long and dark Kes's eyelashes were? I fought an impulse to reach out and touch them, to trace the line of their cheeks, suddenly overwhelmingly aware of how close we were, our limbs tangled in soft sheets, our breath warm against each other. I trembled with the wish that this was something else, that we belonged to each other in this way, that I could roll over and close the distance between us. I sat up abruptly, pulling my hand from theirs.

We were lying in bed in the rear of the private jet we'd stolen from the Huntsmen what seemed like a lifetime ago. This time, it was a far nicer scene, with clean linens and tiers of happy Pothos plants instead of zombie ants and hog-tied mercenaries.

Kes's eyes cracked open. "You're awake," they rasped.

"Look who's talking," I said wryly.

"Did I...was I *sleeping*?" They shook their head. "I must've dozed off for a moment. I've been pretty drained. How are you?"

"Honestly? Weirdly good," I said. "My foot still hurts a bit, but Zo's healing method is so potent that the rest of my pain has temporarily vanished."

"Can I double-check? You need to be able to move in case anything happens." They gestured at my injured limb and I nodded. As they traced cool hands over my skin I wondered with a full-body blush if willbinders could read thoughts in addition to planting them. "Want to try putting weight on it?"

They pulled me up to stand and I let the momentum carry me right into their chest. They put their hands on my lower back to steady me, and I nestled my face into their neck without thinking. "*Mira*—" Kes whispered.

The door flew open as Ramaya called, "Is she awake?"

Kes and I scrambled away from each other.

"Oh, you're *very* much awake, I see," Ramaya said. "Can you two weirdos stop trying to jump each other's bones every time I leave the room for one second? Or is that like your turn—"

"Ramaya!" Kes barked, tackling their friend into a headlock. "I'll never get over how you switch between competent genius and thirteen-year-old at a sleepover."

I watched them tussle good-naturedly while I tried to regain the ability to speak through the crush of embarrassment. Finally, I forced out, "Where's Naomi?"

"In a huddle with the First Owl," Kes answered. "Getting a final intelligence update. Apparently there have been dozens of rumored Confessor sightings all over the world in just the last day. Meaning this whole thing is a giant waste of time and energy. Like I said before, you should be back at Salish Sea Hub resting."

I shrugged. "What will I have to do again?"

"Honestly, just enjoy the party and practice staying calm."

"It's what we magpies call a crash-and-dash," Ramaya added. "Covert surveillance of elites to look for gems that could be siphons."

"It's basically just a shiny excuse for magpies to party on yachts and flirt with socialites," a new voice added. A person in their early twenties with shining purple hair down to their elbows entered the jet bedroom.

"Mira, this is Raj, our peacock for the evening," Kes said. "He's been travelling around North American hubs showing us some of the innovations coming out of South Asian hubs. He joined us when we made a short pitstop outside of DC and we're very lucky to have him." Kes winked at the new man.

I took in Raj's perfectly constructed suit and eyebrows. "You're a...stylist?"

"Don't let the gorgeous eyebrows fool you," said Kes. "Raj is also our weapons outfitter."

"Not that I can add much to Ramaya's kit," Raj said. "Are you gonna let me see those zombie ants sometime?"

"But, um, don't like half the Huntsmen know what I look like?" I said. "From the protest in Seattle?"

"Ah, don't worry, you're not the first to have an epic Awakening," Raj said. "It's a magpie's job to make a scene. And a peacock's job to make sure they don't get caught."

"You'd think it'd be a peacock's job to make a scene," I muttered, not convinced.

Raj laughed. "Fair enough—I get why you're skeptical. Our job *is* getting harder, with cameras and facial recognition everywhere. But we've got something pretty dang cool up our sleeve." Raj pulled something out of his literal sleeve with a flourish, holding up what looked like a can of spray paint.

"When did the peacocks get so corny?" Kes asked, batting their eyelashes.

"I'm going to spray you with the finest threads of mycorrhizal netting—essentially invisible to the naked eye but enough to distort your image. There isn't a facial recognition software in the world that would clock you with Inviso-Net on your face," Raj said proudly.

"*So* corny," Ramaya said.

"May I?" Raj asked.

I nodded and heard a gentle whoosh as Raj circled the spray can around my head, but I couldn't see anything coming out of the cylindrical container.

"You're not going to make a joke about the *Emperor's New Clothes*?" Raj said.

I'd been about to do exactly that. "Too easy."

Kes put a hand on my arm. "There most likely won't be any real Huntsmen at this party. Just the people who benefit from their work, wittingly or unwittingly."

"Oligarchs," Raj said. "Hottie oligarchs. Hotti-garchs."

"Oligarchs?" I asked.

"Anyone with a yacht. Or a private jet."

"Aren't we on a private jet?" I asked.

Ramaya groaned. "Not the weaponized hypocrisy argument. We *stole* the private jet and we're using it to fight the Huntsmen."

"Don't hate the messenger." Naomi stepped into the back of the jet. "But the First Owl just informed me it's a white party."

Ramaya groaned again, letting out a theatrical sigh.

Kes matched Ramaya's groan. "*Another* white party? Isn't it a little on the nose?"

"Nobody said the oligarchs were creative," Naomi answered. "Mira, I know this is all a bit overwhelming. But remember, I am the order's only animimicker and one of its strongest treetalkers." I caught Kes rolling their eyes behind Naomi's back. "I'll monitor your every move from the air through the birds and the bats and from the ground through the roots. The whales have agreed to station me right off the coast so I'll be hidden but have clear access to every point of the island—you'll be under my protection at every moment."

Ramaya's watch vibrated. "We're an hour out—let's get this party started."

Raj eyed each one of us in turn. "I'll do hair and makeup first and then I'll add your Inviso-Net."

"Fine, but I refuse to call it that," Ramaya said. "It sounds like the world's worst infomercial."

An hour later, Kes, Ramaya, and I alighted from the jet in matching white, looking for all the world like a boy band at the peak of our fame. Kes had a fresh buzz, a close-fitting linen suit that matched their casual elegance, and a hint of eyeliner that made their steady gaze even more hypnotic. Ramaya was wearing a pearlescent body suit tucked into an explosion of tulle, a punk rock ballerina. She'd winked and flipped the tulle up to show me a host of gadgets, and vials of seeds, plants, and ants harnessed to her thighs. Raj had talked me into a white and gold brocade suit and slicked my bleach-blue hair tight against my skull.

The three of us crossed the tarmac of the private airfield and waited in a small lounge in the hangar that was as nice as the lobby of a fancy hotel.

"Welcome party's late," Ramaya said. "Rude."

A sound of chopped air drowned out Kes's reply as a military-style tandem-rotor helicopter landed in front of the hangar. Armed guards hopped out and gave us each heavy earmuffs and helped us strap into the hard utilitarian seats. The helicopter took off and zoomed across fields and forests and the occasional lit stripe of a road and then crossed a channel of dark, churning water. We approached what looked like a small city of light on an isolated peninsula and then landed in one of the many lit circles on the perimeter, next to dozens of other helicopters.

As soon as we stepped onto the helipad, waitstaff in identical dark uniforms handed us champagne flutes and ushered us onto a stone path. As the roar of the helicopter diminished, it was replaced by the soothing sound of waves lapping against the shore. Naomi was out there somewhere in the grey vastness, watching. The thought soothed me. We walked along the path, which snaked between dunes and waist-high seagrass, and was lit by twinkling lights. Not until the final turn through the dunes could I see what we were walking towards. When I did, I couldn't help but let out a soft gasp. Ahead of us, lit like the Sydney Opera House, was a white structure built to resemble a giant conch shell. I glanced sideways at Kes and Ramaya, hoping I didn't look as awed as I felt. Ramaya would never let me live it down if she saw how impressed I was. But the two were deep in a whispered conversation and seemed to have forgotten entirely about their surroundings, and indeed, me.

My foot caught on an uneven flagstone and I tripped, launching my champagne into the night air. A hand shot out to catch me. "Is everything OK, miss?" one of the waitstaff asked, emerging seemingly out of nowhere and putting a hand on my elbow. He was young, almost as young as I was, with warm brown eyes that crinkled with secret laughter.

I smiled at him, opening my mouth to speak, but before I could, Kes put a possessive arm around me, unsubtly nudging the waitstaff's hand off of my elbow. "We might've started indulging a little early," they said, slurring their words.

"These two." Ramaya snorted, rolling her eyes. "Can't keep

their hands off each other. At least wait until after the appetizers."

The man tried to hide his smirk. "Of course. The bedrooms on the main floor have been made available for guests to uh… refresh themselves. Very private."

"I bet they are." Ramaya rolled her eyes again, playing the part of the aggrieved third wheel perfectly and peeled off into the night.

"Cheers." Kes nodded to the man. "Shall we?" They pulled me closer so their breath was hot on my neck.

It was easy to pretend, to giggle and let Kes tug me along to where the man had indicated. The tiniest, most idiotic part of me wondered if somehow this was real. If Kes and I were about to tumble into a bed with a billion thread count. Other staff, dozens of them, directed us to a "minimalist" room bigger than the first floor of my house.

As soon as we were inside and the door closed, Kes's smile faded and they pulled their arm out of mine. "Mira, you can't engage with anyone here."

"What do you mean?"

"I saw the way you smiled at that man."

Was Kes…*jealous*?

They continued, "At these parties anyone might be connected to the Huntsmen—we don't know. And any connection you build with them leaves you more vulnerable to being leeched by them. Especially because you haven't learned how to fight somebody else's leeching."

"Ding, ding, ding. I'll take 'things you should've told me before we got here' for two hundred."

"I know. That and a dozen other things." Kes rubbed at their eyes, smearing their eyeliner. My heart skidded in my chest at the sight and I turned my head, pretending to take in the beige on beige décor.

"I'm sorry about this. I don't like putting you in this situation but Naomi's convinced we need you in the field as soon as possible. And for whatever reason the Council is backing her." Kes sighed. "Something big is happening. I can feel it, the shifting ground. But I can't quite see the full picture, I don't know where the real danger lies amidst the chaos. And I'm terrified I'm going to let my loved ones down." They looked up. "Sorry, sorry, I shouldn't put that burden on you. There's enough on your plate already."

"It's OK." I started moving towards them, wanting, needing to comfort them. But they stood abruptly. "Let's get back out there in case Rama needs anything." Kes led me out of the bedroom, through the ground floor and into the eye of the storm.

There were people everywhere. Strings of lights and crystals criss-crossed the party overhead, casting a spray of rainbow over the sea of white fabrics below. Orchids dotted every table. I took in the fake laughter, fake smiles, fake teeth, and forced sneers, feeling like I was in a carnival funhouse.

"Remember when you stepped in front of that speeding car? This is nothing compared to that," Kes whispered, leaning in close. Too close. I ducked away from them, snatching a sparkling lemonade from a passing tray and chugging it.

Kes laughed but I could hear the falseness of it, so corrosive it made my ears burn. I clutched my hands into fists to keep from shoving my fingers in my ears, blocking out this horrifyingly distorted version of the world.

"Mira, *Mira*." Kes's insistence pulled me back to the present. We were sitting in some kind of cabana structure strewn with pillows at the edge of the garden party, although I had no memory of getting there. A black swan glided along the surface of the outdoor grotto next to us.

"Where would they even find a black swan? Nobody's even looking at the pool. Is that actual *gold* tiling?"

Kes snorted. "No doubt flown in by a fleet of private aircraft from some faraway land."

"It's all wrong here."

"I know. It is."

"How do you do it?"

Kes raised their eyebrows. "It?"

I gestured widely at the pool and the party. "Fit into these fake worlds. Talk with, dance with, befriend these people...*flirt* with them."

"You'll understand all of this soon enough, but leeching has to be grounded in a kernel of truth. If you want to chat up someone you loathe in theory, you have to find the part of yourself, no matter how small it is, that wants to befriend that person. And whether I like it or not, some small part of me wants this—the ease, the wealth, the sense of invincibility. It's a small part, but it's there. And I get a sick kind of satisfaction being accepted, adored, desired by a world that rejects so many of my identities."

I nodded. "I get that. Can you teach me more about how to leech?"

"Have you managed to connect to the Rhiza yet?"

I thought about the pod of roots that had sent me crashing through the wall into Edeva's Recollection Room, the field of wild flowers I'd made bloom after Naomi threatened me. "Yeah, I have," I said, leaving out that I'd yet to connect on purpose.

"OK, then *technically* according to order protocol I'm allowed to start teaching you." They ran a finger through their buzzed hair. "Who are you, Mira?"

I stared at them in confusion.

"This is part of the lesson. The more you're grounded in

who you are and what you want, the more you'll be able to bind others' wills to your own. So who are you? What do you crave in this world?"

"Aspen's sister. I want to find Aspen."

"Beautiful. And...?"

I was surprised to find other answers, lots of them, swelling in my chest at the prompt. Surprised and guilty. Kes's steady gaze held mine, permission shining out of their dark eyes and it was as if a dam broke inside of me. I started talking and couldn't stop. "Maybe it's the ADHD, but I *like* being alive, I always have. Even for the dumb stuff—scream-singing in the car with friends, biting into a really flipping good chocolate chip cookie...crushing on a new person. There's so much bad. Like *so* much. But there's also so much to see, and do, and learn. Like did you know dolphins have been observed conducting literal *experiments* in the wild? Stirring up vortexes of bubbles and dropping different objects into the chaos to see what will happen? And when one dolphin gets..." I trailed off as something shifted in Kes's gaze—they stared at me like I was the most interesting, most important thing to ever exist.

"*Don't stop*. I want to live through your awe for the world. I want to swim in it."

I grabbed Kes's hand. "Here, feel it." The awe fizzed inside of me like millions of champagne bubbles. I concentrated, coaxing a handful of bubbles through the invisible links between myself and Kes.

Their pupils dilated and their mouth parted in amazement. "Extraordinary." They scooted close to me on the cabana bed. "What are you thinking right now? What do you want me to do? More than anything else in the world?"

I hesitated.

"The truth, Mira, it has to be born in the truth. It doesn't have to be your whole truth, but you can't leech me if at least a part of you doesn't genuinely want me to act. Not long-term leeching, just what do you want me to do right this moment. Stay grounded in who you are and say it with conviction." They nudged my knee with one of their own.

Kiss me. *Kiss me.* KISS ME. But I didn't want to *make* Kes kiss me. "Uh, give me a high five."

"Is that really what you want me to do?" I felt their knee against my knee. Their body leaned nearer to mine, making the hair on my arms stand on end. "I don't feel the truth in your words."

There was a crashing in the distance. Kes was suddenly alert, soldier-like. "I better go see if that has anything to do with Ramaya. Will you be OK by yourself for a few moments?"

"Don't worry. I know the Huntsmen wouldn't try anything here, not with the fake teeth, and black swan, and real gold..." I trailed off, burrowing into the pillows until only my nose was peeking through.

"That was...profound and poetic, Mira Bracken. You never stop surprising."

I was tempted to jump out of my mountain of pillows and yell "boo" but even I could tell it wasn't the moment. "Right, right, right," I grumbled, a pillow gremlin, as Kes turned back into the storm.

I waited tensely, closing my eyes and trying to take deep breaths. And then I heard a sound that made me open my eyes. I hummed along, not quite able to place the tune.

It's our song, Aspen squealed and I realized the string quartet had moved on to an enthusiastic rendition of Rihanna's *Umbrella*.

"Our songgg," I repeated aloud, pushing my way out of my pillow mountain and getting to my feet. I swayed happily, clapping along, too far away from the action to draw more than a few smirks from the crowd. Something moved in my peripheral vision and I jumped. But it was just the swan. It had come right to the edge of the pool and seemed to be swaying along with me.

"You like Rihanna too, huh? An interspecies queen?" Naomi would know how to talk to the swan. "How did you get here, little bird? Well, not so little, I guess. But are you stuck here, in this world of chlorine and artifice and cages?"

Pain flared in my chest. Like someone had fed my heart into a sewing machine. I clutched it, wondering if I was somehow having a heart attack. Then I locked eyes with the swan and had a terrible realization—this was not my pain; it was the swan's answer. I looked around wildly. How many guests were watching; how could I set the swan free?

But there were too many eyes, eyes everywhere. To set the swan free would risk Kes and Ramaya's safety, the mission, potentially the lives of countless others.

The pain came again, sharp, twisting, and I fled away from the swan, away from the party, towards the sounds of the crashing waves. I scrambled down the rocky outcropping to a sliver of pebbled beach, and the waves came for me, slamming into my shins, my stomach, my chest; maybe they could shake the horror out of my heart, the grief out of my bones. I howled into the salty spray, over and over, desperate for the embrace of my sister, an escape from the pain.

I lost track of time. My limbs became numb and tingly. A wave slammed into me, knocking me back onto the rocks, and the tingling grew more intense. Instead of the pins and needles of blood flow returning, it felt like warm jets of water frothing against my skin. I pushed myself upright and gingerly took a step, unsure if my limbs were too chilled to walk. My leg held. In fact, the tingling sensation fairly propelled me across the rocks and back up to the house. I marvelled at how good my injured foot felt as I sprung from rock to rock. Humming to myself, I skipped towards the gathered crowd, realizing how beautifully the assembled whites and silvers caught the moonlight. Had I thought the crowd looked haughty and aloof before, ridiculous in their all-white? How wrong I was. I hummed louder and saw the black swan in the pool. "How cute," I cooed, blowing the creature a kiss. A sturdy man with freckles caught my eye and smiled. "You look like...my friend Adrian," I whispered dreamily, blowing him a kiss too.

Bodies pressed towards me on either side and I giggled, thrilled at the closeness. Someone slipped an arm around my waist and there was a sharp pain like a needle prick above my hip. I looked up, as if rousing from a deep slumber and found Ramaya's gaze boring into mine. *She'd* stung me. She tilted her head, gesturing for me to look around.

I was back in the light-strung courtyard of the conch shell mansion, at the edge of a crowd of partygoers dressed in white and singing as one voice:

The rich forest, verdant and pure,
Untainted by human greed and gore,
Protected for a thousand years and more,
By the Huntsmen who through it all endure.

The Huntsmen stand proud and free,
Courage, strength, power—they embody the three,
Guardians of all the eye can see,
They know not how to bend the knee.

To be a Huntsman is to choose your own fate,
Bowing to no man, no beast, nor state,
The choice is yours—do not wait,
The die is cast, the hour's late.

Edward fell and William rose,
But evil waited not in repose,
Sins and secrets untold, The Confessor knows,
He'll bring this poisonous chapter of man to a close.

"Sing along," Kes whispered in my ear, "but try to stay present." They squeezed my hand. I felt the tug of the song, of blissful oblivion, but I was pressed between Kes and Ramaya, anchored in reality.

"Good evening, sisters and brothers," the dulcet tones of a GPS navigator crackled through the space and the singing faded to a low hum, but didn't stop. "The Confessor welcomes you."

I shot a furtive look at the crowd, taking in their beaming faces.

"Your jewels please." The voice seemed to come from everywhere at once, unseen speakers, yet all different.

There was a rustling from the crowd as people unclasped necklaces and bracelets, pulled off cuff links and rings. Something spattered across my chest. I turned my neck to see an elderly woman holding heavy gold and emerald earrings, blood streaming down either side of her face. She'd pulled them right out of her ears. Kes squeezed my hand tighter and I squeezed back to let them know I was OK.

A man yelled as he was dragged away by two waitstaff. The crowd's singing swelled to cover the sound of his cries.

"Line up sisters and brothers, it's time to confess your sins." The voice came from right next to me—from the phone in the vest pocket of a stooped older man. It was coming from all the phones at once.

"The singing, we need to interrupt it," Ramaya whispered, under the hum of the crowd's drone.

"On it," Kes whispered back.

Out of the corner of my eye, I saw the familiar netting of the Rhiza climbing up Kes's legs. They were going to disrupt the collective, to stop the singing. The thought made me unspeakably sad. I crouched next to Kes's legs and rent my hands through the netting as if to tear away spider webs. But the silvery threads just climbed onto my hands.

"Mira, stop," Kes hissed. They raised their foot woven with the silvery threads and slammed their heel into the ground.

Chaos erupted around me, but I felt curiously numb to it. The sand dunes undulated up and down like a giant hand had grabbed one edge and was shaking out a rug. Kes tugged me away from the courtyard, but my feet tangled and hesitated, not wanting to leave the sound, the feeling of full-bodied belonging.

It grew harder to see through the darkening cloud of dust and sand scored my skin, leaving it raw and bloody, but still I resisted. Eventually Kes just swung me onto their back. I clung to them, trying to use the solid heft of their body as a talisman again the pull of the song. But I heard myself humming the tune, felt the urge to tumble to the ground and run back to the house.

Kes loped along the beach, the dunes rearing up like a wall between us and the turmoil. "Close your eyes for a second, we're going underground."

I did as I was told, clutching Kes as we tumbled through what felt like a river of sand. Kes eased me off their back and I opened my eyes to a dimly lit tunnel. A moment later the roof of the tunnel shook and a figure dropped catlike to land next to us in the sand.

"No sign of pursuit yet," Ramaya said.

Naomi's voice crackled from Ramaya's middle, "Gadfly to Flying Squirrel, do you copy?"

Ramaya flipped up her tulle skirt and pulled out a hidden GPS phone, answering, "Flying Squirrel here."

Naomi continued, "Owl intel reports an explosion of Huntsmen chatter in the northeast flooding the Rhiza. Active pursuit is imminent. Initiate Mother Tree Protocol. Do you copy?"

Kes snatched the device. "Negative, Gadfly, Mother Tree Protocol is unnecessary."

"Kestrel, Ramaya, initiate Mother Tree Protocol immediately. I'm closing fast on your location and I've called in more back up. "

"Copy that, Gadfly, shutting off all comms now to prevent interception," Ramaya said. "We're going old school."

"Good luck," Naomi replied and I caught the note of worry in her voice.

Ramaya whistled under her breath. "Mother Tree Protocol? What in Godda's name is going on?"

"They're just being precious," Kes said.

"Precious or not, you need to get out of here. Steal one of the helicopters, or go deeper underground. Mira and I will create a distraction."

Kes crossed their arms. "I'm serious. Naomi made the wrong call. We have to protect *Mira,* not me."

"You must know the best way to protect Mira would be to get as far away from her as possible," Ramaya said. "It's *you* they want."

Kes ran a hand through their buzzed hair, their eyes darting around the space as if looking for a physical escape from Ramaya's logic. "These tunnels are shallow but they should provide some protection—this part of the Rhiza has centuries of experience fighting the Huntsmen. You think you can make it to the safe house?"

"I know I can," Ramaya said. "And I'll protect Mira with my life."

"That's what I'm worried about," Kes said.

"Hey," Ramaya said, her voice cracking. "I'll be OK, I always am. Now, get out of this godforsaken hole in the ground before I push you out."

Kes shot me an apologetic look. "Keep safe, Mira." In one smooth movement they flung themself into the wall of the tunnel and the earth swallowed them greedily.

SEVENTEEN

Underground, away from any hint of the singing, my head was beginning to clear. I replayed my attempt to cut Kes off from the Rhiza. It was the song again. Affecting me harder than anyone else. Why?

"We're about two miles from the Newport safehouse," Ramaya said. "Magpies have been coming here for crash-and-dashes for centuries so it's well-stocked and the Rhiza here is trained and ferocious. But the tunnels won't provide nearly as much protection as the safehouse. Can you move?"

"My foot; it's still—"

"We'll go as slow as you need," Ramaya said easily, as if we hadn't just heard Naomi report that half the Huntsmen in North America were descending on our location.

"OK—I follow you." I hoped Ramaya could hear the double promise in the words.

We set off at a brisk walk but I could feel the treachery in my own limbs—ankles trying to roll, feet tripping over one another. Even without the song, the pull of the mansion lingered. I forced myself to keep going.

Trying to distract myself from the pain and fear nipping at my skin, I asked, "What's the Mother Tree Protocol?"

"It's a procedure in place to protect Kes and other direct descendants of Godda. We need to protect them so we can stay on good terms with Silverlight."

"Kes is a direct descendant of Godda herself? The GOAT?"

"I'm surprised Adrian didn't mention it—he usually brings it up at least once every other sentence."

"Why do you need to protect the descendants of Godda? Are they like mascots for the rootbound or something?"

"Silverlight is an ancient oak who joined forces with the original Seven Sisters to help found our order. She holds more than one thousand years of wisdom, and she nurtures the younger mother trees in our network. Silverlight and Godda were rootbound kin, tending and caring for one another. When Godda died, the Seven discovered that her descendants shared a shadow of the original bond between Godda and Silverlight, and thus had a special ability to communicate with and energize her. So we protect Godda's descendants at all costs, to protect our ultimate mother tree."

"Wow. A lot about Kes is making more sense."

"Like their obsessive need to risk their life for their friends?"

"Yeah, like that."

"If they come back for us I'm going to kill them."

Ramaya's words echoed in my head—kill them, kill them, kill them. My mind flashed to the empty pool back at Salish Sea Hub, the dark corner with a freckle-faced little boy collecting his pile of bones. I zoomed in on his freckles, at the contrast between his baby face and the grisly scene. Zoomed in even further on the resemblance between the little boy killer and Adrian. *Adrian.* Dread lodged in my ribcage, squeezing my lungs so tightly I coughed. While I was under the influence of

The Confessor's song earlier, I'd blown a kiss at a man because he looked exactly like Adrian. What if Naomi had guessed right? What if The Confessor was here?

"MIRA." I looked up to find Ramaya gripping my shoulders and staring at me in concern. "Stay with me."

"Sorry, I think The Confessor—"

There was a distant rumbling, like thunder. "Godda's curse —they found us, Mira. RUN."

Ramaya shoved me in one direction, and hurtled in the other, towards the rumbling. I stumbled into a sprint, wincing at the pain in my foot, and rounded a corner to find the tunnel branching in two different directions. Should I go left or right? At the thought, the walls around me seemed to grow brighter. No, just part of the wall. But where was the light coming from? I pushed myself closer to see what looked like thousands of tiny glowing cracks. Roots—the roots were glowing. I edged tentatively in the direction of the light, taking the leftmost passageway.

A mechanical pulsing came from above, shaking the earth around me. And then a voice filled the underground space— soft, goading. "Members of the Seven, you fight well, but you cannot hold out much longer. Surrender peacefully and we will not harm you, nor the other brave members we intercepted outside of Providence, presumably on their way to your aid. Sacrifice your lives if you must, but don't sacrifice theirs."

The tunnel went dark, the roots had stopped glowing. I held my breath in the pitch black.

"Really. No thought for your friends? You will not spare them a painful death? Perhaps The Confessor is wrong. Perhaps you are just as selfish as the Huntsmen have become, corroded by greed so that they forget our true purpose. We have been...cleaning house, carving out the gangrene.

"A time of renewal, of rebirth, is upon us. And in the spirit of that rebirth, The Confessor has generously offered a cease-fire between our orders, an end to our millennium-long feud. Surrender peacefully and we will parley. Continue fighting... and these tunnels will become your grave. The destruction of the Seven will be laid at your feet, Kestrel, descendant of Godda."

"It's lies, all lies, more of the Huntsmen's propaganda," I chanted like a mantra to myself. Please keep running, Kes, please don't listen. Somehow the Huntsmen knew Kes's deepest vulnerability—was this whole night some giant trap to get to them? I felt the net closing in.

The roots began to blink on and off, faster and faster, reminding me of the flashing lights of a highway construction sign at night. They strobed violently and then settled into a hazy, ghoulish glow.

A figure stepped out from behind a shadowed curve. The man looked remarkably normal—medium height and build, freckles, blue eyes. A grown-up version of the kid holding the bones I'd seen in the pool graffiti.

The Confessor.

"Beautiful, isn't it?" The man gestured at the glowing roots. As he pointed, his sleeve lifted to show a hint of red gem.

I fought back bile at the literal blood that had been shed to get it. Was mine next? Would he bleed my life force into a jewel?

"I'd introduce myself but you already seem to know who I am. Clever. *Like your sister*."

I was halfway across the distance between us before I even realized I'd moved, hands tensed like claws in front of me to tear at his face.

"Freeze," he said, easily.

I froze—tendons, muscles, bones jerking out of movement into stillness—rocketing face-first to the ground. I couldn't shift to break my fall and I landed hard against my face. Blood filled my mouth from where my lips had cut against my teeth. My body had felt a lot like a prison over the last year and a half, but never more so than now. Every primal urge in my body was begging me to retreat, to run, to get far away from the looming presence. But the flight instinct had nowhere to go. It just bounced off my frozen limbs, growing louder and more desperate, making my head feel like too many birds flying in a cage. I tried to quiet the noise, to focus, and realized The Confessor was standing directly over me. He flipped me over. Blood dribbled down my chin from the cuts in my lips and he grimaced, as if he didn't like the sight of gore, this man who had ordered the death of so many.

"It feels good to lie down doesn't it, Mira?" He was leeching me. To stop caring. To stop fighting. "That's it," he said, his voice gentle, almost loving. "Give up."

Give up. The words were like a heated robe after a cold shower. I slid into them, breathing a sigh of relief. This was what the song had been leading me towards. This nothingness, this blissful surrender.

I saw myself in fourth grade, body clenched in fear as I learned about our heating world. I stared at my teacher Ms. Martin feeling a sense of betrayal more profound than any I'd known before. How had she, my beloved teacher, my parents, my government, the adults of the world let this happen? How had they not done more to protect us? *Give up.*

Sixth grade. Aspen and I had organized a Meatless Mondays club at our middle school. Kyle Morgan tore down one of our posters, making a big deal of crumpling it into a ball and arcing it into a trashcan in front of his snickering friends. I yelled at him and he shrugged, laughing that it didn't matter because we were all gonna die in the apocalypse anyways. *Give up.*

I sat in the principal's office next to Aspen, burning with shame as Dr. Fowler lectured us on how "naïve and inappropriate" it was to disrupt the school board meeting to broadcast our divestment demands. How he couldn't "in good conscience" write us a college reference letter. I stared at the giant poster of a Dr. Martin Luther King Jr. speech above his desk while he droned on, his cheeks getting more and more ruddy as he worked himself into indignation. *Give up.*

Aspen and Dad were arguing at the dinner table again, Dad ranting about the threat to people and planet of one of the presidential candidates. And Aspen challenging him to do more, to donate his time and money to the election instead of "just whining in the suburbs." Dad roared at Aspen. I shrunk in on myself, silent, complicit, as my sister fled the table sobbing. *Give up.*

I asked another rushed passerby to stop for a moment and listen to my story. To care about me, to care about my missing sister. She brushed past me, knocking my shoulder as she went, and my flyers flew in the air. *Give up.*

My thoughts slowed with my pulse.

Slower...slower...slower. Until I realized I might never stand up again. My mind was a map, zooming further and further out of my own life. I saw myself lying peacefully on the floor of the tunnel, red blood mixing with the blond and blue of my hair, a Picasso painting. I saw the beach from above, no trace of the violence unfolding beneath the white sand. I saw the island, a speck of green against the grey patchwork of the ocean.

I saw two orbs staring at me like twin suns, bathing me in warmth. I stopped zooming out, those orbs pulling me with their own impossible gravity.

I stared into that steady gaze, feeling something cracking open inside of me, a longing to see and be seen, to *live*, if even for one more moment. That steady gaze stared back. Hands cradled my face. "The caring is the point, Mira. It sucks, but it's true. *The caring is the point.* Remember who you are."

I felt the familiar sense of warm water rushing down my back, of infinite safety, and realized Kes was binding me. I felt their binding battling with The Confessor's leeching and hurtled back to the present as if reawakening behind my own eyes. Sensations rushed back to me. The clank of something cold and foreign falling against my teeth. The scent of oak and lavender. The sight of Kes's face, mouthing something I couldn't quite understand.

And I watched, unable to scream, unable even to blink, as The Confessor lurched behind Kes and slipped a chain of rubies over their head, tightening it across their throat like a bloody collar. He tugged the teen backwards, until they were at the very edge of my vision. Kes began to vibrate.

"Thank you for coming back for your friends, Kestrel, descendant of Godda," said The Confessor.

Kes vibrated more violently. Their jaw clenched and their muscles corded and strained. "Leave...leave them out of it," they panted, clearly in terrible pain. "Take me."

"Always the savior, just like your kin before you."

Kes let out an animal whine, bucking and writhing. I shrunk inside of myself watching Kes be tortured. I wanted to slip back into the warm robe of the whispered words. *Give up.* But I couldn't. Something was burning in my mouth like I'd swallowed an ember from a campfire. What felt like a horde of wasps stung my throat and mouth. Pain and heat erupted from the site, consuming my face, core, arms, and legs.

I could feel something growing as the pain grew, tentacles pushing against my locked jaw. My blood was magma boiling against my skin, cooking me from the inside out. Kes had dropped something in my mouth—*a seed.* What had they whispered to me? My brain did cartwheels as I tried to piece it together, and then I felt my neck jerk with the effort. *The only way out is through*—that's what they'd said! Kes's binding and the pain were freeing me from The Confessor's leeching.

But not enough, I realized, as I tried to flex a finger. After a long moment of effort I managed to wiggle my toes, but I still couldn't lift my arms or legs. I had endured, this body had endured the unimaginable. Again. But it wasn't enough to save Kes.

A figure hurtled through the air at The Confessor.

"Freeze," he called, lazy, uncaring, secure in his invincibility.

Ramaya slowed at the command but didn't stop. Moving as if fighting her way down a wind tunnel, she kept creeping towards The Confessor.

His eyes narrowed, first in surprise, and then in hunger. "Remarkable. Nobody has tried to resist me in a very long time."

Ramaya circled her arms, fighting to keep her forward momentum against the force of the leeching. She wasn't totally bound, but she *was* a sitting duck. I needed more pain to free myself. Aspen? I whispered. Will you come with me? I waited, not wanting to go any deeper into the pain without my sister. Aspen! I said again. Aspen! I screamed into the abyss of my mind. The pain and the heat and the grief converged into an inferno, and I was lost to it. I forgot my name, my purpose; I forgot if I had a body or a mind or if I was pain incarnate. After a second, an hour, a year, the inferno burned itself out. I spat out a flower that was hot as flame and tasted of copper.

"—how did you hone your will into such a knife point?" The Confessor held up an opal; he meant to bind Ramaya's will to a siphon. He strode towards the woman, leaving Kes momentarily forgotten.

Something the size of a football launched itself out of the darkness to collide with The Confessor's hand, knocking the opal away. Another object slammed into the back of his head. And another. Bats. Thousands of them exploded down the tunnel. Roots clawed their way out of the wall to wrap around The Confessor's limbs. Naomi sprinted towards us, her black coat lifting like a cape.

"Now, Mira! To Kes!" Ramaya forced out.

I launched myself at the leash while The Confessor was distracted, yanking it out of his hands and pulling it up and over Kes's neck so they were free. They slumped against me and I had a moment to exhale before my body screamed at the wrongness.

Kes's heart wasn't beating.

Violence unfolded around me, but I watched it as if it was a movie on fast forward. The metal drill piercing through the roof of the tunnel. The swarm of men cutting The Confessor free of the roots and dragging him away. Naomi wielding the Rhiza to shield us from a hail of gunfire and launching herself fearlessly after them, thousands of bats at her back.

Ramaya crawled over to us, letting out an animal howl when she saw what I already knew. Without thinking I reached out an arm to her and jerked like a live wire at the rush of love and grief that poured through me. Kes jerked too.

"They're still in there, Mira! Kes is still in there!"

But I wasn't listening. I'd seen it too. Immediately I started feeling for the tiny threads of connection running between Ramaya and Kes, between Kes and me. At the same time, I focused on grounding into myself, calling up favorite memories—Adrian and I dancing in a sweaty tangle at the welcome party. Ramaya standing up for me when Naomi went too hard in training. Tai hugging me deeply in the sick bay. Kes sitting next to me at the cabana just a few hours ago, staring at me like I was something sacred.

As I grounded, the threads of connection became clearer and clearer; there were thousands, millions of them between Kes and Ramaya. To my surprise there was also a thick, glowing channel of connection between Kes and me, as if hundreds of little whisps had fused into one superconductor, a mystery I had no time to puzzle over at the moment. I sent a surge of love and energy through every little channel of connection I could find. The links began to swell and glow, brighter and brighter. At the peak of their brilliance I commanded with as much force as I could muster, "Stay with us, Kes."

CHAPTER

EIGHTEEN

I drifted in and out of consciousness, aware only that Kes's hand was still clutched in mine and that we were being transported somewhere with great urgency. The faces peering down at me changed but their desperate pleas were the same—*hold on*. The last face I saw before collapsing into deeper unknowing stood out from the rest—an older woman with a warm, lined face like the bark of a tree and a shock of purple hair.

"Mira," Teddy called to me out of the darkness. "You can let go." She tried to force my hand open. The hand that had clung to Kes's across land and sea.

"No," I hissed, grasping tighter, muscles screaming for release.

"Such determination," Teddy said tenderly. "I can see you won't rest until Kes is safe. May I show you?"

I nodded, still unsure if this was dream or reality. A warm, wrinkled hand folded over mine and Kes's.

Suddenly I was lying against wet pavement. I felt the bite of the surface against my cheek, felt light rain falling against my bare arms. Out of the corner of my eye a missing person flyer with Aspen's smile flapped in the breeze. Seattle. The protest. The day I met Kes. The day it all started.

Gentle hands pulled me upright and I turned to see familiar eyes, so steady and so warm. Staring into that steady gaze I felt safety wash over me like hot water streaming down my back.

"Are you OK?"

"Asks the girl who just face-planted into pavement. Are *you* OK?"

I brushed their question away. "Can I hug you?" I needed to feel them in my arms.

They tilted their head like a dog and shrugged. "When a beautiful mystery girl asks you for a hug, I guess you hug them."

I latched onto them, an octopus, tucking my head into the crook of their neck, breathing in their scent of oak and soil. Wrapping my arms still tighter, I felt the thrum of their heartbeat against my own.

Finally, I let go.

"That's it, Mira." The same wrinkled hand slipped into mine, replacing Kes's for a momentary squeeze. "Can you try opening your eyes for me?"

I did as I was asked, pushing myself shakily upright to find that I was on a simple cot. Kes lay next to me in a twin cot, roots wound around them like a tangle of IVs and wires in the hospital. I followed the path of the roots to a tree, which stood fifteen-feet tall, its upper boughs pushing against the vaulted stone ceilings of what looked like some sort of castle.

"A nursery tree," Teddy explained. "The tree is keeping a constant read on Kes's vitals and giving them the energy they need to heal." As the woman spoke, I had the sense she'd held vigil at many a bedside. Something in me that had begun to release let go even further.

"Have they...woken up yet?" I knew the answer but felt the need to ask anyway.

"Not yet. But we're close." Teddy nodded in the direction of the nursey tree and I realized that her calves were wrapped so thickly in the roots of the tree, it looked like she was wearing gnarled boots. For a strange moment, I thought the roots were coming right out of Teddy's skin, as if she was woman on top and tree on bottom.

"And the others? Ramaya, Naomi? The rootbound who came to help us?"

"Everyone is fine, dear."

"Oh thank, God—Godda."

A dark look crossed Teddy's kind face, so quickly I might have imagined it. "I was just telling Kes one of their favorite stories," she said. "The one I told at the Salish Sea Hub root-binding—about Edric the Wild stealing away with Godda, and her Sisters and the trees rushing to her aid."

"Oh, tell it again, please."

Teddy smiled. "Of course, anything for you, Mira. Once again, we owe you a great debt, just like when you saved those protesters in Seattle."

The archivist told the story again, adding even more details and embellishments than she had at the rootbinding. A root handed me a mug and a plate of cookies. I was so engrossed I took a swig of tea without checking the temperature, spitting the scalding liquid all over the stone flood.

Teddy clucked. "Are you OK, dear?" The root wrapped around the woman's shoulders, clearly apologetic. She held it as if holding a hand.

"I'm fine."

"Are you sure? I don't want to bore you with ancient tales."

"No, please—oh, you're teasing me."

"I *am* a terrible tease.

"What happened next?" I asked eagerly. "After the Sisters joined with the trees?"

"There's all kinds of wild stories, like that each of the Seven fed their bodies to the Rhiza so they could always be part of the web. It's possible—fungi will eat *anything*. But my favorite myth is that they dispersed around the world in their twilight years, finding mother trees of their own, connections like that of Godda and Silverlight, and nourished their own small communities of human and tree kin."

"Would you do it? Feed yourself into the Rhiza? To stay connected to the ones you love?"

Teddy shivered, and the tree branch wrapped more tightly around her shoulders. "I don't think so—it would be such a hollow existence. Would you?"

"A couple of weeks ago I would've said yes, without hesitation. If there was any path in the world, as desperate or as painful as it might be, I would take it to be reunited with my sister. But now..." I thought of all the people I'd have to leave behind to be with Aspen—Kes, Ramaya, Tai, even Naomi.

"Can I ask you something, dear? Why do you feel so much pressure to find your sister? Why shoulder such an immense burden when even your parents have let themselves grieve and begin to move on?"

"I...failed her. She took on so much. I went through the motions of activism, but my heart was never in it, not like Aspen. And I was always afraid of getting into trouble, always holding back."

"So now you fling yourself into danger? What if you valued your own life as much as you valued Aspen's? What if you let yourself feel joy and love without guilt?" Teddy had a faraway look in her eyes.

"You feel guilty too? About...about someone you love?"

Teddy collapsed in on herself, looking suddenly ancient.

"I'll try...if you try." I put a hand on hers and she slowly bloomed again, a flower set into water. I realized too late that I was leeching Teddy and snatched my hand away, hoping the kindly archivist hadn't noticed. I was still lying to Teddy and the others about my abilities, still afraid they'd ostracize me if they knew the truth about who I was.

Kes groaned in their sleep. Teddy moved to their side, and the roots began poking, prodding, soothing all over Kes's body. "Mira, I must ask you to take good care of yourself in the coming days—eat, sleep, connect with the others. And stay close. For Kes is not out of the woods yet—what an ironic expression—and we may still need you."

"Of course, I'll do anything. I'll eat my weight in kelp, I'll—"

"Child, do what feels good and it will nourish you. Catherine here will show you around and see that you're taken care of." In a stage whisper she added, "Silverlight gets all the glory, but Catherine's the real boss of the castle."

I turned to see a fresh-faced woman with brown hair, glasses, and striking metalwork jewelry around her neck. She grinned and waved. "Delighted to meet you, Mira. I imagine hot food and a shower top your list of needs at the moment?" She hooked her elbow through mine, pulling me from the room.

"Is that real sunlight?" I pointed at the dusty rays of light shining through the arrow slits in the granite wall.

"That mythical sun everyone is always talking about occasionally makes an appearance in England too."

"No, no, it's just that the last hub I was in had fake windows. But we're above ground, in some kind of castle?"

"We are above ground. And, well, as for the castle part—it *is* England."

I wasn't listening anymore. I stepped towards a window and gaped at the massive tree that filled almost the entire courtyard. Its bark was a thousand different colors of grey and silver and the sunlight gave it a liquid metal sheen. Its trunk rose like the tower of a keep.

"That's our mother tree," Catherine said. "Or I should say *the* mother tree. Silverlight."

"*Silverlight*," I whispered, the name holding new meaning.

"I know, right?" Catherine answered, matching my reverential tone. "There are mothers all over the world but this one struck the blow that saved Godda a thousand years ago, or so says Teddy." She paused to sniff the air. "It's your lucky day. From the divine smell wafting up from the kitchen, it looks like we're getting vegan shepherd's pie and chips for lunch. Food before bath?"

"Food before bath," I agreed with a grin.

Catherine, or Kate as she insisted I call her, made good on Teddy's promise to nourish me. After a feast of potatoes served every way imaginable she led me on a chirpy tour of the castle, winding me down beneath the cellar, to the underground hot springs. I soaked in their lavender warmth while Kate filled me in on order gossip, at least a quarter of which seemed to involve Kes. When I was so relaxed I could barely hold my head up, Kate half-led, half-carried me back to the infirmary. Teddy was still holding gentle vigil over Kes, whispering another story in that rich, lilting voice. I tried to listen, eyes fluttering, but almost immediately fell asleep.

CHAPTER
NINETEEN

Someone shook me awake in the pre-dawn light and adrenaline rocketed through me. "Is it Kes? Are they— Naomi!"

Naomi held a finger to her lips. There were great dark circles under her eyes but they still burned with their usual fire. She motioned for me to get dressed and follow her out of the infirmary. Teddy was gone but the roots cradled Kes's still figure and their breathing sounded steadier than before.

"I know it's early, but I wanted to come see you as soon as I arrived."

I couldn't help wishing she *had* waited to come see me. Thinking longingly of my warm bed in the cozy infirmary, I yawned widely. "Maybe we could get some coffee?"

"Better not."

I'd been following Naomi down stairs and around corners without thinking but stopped when I realized we were about to exit the castle.

Naomi raised her eyebrows. "What's up?"

"Uh..." I started. "Teddy asked me to stay close to Kes...in case they need me again."

The First Magpie fixed me with a hard stare. "Teddy is the one who asked me to take you out onto the grounds for training. It's like a playground for the Seven—they're re-wilding the whole estate. The trees are having a party."

"I don't think...I'm not sure if I'm up for that right—"

Naomi cut me off, "What happened on the mission was you got lucky. The next time you face the Huntsmen, do you want to hope you get lucky again? Or do you want to know how to protect yourself? To protect Kes." She pushed hard against a circular oak door, beckoning me to join her outside.

I stood in the doorway, still hesitant. The kaleidoscope of green scenery—shrubs, trees, vines—was disappearing into the mouth of a fast-moving fog. My body trembled with the exertion of moving after being static for so long. But at least I could move. Kes was still stuck in that bed. I looked down at the flannel PJs covered in rose buds Kate had given me to wear after the bath. "I guess mud will wash out of flannel?"

"That's the spirit," Naomi said with what seemed like forced cheer, and I followed her into the fog that was now billowing towards us. I caught glimpses of the castle grounds as we trudged deeper and deeper into the woods. Naomi pointed out various features but I was so tired I could barely concentrate.

"—those roses date back to a sixteenth century courtship between a magpie and a lark—"

"—a Huntsmen lackey was staked in the heart in the middle of that maze—"

"—legend has it that Godda's ashes are sprinkled in that pond; it's why those lily pads bloom all year round—"

"—the fog is actually a perfect metaphor for wealth in England. If you keep your riches secret, you keep them safe—"

We stopped at a thick growth of moss and loam, ringed by red and white toadstools. I was relieved when Naomi told me to take my usual position lying in the dirt. My eyes fluttered as she reminded me to breathe in the spicy, decaying scent around me, to feel the tickle of the breeze, to sense the solidity of the ground beneath my back. I readied myself for the long, frustrating wait for the roots to respond to my openness, but to my surprise, they fairly sprung out of the ground, slithering around me. I went to high five one of the roots but it glanced off my palm and circled my wrist instead. "Hey, be gentle please," I chided, as if talking to a puppy.

But the root was not gentle. It jerked my now trapped wrist up and over my head before plunging back into the dirt. I yelped as my shoulder twisted unnaturally. "Help, Naomi!"

No response.

The assault kept coming. Roots bound my other wrist and both my ankles. The smell of the earth, once inviting, turned sour, like moldering flesh.

"What's going on, Naomi? Is this some kind of test? I'm not really up for tests at the moment."

No response.

"OK, I get it. You're replicating the other times I was able to connect to the Rhiza, when I was in danger. But I'm not actually scared."

"You should be," a voice whispered roughly and it took me a moment to realize it was Naomi.

"Naomi—"

"Enough, imposter, enough. The trees will see the lies that hang off of you. You stink of deception." Roots wound more tightly across my chest, pushing against my diaphragm.

"What lies?"

"What were you doing at the protest? When you just happened to bump into Kestrel, descendant of Godda."

"What? No! Kes bumped into me. I was upset, in pain after hours of looking for my sister. And Kes...they helped me." A tree root pulled tighter across my throat. I tried to tell Naomi but I could only gurgle.

Naomi's voice got higher and her words tumbled out, "The Huntsmen have been trying to corrupt treetalkers for centuries. It was only a matter of time before they succeeded."

I gurgled again, more insistently. I was running out of air.

"And the Huntsmen knew exactly where to find you and Kes. Now you've put them, all of us, our mother tree in danger."

I flickered in and out of consciousness, relieved every time the world went black.

"Say something! Say something so the Rhiza can witness your lies."

"Release her," a new voice commanded. *Ramaya.*

"Ramaya, Ramaya," Naomi said, her voice cracking. "We're in terrible danger; I can feel it rushing towards us."

"I know, but not from Mira," Ramaya soothed, and the roots loosened their grip against my throat. I gasped for air. Naomi dropped in the mud next to me, her face stricken. "Mira." She reached a hand towards me and I shrank away.

"I don't understand." Naomi shook her head, repeating the words over and over.

"It's OK." Ramaya knelt next to the woman and put an arm around her.

"The Rhiza detected no lies, but...how?" Naomi said.

"Because she's not lying," Ramaya answered.

Naomi shook her head sadly. "She'll be the death of us all. She's connected to The Confessor. To his cursed song. And you'll say I didn't warn you. You'll say I was root-mad, lost to the world—" She stopped abruptly, slumping against Ramaya, who laid her carefully on the ground. The roots imprisoning me retracted into the soil, leaving no trace of their presence aside from the red welts across my skin.

"You just can't get enough excitement," Ramaya clucked, helping me to my feet.

"That's the second time you've saved me," I rasped.

"Third by my count, but who's counting? And anyway, back in Rhode Island—it was you who saved Kes. *Thank you.*" Ramaya's voice faltered and she pulled me into a quick side hug. "Let's get some tea and honey for your throat."

I held back, eyeing Naomi's form splayed against green moss. Silver tendrils fine as lace were knitting over her skin.

"What's...what's happening to her?"

"Silverlight is probably not thrilled with her interrogating you like that. Naomi's always been intense, but that was a step too far. The Rhiza is putting her into a torpor to try and heal her."

"Heal her?"

"I'll explain later, but let's get you fixed up."

Ramaya had already turned the kitchen into her makeshift lab. She ushered me to a wooden stool by the hearth to warm up and insisted on rubbing a foul-smelling ointment over my bruised throat and the red welts on my wrists and ankles. Then the kitchen crew made me the "perfect cuppa"—a nice hot tea. The only hint of my near-death experience was a voice that sounded like I had a mild cold. It was maddening how unscathed my body looked compared to how my mind felt.

Ramaya led me into a cozy sitting room off of the kitchen. It was filled with mismatched velvet furniture in rose and emerald hues and shadowed by an overgrown lemon tree with lemons the size of my fists. "I'm sorry about that."

"Not your fault."

"No, not exactly. But the order should feel safe for all who serve it. It's not an easy life for any of us, but you've had an exceptionally rough go of it the last couple of weeks."

"Again, not your fault. In fact, they would've been a lot rougher without you."

"Naomi's been acting off for months. She was a little too obsessed with training you. Somebody should've see the signs. I should've seen the signs—"

"That Naomi was...root-mad?"

"People call it that, but they shouldn't. Oversaturated or OS is the better term. It's when all the violence and horror of the world the Huntsmen built overcomes a person's faculties and they start to mirror that world in their actions. They usually aren't aware of it. It's why we have over-stim days."

I rubbed my garroted throat. "I thought Naomi was going to kill me."

"I don't think she would have. She wasn't hurting you on purpose. I think sending you on that mission and then having Kes almost...having Kes get hurt—it pushed her over the edge. Ten to one she'll be devastated when she realizes what she's done. Honestly it's a miracle more of us aren't OS."

"Cause so many of us are neurodivergent?"

"Cause so many of us care. Feel it all. Feel it ALL. You know what I mean?"

I thought about holding Aspen when she'd wake screaming in the night, living whatever climate disaster she'd seen on the news, sobbing about children washed away by raging waters, refugees imprisoned behind barbed wire. Aspen had felt it all. I'd been terrified by the power of her empathy, the toll of it. I nodded, although I wasn't sure if I really did. Not the way Ramaya or Aspen or Naomi did.

"Some say the willbinders and the treetalkers have it the worst—being linked in to so much suffering human and non-human. But I'm not so sure." Ramaya took a long sip of tea and

I noticed her hand was shaking. "I do know Naomi has it particularly bad. Because she's a treetalker *and* an animimicker. Because of her bond with animals. She tried to tell us a few times, when she'd passed too close to a factory farm, feeling the fear and the pain of hundreds of thousands of beings all at once. Pigs, chickens, cows, separated from their families, stuck in cages so small they couldn't turn around. But we couldn't listen. Didn't want to. Didn't want to imagine what we couldn't fix."

"Aspen was like that," I whispered. "With people, with trees, with animals. I worried sometimes that she might split right open with the hurt of it all. But she just channelled it into action. The worse the world was, the better she had to be. And I shut her out sometimes. I didn't want to hear how many children had died in school shootings that month. Or how many kids were in adult prisons. I shut her out. I shut it out. Me—her own sister. I left her to carry the burdens of the world on her own."

Ramaya didn't say anything, there was nothing to say, but she held my gaze. And I held hers. And we sipped our tea. Finally she stood and began to rummage through her work space, sorting through vials, plant trimmings, old computer hardware. "Can I show you something?"

I nodded and Ramaya handed me a gadget that looked like a grocery store scanner. "What is it?"

"Only a prototype for now. But one day it will let non-treetalkers connect to the Rhiza in rudimentary ways. I started working on it for Adrian."

"Because he wants to be a magpie?"

"And you can't be a magpie if you're not a strong treetalker, no matter how brave or clever or charismatic you are." Ramaya held my gaze deliberately.

My heart suddenly felt two sizes two big, slamming against

my ribcage like a basketball, and my mouth went dry. "Why did you...why are you showing it to me?"

"What you did at the white party, how you saved Kes—I've never seen such powerful willbinding."

I wanted to feel pride at the awe in Ramaya's tone but I couldn't breathe for the fear that my secret was about to be exposed. Would I be expelled from the rootbound, ripped from this world I was starting to belong to?

Ramaya put a hand on my shoulder. "In my debrief, I told the First Owl and the Council that you called on the Rhiza to save Kes."

I exhaled in a sharp whistle, grabbing her hand in silent thanks, too overwhelmed to speak.

Before Ramaya could say anything more, Kate ran into the room, glasses fogged up and hair askew. "Kes is awake! And they want to see you."

TWENTY

"See, I told you, she's safe and sound," Teddy said to Kes, presenting me like a trophy at their bedside. The archivist gave Ramaya and me a pointed look; she had clearly heard of the morning's excitement and didn't want us to mention it to Kes.

"Liars! You're all liars!" Kes rasped. "And you, Teddy, with the poker face of a toddler. But I'm happy to see you." They looked at me, then Ramaya and quickly added, "Both."

Ramaya snorted but didn't say anything. I felt suddenly shy. Teddy giggled. "I know, I know. Why do you think they never let me out of the castle? I'd be babbling about the Huntsmen to every milkman I met."

"You really haven't been out of the castle in a while," Kate said, putting an affectionate hand on the older woman's shoulder.

"And I haven't been out of this room in even longer. Time for me to get some breakfast I think. Join me, Ramaya, Kate?"

The others departed and I made my way over to Kes's bedside, still tip-toeing as if not to wake them. I scanned their form, drinking in the pink flush in their cheeks, the alertness in their gaze. They were alive, *awake*.

"So..." Kes started with a grin.

"So..." I grinned back.

"What actually happened to you this morning? Your fear flooding through the Rhiza woke me."

My grin faded. "Sorry, I should let you rest."

They grabbed my hand. "I rest better when you're here."

I thought about what to say. Naomi assaulted me. Naomi tried to kill me. Naomi betrayed me. But I could see, more than ever, the immense burden shouldered by the rootbound, the pressure of protecting so many. All of them were struggling. All of them were just trying to keep it together. Even though my throat burned, I found it hard to feel any anger or even fear towards Naomi. Just sadness.

"Naomi was overstimulated," I said. "And confronted me in an...unpleasant way."

Kes snorted. "Figures Naomi would go OS on you. It's always death, doom, apocalypse with her."

"She said I would kill you all."

Kes groaned, leaning back against their mound of pillows. A root emerged from the wall, wrapping gently around their forehead. Kes batted it away. "This tree won't stop checking my temperature. Teddy has them trained to be just as overprotective as she is. Hard to tell where the roots end and Teddy begins—she's part of the castle."

"Is she...your grandma?" I thought of how tenderly she looked at Kes.

Kes let out a guffaw that quickly turned into a cough. Automatically I put my hands on their chest, as if I could pull the hurt out of their lungs. They looked at me, giving me the patented Steady Gaze except this time there was something else flickering there, something that made my stomach tighten. "Teddy? My grandma? No, thank goodness. Although I guess we are related, very distantly."

"She's also...a descendant of Godda?"

Kes flushed. "Yeah, but I mean, it's been a thousand years so we're like her great-great-great-great—you get the idea—grandchildren."

"Still, it means something to the order," I pushed back.

"More than it should, probably. We, me, Teddy, and a handful of others, we have a special bond with Silverlight. We can share with her—energy, information, love. Silverlight is kind of the beating heart of the Seven. She teaches the other trees to trust us, to talk to us so that we can listen. Her root system is so ancient and so massive that she can push energy halfway around the globe through the Rhiza. I can feel her when I'm in Vancouver or Seattle on a mission, always making my way a little easier, introducing me to the local trees."

"Sounds important to me," I said. "You have a whole protocol to protect you."

"The Mother Tree Protocol is more about protecting Silverlight. It's theorized that if someone with my connection were leeched, the Huntsmen might be able to find Silverlight and approach through all of our defenses."

"That would be bad."

"Really bad. We're not sure what will happen if Silverlight dies, if we'll still be able to talk and listen to the trees like we have since Godda and Silverlight became bound so many centuries ago. It's why we protect the identities of those descended from Godda so carefully. But somehow The Confessor found me out."

"Naomi thought I told him."

Kes snorted so hard their head hit the back of the cot.

"What—you don't think me capable of international espionage?"

"Don't sound so disappointed." Kes rubbed a hand over the spot where they'd hit their head. "The point is, Silverlight protects thousands, millions of other plants and animals—most of whom are struggling to adapt to warmer temperatures and more extreme weather. She gives her energy to them and we...give our energy to her. And if I'm not, if we're not, around to give her energy, she may fail."

"So the Seven protect your lives over others, and, let me guess, you *love* that."

Kes swatted me. "Merciless. Here I am baring my soul to you..."

"I'm sorry, I'm sorry. I'll be serious. Look." I pointed at my face. "It sounds very hard to be loved and cherished by a global community."

Kes groaned again. "Nurse, nurse—Teddy!" they whisper-called. "She's hurting me, ripping my poor heart right out of my chest."

"Don't! STOP!" I clambered on top of Kes to quiet them. "Naomi literally accused me of that this morning. Teddy will probably run in here with a spear or something."

"I like it when you hold me down," Kes said, gravel in their voice. The Gaze was back. It held me, a question, an invitation, a plea. I drew in a shaky breath, letting my body sink against theirs, bringing my mouth towards their mouth.

"Brought you some clear broth," Teddy said, clattering though the door. I rolled so quickly I landed on the stone floor.

"You're lucky no one else saw that. And you, Kestrel, you're not supposed to be overexerting yourself," Teddy chided. "Give us a minute, dear," she said to me and I scrambled away to the balcony, hot and red all over, and not just from embarrassment.

CHAPTER

TWENTY-ONE

I spent the next week in the infirmary with Kes, napping when they napped and keeping them company when they were awake. Ramaya and Kate dropped off our meals and visited. Nobody tried to get me to open my heart or mind or soul to the trees. It was a blissful little sanctuary.

But I knew it couldn't last, especially as Ramaya and Kate's visits got shorter and shorter and their faces more and more tired. I half-heartedly asked them what was happening, but they shrugged off my questions, rightly guessing that I didn't really want to know the answers. There were people massing at the castle, a lot of people, that much I could see from looking out the window. They moved like ants, coordinated and purposeful. I could also *feel* their energy, the castle hummed with it, especially when I held Kes's hand. It was amplified a hundred times over—I could pick out the individual strands of anticipation, feel the nerves bubble in my stomach like a freshly popped can of ginger ale.

Finally my brain couldn't tamp down the curiosity any longer. While Kes was snoring, I gently snuck over to the infirmary door, feeling like a thief. My heart did a polka in my chest and I searched internally for the source of my sudden anxiety. *Naomi.* The blissful bubble hadn't just been about staying near Kes, but also away from the First Magpie. Ramaya, Kate, and Teddy had all assured me that she was better—getting the treatment she needed and feeling terrible about what she'd done to me. But they hadn't been there. Hadn't heard her whisper with the confidence of an oracle that I would kill them all while letting the roots steal my final breaths.

I waited for Aspen's encouragement but it didn't come. She'd rarely visited me these last few days. "Fine," I said aloud, "I'll psych myself up—you got this, Mira. Who cares if there's a vengeful, homicidal beast who's so intense she can scare sharks off with a look on the other side of the door? You're, you know, kind of smart and have now escaped several near-death experiences."

There was a grunt of amusement from behind me. "Just do it," Kes whispered.

"Thanks, Nike," I shot back, but I pushed through the door out into...the same stone corridor that I'd seen the week before. The space was decorated with tapestries and abstract paintings—apparently created by Silverlight herself. The warm smiles of order members bustling past and the shouts of feasting and laughter echoing from other wings lent speed to my steps. But where exactly was I going? Teddy—I wanted to see Teddy. Kes had told me the castle was so attuned to the older woman that I could say her name aloud and the building would guide me to her. But maybe they'd been teasing me; they liked to do that. I flushed, thinking about their less innocent teasing, whispered in our few moments of alone time.

Shaking my head before I went further down that road, that very appealing road, I put my hands against the wall with a flourish. "I need to find Teddy." Nothing happened. "Teddy," I said louder, trying not to feel as foolish as I looked.

"Searching for Teddy?" A teen with a stylish mullet and Scottish brogue asked, pausing from their dash.

I nodded, too embarrassed to speak.

"She's in the archives."

I looked blankly at them.

"Go down six flights of stairs, follow the sloping tunnel and take a right—look for the room full of books. It's impossible to miss."

I smiled my thanks and followed the teen's directions, silently cursing Kes with every step. Twenty minutes later I was forced to admit I had done the "impossible" and missed the archives. Instead I wandered the bowels of the castle, somehow winding deeper every time I tried to get back up towards the infirmary. I passed an ancient oak door with a carved raven's head for a handle and felt an overwhelming urge to go through it. The bird looked so lifelike I swore it winked at me. I grabbed the handle, expecting it to be locked, and almost tripped as it swung open at my touch and I hurtled through after it, right into the midst of a room full of people.

"Sorry—" I trailed off, shivering. The room wasn't full of people; it was full of statues, carved out of stone and wood. They all had the same weirdly life-like quality of the raven door handle, as if they had once been living beings turned to stillness. And they were all of the same person. Those fierce eyes, the long hair, the birds standing to attention on the stat-ues' shoulders—it had to be Edeva. I moved closer to a lumi-nous marble carving of two women embracing, flowers woven across their brows and around their waists. A dusty plaque read "Godda and Edeva, circa 1204."

Find me, sis, Aspen whispered and I jumped, sure that I'd felt the tickle of her breath on my neck. I spun around, but found only another statue of Edeva, this one holding a basket of eyeballs.

Over here, Mira, Aspen's voice called from the other end of the room.

I scrambled to follow the sound as fast as my aching limbs would allow, finding only a blank dirt wall. Just in case, I traced my hands along the rough surface, surprised to feel it vibrating. A guttural rumble sounded and I had a second to throw myself backwards before two figures exploded out of the structure. Naomi stood before me wild-eyed in black silk pyjamas as Ramaya grappled her around the waist, holding her back.

The First Magpie reached for me, and I ducked behind the closest statue, crouching, heart thundering. "I'm sorry, Mira," she cried.

"Mira," came Ramaya's voice, soothing, calming, "Naomi's not here to hurt you. She wanted to apologize so badly she destroyed half my lab to get here."

"I'm sorry," Naomi said again, her voice softer, full of surrender. "Will you let me explain?"

Don't! You owe her nothing! Aspen hissed.

But how many times did I listen to you, Asp? How many nights did you creep into my bed to apologize for being too harsh, for going too far? Ignoring my sister's voice in my head, I stepped out from behind the statue to find Naomi half-slumped in Ramaya's arms. "You have five minutes."

Ramaya unsubtly edged her way between us, still supporting Naomi with one hand.

"I've gone over and over it in my head." The First Magpie's chin trembled. "The animals kept telling me you stunk of deception and they've never been wrong before. And Teddy thought so too."

"Teddy suspected me too? All this time?"

"Teddy and I felt your unusual energy at the rootbinding and we both agreed it would be best for me to investigate. But I must be losing my edge, losing my grip on reality…" Naomi ran her hands through her hair. She'd chewed her fingernails down to the quick and the skin around the nails was raw and scabbed.

It was painful to see the First Magpie so diminished, literally gnawing away at herself as she stewed in guilt and self-doubt. I knew only too well what she was feeling, and I hated that my deception was driving Naomi's pain. Ramaya caught my eye, shaking her head as if she knew exactly what I was about to do.

"I was lying," I admitted. "But not about what you thought."

"What do you mean?"

I explained what Kes and I had done, how I'd been deceiving everyone. "So I haven't connected to the trees on purpose. Not yet. And at this point, I can't say I want to—they keep trying to kill me."

Before Naomi could speak, Ramaya rushed out, "If you're going to punish Mira for lying, you'll have to punish Kes. And me. Kes is the one who *told* Mira to lie, something she kindly left out of the story just now. And I've known since the white party in Rhode Island and intentionally lied to the First Owl and the Council in my debrief. As soon as Kes woke this week, we consulted and decided we would do anything it took to keep Mira in the order."

I flushed with warmth, as if I'd suddenly slipped into the hot springs beneath the keep.

"*Ramaya*, you've never broken an order rule in your life, no matter how much you joke." The First Magpie looked between us, picking at a scab on her thumb until it bled. A bat swooped through the hole in the wall, gently wrapping around Naomi's hand so she couldn't pick anymore. Finally, she said, "It would be a devastating blow to lose the two—three of you from active duty in this moment of heightened danger. I won't say anything for now."

"Thank you!" Ramaya and I said at the same time, trading relieved smiles.

"But you must know your secret is unsustainable. It will become ever more obvious what you can, and *cannot*, do, Mira."

"We'll lobby to change the rule," Ramaya said confidently. "The Huntsmen know the importance of human persuasion; they literally invested all of their firepower into a *song*. And we're out here gatekeeping our order from folks like Mira—one of the very few of us who genuinely likes humans and is any good at connecting to them."

"I agree with you," Naomi said. "But many will not. And they'll do anything to protect what they hold dear."

"That I understand," I murmured, my eyes drawn once more to the statue of Edeva and Godda, the way the carving made the two sisters look like one being bound together for eternity.

TWENTY-TWO

Someone knocked on the infirmary door late that night. Not wanting to wake Kes, I rolled out of bed and peered into the empty hallway. I caught a figure disappearing around the corner and hurried after them.

"Wait," I whispered. What if they had something for Kes? "Wait," I called again.

Hurry up, sis, don't want to get left behind, Aspen teased.

"ASPEN!"

This castle is way creepier at night. Where are all the people?

My sister chatted animatedly to me while I wound down flight after flight of stairs, heart pounding from exertion, fear, and...hope. I knew that skipping stride, that toss of the hair. My sister. My sister was in the castle. I pulled up, realizing how dark it had become. We were deep below the keep now in the warren of tunnels common to any hub of the Seven. Aspen had disappeared into the maze. I drew in a breath to call for her and suddenly she was there—pale, solemn, and with a finger to her lips, shushing me. I lunged towards her, but she shook her head, darting away, leading me deeper into the ground.

The tunnels got smaller and smaller until I was crawling on my hands and knees. I hadn't seen Aspen in what felt like hours, but I could feel her everywhere, I knew I was still on her tail. But my body was giving out on me. Crawling was making my wrists and ankles swell and every shift of soil or brush of a root brought me back to the panic of Naomi's ambush.

I stayed quiet as long as I could, remembering Aspen's plea for silence but the soil was starting to shift and give way. It fell on my face, mixing with my tears so I was crying mud. "Aspen, I can't go any further, please. Come back, come back to me!"

"Mira! Is that you?" a voice echoed faintly.

"Aspen," I hissed. "Should I wait here for—" A hunk of dirt hit me in the face. If I stayed here much longer I'd be buried alive.

"Mira," the voice came again, closer, more urgent.

"Here," I whispered, waiting for Aspen to shush me. "Here," I said, louder, shifting towards the voice.

"Stay as still as you can, the soil's not stable down here."

Kes.

"Now I'm going to grab your hand and Silverlight is going to pull us up to firm ground. Close your eyes and mouth as tight as you can and try not to inhale."

A hand emerged from the soil above me, reaching, searching. I stared at it in resentment, curling tighter into myself. Dirt shifted and fell around me as the earth seemed to shudder.

"Hurry, Mira." Kes's hand found my shoulder. I tried to pull away but another hand plunged out of the dirt grabbing my other side. Suddenly I was being dragged roughly up a narrow channel, my limbs glancing off rock and root, and Godda knows what else.

Kes hauled me out of the tunnel, hefting my body onto safe ground. I couldn't see through the dirt caked thick across my eyes but I spun towards where I thought they were and cursed at them. "Why'd you do that? Take me back!" I demanded, rubbing my eyes with no result. Kes put a scrap of something soft in my hand and I managed to wipe enough muck away to pry my eyes open. The first thing I saw was Kes's bare arms and chest, also covered in dirt, but not enough to cover their muscles. They were shivering, sweaty from exertion and I remembered how fragile they were.

"I saw Aspen, I was following her."

Kes shook their head. "There was nobody else there. You were dozens of meters underground, nearly deeper than Silverlight's roots. I don't even know how you got there—it would've taken some serious treetalking—"

"It was Aspen!" I cut in. "She led me there."

"Yeah, well then she led you to a tomb. Your tomb. Why would she do that?"

"No, she wouldn't hurt me. She comes to me clearest when I'm in danger, and she saves me."

Kes gave me a look of naked pity. "Maybe—"

"Don't say it. Don't say that it's just my brain, my survival instinct, calling up a shadow of Aspen when I need a push."

Kes didn't speak; they just moved closer. "May I?" They held their arms open for a hug.

I nodded, sobbing into their warm chest. They held me for so long I lost count, only coming back to the present when they shivered beneath me. "Are you OK? Should we get you back to the infirmary?"

"No, I'll be fine. I just need to warm up." They looked over their shoulder and I saw a billow of steam.

"Are we at the hot springs?" I looked around at the cavernous space, trying to match it to that first night at the castle.

"These are more *private* hot springs."

Kes shivered again and I grabbed their hand. Wordlessly

we walked towards the steam. Sloped stairs cut into the earth led to a natural spring. The steam got thicker as we approached, loosening the grime caked over me, loosening the muscles underneath. I sighed at the embrace of the water and dirt fell away from me in great sheets like I was a snake shedding my skin.

"Better?" Kes asked from somewhere to my left, behind a curtain of steam.

"I think I live here now; I may never leave. You?"

"Getting there."

"Anything I can help with?" I was shocked at how flirtatious my voice sounded.

Kes groaned.

"What?" I would've blushed but my face was already too warm from the steam.

"It's just..." Their voice had that same gravelly tightness as before, when Teddy interrupted us. "Nothing."

We lapsed into a long silence at our opposite ends of the pool.

"Do you hate me?"

Kes's question startled me out of my fantasy, starring *them*, and I couldn't help but giggle at the irony. "To borrow a classic Teddy expression—why on Godda's green earth would I hate you?"

"I...I dragged you into this whole mess, and I can see how much you're hurting—"

I put a hand up even though they couldn't see it. "I literally made you drag me into this mess. Or has the great Kestrel forgotten that I leeched you without even trying?"

They didn't answer and I worried that I'd gone too far. Why did I always have to deflect, why couldn't I just let them be vulnerable? I pushed through the steam and found them, draped across a rock cropping like a Renaissance painting, eyes closed. I drank them in, the lean muscle, the tattoos of the Rhiza, made from hundreds of tiny lines like a Degas sketch, the twin scars on their chest. There was an angry red line across their neck from where the gem garrote had bound them.

Kes caught me looking at them.

"Does it still hurt?" I forced out, my mouth suddenly feeling like it was full of peanut butter.

Kes ran a finger over the healing skin. "No more than the others." I fought the urge to scan their body again, searching for the other scars, and met their gaze instead. Their eyes twinkled; they were enjoying this.

A month ago I would have turned tail and fled. But now, now I glided through the water towards Kes, getting a delicious full-body jolt as the grin slid off their face. As that steady gaze turned questioning, hopeful. They unfurled back into the pool, reaching for me. The water seemed to push me forwards into their arms. They looked at me intently, their warm hands tracing the line of my jaw and it was my turn to shiver.

"Are you sure?" they whispered, voice ragged, and I kissed them, trying to catch that hunger in my mouth. That hunger for *me*.

Kes kissed me back, and I felt their emotions rushing into me, the force of their affection humming through my body, loosening the last bits of tension. Kes's heart beat into mine and I forgot where we ended and the water began.

Someone wolf whistled. At first I thought it was Aspen but when it came again I realized the sound was echoing from somewhere in the cavern. I broke away from Kes reluctantly just as the clapping started.

"I see you, Mira Bracken, you got game," Adrian called, coming into sight with Tai close behind. I jumped towards my friends, forgetting I was in the water and splashing Kes directly in the face. They sputtered. So much for having game.

Kes recovered, bounding out of the hot springs and shaking like a dog in front of Adrian and Tai until the two were drenched. I followed in sodden PJs and gratefully took the towel Adrian handed me.

"Here we were, stopping by to visit our poor, bedridden friend for a quick hug..." Adrian trailed off, shaking his head in mock dismay.

"What are you even doing in this part of the world?" Kes asked. "Is this for the London climate march?"

"They're predicting *two* million in the streets." Adrian leaned into Kes's side.

"It's all hands on deck." Tai leaned into Kes's other side. "Zo had a really bad feeling about this one; they insisted on having a few more eyes from Salish Sea Hub on the ground. The Confessor's too flashy, too unpredictable—who knows how many civilians he'd be willing to sacrifice."

"And you folks are first to go out in the field?" Kes pulled their friends tight. "Intrepid larks."

"You really have been out of the loop—" Tai started.

"Or distracted by more...*visceral* pursuits." Adrian smirked.

"We're the last to go out," Tai finished. "Just stopping here for a quick resupply and then we'll head to London with the others."

"What for?" I asked.

"We want to be prepared for whatever's coming, especially with the counter-protesters massing."

"Not that again." Kes rolled their eyes.

"It's worse than usual. Somebody's pumping millions of dollars into it."

"Into protesting?" I asked.

"Counter-protesting, staged and funded by corporations to make it look like their anti-climate action has grassroots support."

"They can do that?"

"Oh, that's child's play for Big Oil."

"But what are the larks going to do at the protest?" I asked.

"We're organizing a massive, joyful dance party to build morale for the climate protesters, gather intel, and charge the Rhiza with energy for anyone on our side who will need it. Want to join? We scored Billie Eilish as our secret headliner."

Kes's eyes lit up. "I'm in."

"Oh no you're not." Ramaya strode into the hot springs. "You're not going anywhere. You're on recupe duty."

"This is dancing. What could be more restful?" Kes replied.

"Ramaya," the twins called, pulling the woman into our circle of entangled limbs.

"I'm playing chaperone today." Ramaya grimaced.

Adrian shook his head. "I know for a fact that you've been to six Billie Eilish concerts and that you personally requested doing security for us today."

Ramaya grinned. "Seven, actually. And I liked her before she was famous."

"Rama, let me tag along. Please, pretty please?" Kes hung off of his friend.

"You little hypocrite, always talking about how rest *is* work and how the order has to enforce recuperation more. What was it you told me last month? We need five weeks mandatory leave—no missions, no exceptions. You've lasted what? A week? Two?"

"You know you're going to let me," Kes crooned, grabbing Ramaya in an affectionate side hug.

She heaved a fake sigh and looked at me. "What do you say? Want to watch these idiots dance, poorly, in the name of climate justice?"

"Who could resist—" I stopped, my fingers brushing against something soft and foreign in my pocket. I pulled it out to see a raven's feather. One that hadn't been there before. *Aspen*. She was really in the castle. She'd left me a sign, like the ravens from her room.

"What's that?" Kes asked.

I hesitated, on the brink of telling them the truth.

No, hissed Aspen.

"A little keepsake from Salish Sea Hub," I lied, blushing. "I think I better stay here and rest a little—"

My words were swallowed by the sound of the ground shaking. Dozens of roots shot out of the walls, wrapping around Kes and Ramaya, their message clearly urgent. Other roots began to glow on and off, strobing a silent warning to us. My friends' eyes widened, and I watched in awe as the two magpies snapped into coiled focus. Adrian and Tai however looked how I felt—like bear cubs scared by our own shadows.

"Our perimeter has been breached," Kes explained. "Silverlight is evacuating the castle."

"Follow me," Ramaya commanded. And we did, falling silently into line behind her. She led us quickly back up the winding staircases. I stroked the feather in my pocket, praying I could get the timing just right. There'd be only one chance.

I waited until we were almost at the main floor, when the root updates were coming even faster, and the others' attention had clearly turned to whatever threat awaited us in the castle. And then I slowed just as everyone turned the last corner, slipping quietly back down into the warren of tunnels. I tried to remember the way I'd gone earlier when I'd stumbled upon the room full of carved stone bodies frozen in their silent dance. Aspen had whispered to me from amongst the statues and my gut told me to return. I pushed open a doorway only to find myself in some kind of pantry. A root shot out of the wall at me and I ducked and threw myself backwards, slamming the door in a hurry. I recounted my steps, running now, and took a different turn. There—the door with the raven's head. The bird seemed to wink at me as I shoved it open.

I didn't see her at first, she was hidden almost perfectly behind a figure of Edeva—how had I not noticed how similar they looked? The fierce eyes and determined jaw. My sister. My sister was in the same room as me. Alive. Energy knocked into me like a tidal wave—fear, love, hope, every pore flooded. There was the face I'd been searching for with every breath the last eighteen months. The eyes that had stared up at me from a million missing person flyers—laughing, full of mischief.

They weren't laughing now.

I threw myself at my sister and she caught me—a real, solid person, not a ghost of my imagination. The echo of a million other hugs like this washed over me. We were back together. All was right with the world.

Except all was not right with the world. I pulled back and took in my sister's appearance—the bruises on her arms, as if she'd been battling a pack of snakes. The eyes not shining with fire, but confusion, terror.

"Sissy, where am I? I've been stuck in a bad place." Aspen repeated herself, whispering, "Stuck, stuck, stuck."

"If they've harmed one hair on your head, I'll..." I trailed off. It was clear the Huntsmen had done far more than that. Aspen's energy felt corrupted, wrong. But at least we were together.

She took my hand, tugging me towards another set of stairs, one leading deeper into the underground maze of tunnels. I resisted. "I've got to get you back to my friends. They can help. They're the best we have—"

"Take me away, please," Aspen begged. "Sissy, please, I'm so afraid." She tugged me again and I was surprised at her strength. I tumbled forwards and my sister grabbed me towards her. Roots reached out of the ground, wrapping around the both of us. *"Finally,"* Aspen whispered, her eyes illuminated by a strange light.

"UNHAND HER," Teddy called, stepping through the door. She didn't look like a kindly old woman anymore—more like a witch out of a fairy tale. Her grey-purple hair fluttered in a self-made breeze; her eyes shone with lethal intensity. She was flanked by Ramaya, Kes, Naomi, Kate, Tai, and Adrian, each looking solemn.

"This is Aspen, my sister." I strained my neck towards them, trying to explain, but their faces didn't relax. Indeed, Adrian turned pale in horror. I whipped my head back around to see Aspen's face transformed, a red glimmer in her eyes as if they were made of scarlet gems. My friends strode towards us, moving in lockstep, and Aspen spun away from them, away from me. She dove as if jumping into a pool and arced downward—right through the dirt floor, hurtling deep underground, propelled by a network of roots.

There were hands all over me, dragging me, pulling me.

"Get Mira to safety," Ramaya barked. "That thing is coming back." I was bundled between Teddy and Naomi and towed somewhere, forever at the whim of somebody else's choices. The others split off, presumably to battle Aspen, or the demonic force inhabiting her body. Our trio launched through a final door into the courtyard of the castle. I gulped for air, desperate to hold back the bile surging in my throat at the thought of Aspen being puppeteered by the Huntsmen and targeted by my friends.

Silverlight scooped us up and set us down in an open-air rotunda perched on the castle ramparts with a view out to the grounds and into the courtyard. Teddy grabbed my hand, speaking quickly, "Mira, please stay here and be as quiet as you can. Kate will be up in a moment to explain more. The rest of us will fan out to protect you and help your sister."

I grabbed Teddy's arm before she could climb back over the rampart wall into Silverlight's waiting embrace. "NO. No. If you want me to do as you say, you owe me more than that. How in the world is Aspen here, in the castle?"

"You can feel her, can't you? Hear her? Sense her energy everywhere?"

"How did you—"

"So it always is for those who have been rootbound to one another."

"Aspen and I aren't..." I trailed off, feeling the lie in my words. "But...but how? We never had a ceremony..."

"Are you sure? It's possible she bound you in your sleep, or leeched you to forget the ceremony. I should have seen it earlier, what we all should have seen. I couldn't understand where your power came from. You seemed to have none of the natural affinity for trees that engendered the connection between rootbound and Rhiza. Naomi was also puzzled—why could you only use your powers when threatened? But now I see. You and Aspen are rootbound. When you're in danger Aspen senses it through the Rhiza and instinctually sends you her power."

"So...Aspen has been protecting me? It's her treetalking power I'm getting through the Rhiza...but then why wouldn't she come talk to me?"

Teddy's eyes widened and I swung around to see a thin column of smoke rising in the forest several miles away. Silverlight wrapped a branch around Teddy's wrist and she gasped. "*Aspen did not come alone.*"

"Greetings, rootbound," a robotic voice blasted through the air. "The Confessor has a message for you."

I leaned against the older woman, trying to use her as an anchor against the memory of the sandy-haired man whispering my bloody, frozen body into oblivion. The Confessor was here, in the heart of the rootbound, at the same time as my sister. What in Godda's name was going on?

The Confessor boomed, "You've no doubt seen the smoke rising in the distance. I've set a small fire. It's contained for now, but with our new chemical accelerant I could ensure every last tree in this forest of a thousand acres burns to the ground." Another column of smoke rose a little to the left of the first, and another. "I propose a Test of Wills so we may finally speak of truce. Does one among you accept? Or will you let your tree kin BURN?"

Silverlight began to tremble and sway, creaking her branches in agony. I remembered what Ramaya and Naomi had said, how mother trees could feel the suffering of the plants in their network. Silverlight was sensing her kin being burned alive.

Without hesitation, Teddy called, "I do." The Rhiza amplified her words, every branch and root echoing her voice for miles.

"Excellent. And you will allow me to enter unharmed to begin the ritual?"

More plumes of smoke snaked into the air, blocking out the sun. Teddy clutched at the branch in her hand, stroking the bark with her thumb. "Douse the flames and you may enter."

Silverlight swept the archivist off the rampart. Suddenly I was alone, waiting for the murderous blond man to enter our safe haven and aching for my sister, always just out of reach.

CHAPTER

TWENTY-THREE

The smoke columns in the distance slowly thinned and disappeared. A few minutes of eerie quiet later Kate scurried across the parapet connecting the turret to the rest of the castle and pulled me into a tight, wordless hug. "Here." She twirled a finger and a curling green shoot wound up from the lichen-covered stone. "This is connected to Silverlight. Wind it around your ears, like so, and you'll be able to hear what the rest of us are saying through the Rhiza."

"What's going on?"

"Teddy is preparing for the Test of Wills. Ramaya and Kes are tracking your sister—she is quite a proficient treetalker and a slippery target, but they've vowed to take her unharmed." I let out the breath I'd been holding; I trusted Kes and Ramaya to do just that. "The others are doing recon on the enemy's position and communicating with reinforcements."

A black SUV snaked its way down the winding road to the castle and through the open gates. The Confessor emerged from the vehicle. I expected him to be draped in glowing jewels like a psychedelic version of a king on coronation day, but he looked for all the world like a member of the Seven in a fleece and joggers.

"When I tell you to, turn around, and don't turn back until I signal. During the Test, two master willbinders open their minds to each other. It's very rare nowadays, but if it goes right, they can bind each other to tell the truth. And vow to do no bodily harm to one another."

"And if it goes wrong?"

Kate took a moment before she answered. "One willbinder can emerge in total control of the other. Like they're root-bound, sharing powers, sharing energy, but one is bound in servitude to the other. And if we hear or see the vows we risk being bound as well. *Turn*."

I did as Kate directed. The plant shoots nestled gently over my ears suddenly plunged deep into my ear canals, blocking out all sound. I couldn't help but think of Ramaya's zombie ants, how fungi had hacked their bodies, allowing them to be controlled through the Rhiza. I shivered, worrying the plant might somehow lodge itself in my brain, taking control of me. But just as soon as I had the thought, the tendrils withdrew, returning to their spot wrapped around my earlobes.

"It's done—they have commenced the Test of Wills. Remember, The Confessor cannot hurt Teddy while they're bound," Kate whispered. "Magpie reinforcements are attempting to communicate through the Rhiza. I must go update them. Stay here, and please, for the love of Godda, don't do anything foolish."

Kate disappeared and I peeked through the slit in the rampart, straining to get a better view without being seen. The Confessor had joined Teddy at a table placed beneath Silverlight's boughs and set with two steaming bowls of soup.

Teddy spoke first, "I can guarantee us thirty minutes of unbroken conversation at most. The rest will not be so understanding. Too many friends, children, rootbound kin have died at your command."

"I know," The Confessor said. "That's why I'm here. I don't want any more rootbound to die—it's such an unnecessary waste." It sounded like he was talking about paper towels or grain, not human lives.

"You want us to ally with you?"

"In an ideal world. We both want the same thing."

"Which is?"

"Clean air, fresh water, rich forests. I'm trying to remind the Huntsmen of our original purpose—we were the guardians of the forest."

"Yet the Rhiza rejects you."

The Confessor's eyes flashed. "Are you sure?" After a moment, he shrugged. "I'd settle for the Seven staying out of my way. Just stand back and let me take control of the Huntsmen. Once in full control, we can build a new world, unsullied by the ills of this one."

Teddy didn't say anything. She began to sing, "The rich man in his castle, the poor man at his gate—"

"You have a beautiful voice," The Confessor said mildly.

"Do you believe it,? The words of the song. That the rich are destined to rule the poor?"

"You haven't figured it out yet, have you?" He dipped his spoon in the soup.

"Figured what out? That you're orchestrating a mass intergenerational leeching. That you're seeding the song in the deepest recesses of the brains of young and old alike and using it as a hook to leech them into mindless servitude. It's ingenious."

"Do I believe the song?" The Confessor shrugged. "It doesn't matter what I believe. It's what they believe."

"*They?*"

"People. Deep down, in the darkest corners of their soul, they believe that they're better, more human, more deserving of a good life. All we do is amplify that voice."

"No. You plant that voice. And you're stealing from school-children. Stealing their hope, their very will to grow, to thrive, to live."

"Let's not waste precious time on semantics."

"Fine. Tell me *how* you did it, how you planted the song. As a sign of good faith. I've been looking everywhere."

"Maybe you should have been *listening*."

"Using riddles to evade the binding of the ritual? Naughty, naughty."

A crow landed in Silverlight's branches. Another swooped to rest on the table, narrowly missing the bowls of soup. They sat very still as if they too were listening to the conversation.

The blond man whistled to the bird in front of him. The crow whistled back, The Confessor's song unmistakable in its trill.

Teddy stared at the bird. "No. The leeching is *in* the bird-song? The Huntsmen have corrupted an animimicker to do their cruel work? *Who?*"

"You know who." The Confessor nodded at the crow. It fluttered to Teddy's shoulder, brushing its head against her neck as if to nuzzle her. Another crow swooped down to land on her other shoulder, giving Teddy the illusion of towering, feathered shoulder pads. I'd seen that imagery once before—a painting of a woman hidden away in a dusty shrine. A painting of Edeva. "Your dearest Sister," the man purred.

The blood drained from Teddy's face. "It cannot be. I watched Edeva die."

I gasped, my mind jumping to the marble carving of Edeva and Godda wrapped in an infinite embrace. If Teddy had known Edeva, had been her dearest Sister, that would make the petite, purple-haired woman below me...

Godda.

Teddy was Godda, the one-thousand-year-old living heartbeat of the rootbound.

The crows began to shriek. Flocks of them flew across the sky in black masses.

"If it's true, let me speak to her," Teddy said. "Let me speak to my Sister!"

"You don't believe me? She said you wouldn't, not unless I told you the whole story." The blond man sighed, as if the words bored him. "Haven't you heard the tales of the man-eating bog in the forests of Ceredigion? Where hikers enter but do not leave."

"Why are you bringing up that childish..."

"There you go, you're starting to catch on, aren't you?" The castle shook in warning at The Confessor's patronizing tone. "Where did you last see your dearest Sister? Where did you betray her in her moment of deepest need?"

"Enough of these lies."

"You know they're not lies. I'm just surprised you didn't put the pieces together before me, the storied Godda, sacred kin of Silverlight. I've studied you and your Sister since childhood. All Huntsmen learn about the ambush of Ceredigion, where our most powerful willbinders were attacked while they slept—their eyes plucked out by the ravens, their hearts staked through by the trees. A massacre carried off by one woman. *Edeva.* And just as she celebrated her victory, she was slain by her sister, Godda, and left to rot in a blood-filled bog."

"So many dead. So many bodies. Children killed while they dreamt. Blood everywhere. And the birds and the trees were mad for it, they lusted for more, for revenge against all of humanity under Edeva's sway."

"And revenge they shall have," The Confessor announced. "Edeva didn't die the day you betrayed her those many centuries ago. The Rhiza saved her, preserved her. And it was I who found her. Who heard the reports of the missing hikers near Ceredigion and thought maybe, just maybe, the woman who nearly bested the Huntsmen had found a way to cheat death itself."

"Why would you, a Huntsman, want to resurrect Edeva, the worst nightmare of your kin?"

"The Huntsmen have lost their way. A thousand years ago, we noble families were gifted a sacred task. To protect the forest from human overreach, to steward the wonders of this planet for millennia to come."

"What a pretty way of saying you maimed starving people who crept onto your forests to feed their families. But there is something else you're not telling me. *Say it*. What else do you want from Edeva?"

"Edeva promised me something. Something I've wanted for a very long time, since I was a little boy. The power to command the trees." The Confessor put a hand on Silverlight's trunk. The bark began to climb up his skin, pulling his arm inwards as if into a hungry maw, and he yanked it free, just in time to avoid the branch that speared downwards at his exposed neck.

"You just murdered a dozen trees for sport, set them alight without a moment's thought. The Rhiza will never accept you—"

"It will if I'm rootbound to Edeva."

Teddy's spoon trembled in her hand and I hoped The Confessor was too busy recovering from Silverlight's assault to notice. "Now we get to the heart of this whole loathsome puzzle. You want *power*. Power over the public, the Huntsmen, and now the trees. And you dragged Edeva out of the grave to give you more." She set the utensil down. "So Edeva has helped you spread your song, leeching thousands, millions through birdsong, leeching even other Huntsmen. Commanding them to give up, to stop questioning the status quo, to stop caring."

"A 'doombind' I call it," The Confessor said proudly. "To make the weak-minded and weak-willed surrender and let the mighty rule and protect once more."

"And Edeva has promised to give you power over the trees. Although Silverlight tells me you're no friend to the Rhiza, so you're not yet bound. Edeva's not playing by the rules?"

The Confessor clenched his jaw, as if trying not to answer. After a few moments, he growled in frustration, "She'll bind me once I make peace with the rootbound. With *you*. Imagine —all of this fuss for a tired old woman in a decrepit castle. But like me, Edeva is growing tired of your hesitation." He leaned back, clasping his hands behind his head and his sleeves lifted to show rows of glowing gems in cuffs on his forearms.

"I wondered why you were so obsessed with a truce. So that's what you're getting out of the alliance with Edeva. What is Edeva getting?"

"Don't make me spell it out for you."

Teddy waited silently.

The Confessor sighed. "A decade ago, I used siphons to bring Edeva back from the brink, to help her anchor her power and take tangible form once again. But we needed more, so many more. Every leech on the planet knows which wills are the most potent. The most...enlivening. The young—so full of big dreams, so obsessed with ideals, so stirred by their passions."

"That's where the kidnapped youth climate strikers are going? To Edeva?"

"It's a small trade—a few hundred lives to finally purge the worst aspects of humanity, to draw out the poison."

"Show me. Prove it. Prove this is not all an elaborate trick."

"We are bound. I cannot lie."

"Prove it," Teddy snarled.

A figure spun out of the ground, long hair fanning out in a halo. Aspen looked for all the world like an Olympic ice skater mid-jump. She rasped, "He speaks the truth." It was Aspen's voice but not; there was something ancient, something evil about the sound. Edeva was speaking through Aspen—they were bound in some way. *"It's been too long, dear Sister."*

"NO! Edeva, you let them torture the brave youth fighting for our future? You let them murder those children? *More children.*" Teddy's eyes looked very far away, as if she'd been sucked back into the trauma of whatever happened in Wales. "So many dead. So many bodies. Blood everywhere. The mud was caked with it for weeks."

The Confessor's eyes narrowed in a predatory gleam. "You're mine, Godda. Submit to me."

Teddy slumped against the table. I waited for Silverlight to respond but the mother tree seemed as frozen as Teddy. The man pulled the older woman roughly to her feet, dragging her towards the front gate of the castle. "Protect us until we reach the troops gathered at the boundary," he called to Aspen and she nodded, melting back into the ground.

The Confessor and Teddy began walking down the winding road arm-in-arm. The beating heart of the Seven was going to stroll out of the castle with her greatest foe essentially unchallenged.

Geysers of dirt sprayed up around the walking pair and a figure rocketed out from the cover of the dirt volcanoes, Naomi exploding into the sky like some kind of creature of the night. Bats, hundreds of them, held the woman aloft, claws digging into her trench coat and pulling it taut to make her look winged. She shrieked in a language I didn't understand

and the bats began peeling off to dive-bomb at the fleeing duo.

Hawks launched out of the cover of the forest to collide with the plummeting bats in a tangle of exploding feathers. Hundreds of birds and bats fought each other, rending and tearing.

"See how unnatural it is that we fight," The Confessor's voice boomed over the din. "Bird against bird, tree against tree, kin against kin! Stop this futile madness once and for all—join us, and unite the Sisters!"

A raven broke through the protective bubble of hawks and managed to rake its talon across the blond man's face, leaving a gash of red. He grinned, a terrible bloody grin, and whispered something in Teddy's ear.

Teddy made a gesture with her hand and the earth beneath the two of them punched upwards, forming a miniature tower with impossibly steep edges. The summit brought them almost face-to-face with Naomi. Her platoon of bats tried to drag her backwards and away but The Confessor was already talking, his voice silky, insidious, "You failed your friends, Naomi Squall, you failed your order. GIVE UP!"

Naomi unzipped her trench coat and slid out of it, plummeting away from the bats that had held her aloft. They dove at her frantically from above, shrieking in panic, just as roots shot out of the ground to catch her from below. I held my breath, waiting for root and bat to arrest her plummet, but Naomi knocked them away, spinning and turning from their grasp. She landed with a sickening thud and lay unmoving.

"No!" called an anguished voice. Ramaya launched out of another dirt geyser, somersaulting to land on the earthen tower and slinging mycelium webs as she hauled herself up the pillar towards Teddy and The Confessor. I threw myself at the stairs, practically falling as I hurtled down them, and crept to a side door in the castle gate. I emerged just in time to see Teddy command a root to shoot out of the dirt summit like a Jenga block, jack-hammering into Ramaya's chest. She fell backwards but jerked to a stop after a few feet as the mycelium caught her and held, like a rope in a climbing gym. She threw herself back at the pillar, undaunted. Another root slithered out of the tower, thick as a python, and wrapped around her neck, dragging her back into the dirt so she disappeared completely. I pictured the root squeezing the life from my friend, suffocating her in the dark.

The pillar shifted perilously and began to tip, crashing back down to earth like a wave in my direction. I scrambled backwards, throwing my hands up just in time as the churning mass swept me up in its path and sent me tumbling. I stumbled to my feet, clawing dirt out of my eyes and scanning for Ramaya and the others. There—a shock of purple amongst a sea of brown. Teddy lay face down in the dirt next to another still figure. *Ramaya.* The Confessor stalked towards them, grimy, bloody, and very angry.

I crouched low, ignoring the burst of protest from my knees, and started towards the three of them. I didn't have the slightest idea what I was going to do against the power of The Confessor and his siphons, but I couldn't stand by and watch another friend be murdered in cold blood. The blond man kicked at Ramaya's inert form, hissing at the woman, "Your limbs are numb, your mouth is sealed, you cannot speak to the Rhiza." The pull of his leeching wound around my limbs even though it wasn't directed at me, and I rubbed my hands to keep my circulation flowing against his command.

"Ramaya Astre, your will shines as bright as any I've ever seen—so much strength, so much clarity of purpose. And yet, your power never got the recognition it deserved by the rootbound."

Something small scurried out of The Confessor's pocket, up his torso, and into his open palm. A siphon with a diamond body the size of a quarter. The tick-like creature rubbed its legs together, chittering loudly, clearly excited. Excited to sink its head into Ramaya's body, to drain her essence. Crawling closer, I stayed as low as I could and hoped my muck-smeared skin and clothes would give me enough cover. The Confessor crouched over my friend, cutting off her face from view. I dug my nails into my palms, drawing blood. Teddy's words came back to me: *When you're in danger Aspen senses it through the Rhiza and instinctually sends you her power.* Any treetalking I had managed in the past had come from my sister; she was the magical one. I had not a martial skill in the world.

Nothing but my voice.

"False Confessor!" I called, as loudly as I could, pulse pounding in my ears. "Fool! You really thought Aspen and Edeva would choose you over me and Godda? They betrayed you!" I lied. "They fed me their powers, *your* powers!"

The blond man glanced my way.

I opened my mouth to yell again, desperate to draw his attention even further from my friend, but I never got the chance. Like a loaded spring, Ramaya jerked upright and slammed her forehead into the side of The Confessor's face. There was a sound of shattering bone and the man fell backwards with a groan.

Ramaya had resisted the power of The Confessor's siphons. How could it possibly be?

I sprinted towards her, giving a wide berth to the blond man's form slumped in the dirt, blood streaming from his nose and black eyes beginning to bloom. Ramaya still sat on the ground, trembling with the effort of holding herself up. I rushed to support her and she leaned against me. What had happened to her? Had the python-root suffocated her?

Groaning with the effort, she lifted her arms to flip up the back of her hair and I let out a scream. Like bolts in the neck of Frankenstein, two siphons were buried in either side of her skull, their heads lodged deep into her skin. No, not siphons—

Two of Ramaya's zombie ants!

Ramaya pointed at her pocket and then collapsed unconscious in my arms. Quickly I felt where my friend had pointed, finding a small object that looked like a tube of lipstick. I remembered Ramaya spraying something similar to calm the zombie ants attacking the Huntsman on the plane in Seattle.

Before I could figure out how to activate the tube, the two of us started sinking through the ground, as if the dirt had turned to quicksand. I cradled my friend's head in my arms as we dropped through earthen level after level, finally landing in a nest of roots in one of the infinite tunnels beneath the castle grounds.

Aspen stepped towards me, her blood-red eyes luminous in the semi-dark. I scrambled to my feet, instinctively moving between my sister and Ramaya. She held her hands up to embrace me. Every fiber in my body tensed to shrink away, but this was my one, perhaps my only, chance to talk to my sister alone. And the longer she was with me, distracted, the safer Ramaya and my other friends were from the ancient evil lurking within her. So I let her hug me. When she pulled back to stare at me hungrily, I met those crimson eyes. "Edeva, let me speak to my sister alone."

Aspen barked with laughter. I had loved her laugh, had done so many stupid, embarrassing things to draw out the sound, like a rushing rapid or a bursting dam. But this laugh was grating, humorless. "Impertinent," she hissed, the threat in her tone and posture clear.

Aspen might still love me, but Edeva clearly did not. The thought terrified me, but it also gave me an idea. It was a fool's chance, but I was a fool. As far as Aspen had strayed, she'd proven again and again that she would stop at nothing to protect me from certain violence. And I would bet that once Aspen had set her mind on something, not even a force as strong as Edeva and her siphons could stop her. Across oceans and continents my sister had poured her love into me through the Rhiza, coming to me clearest when I was in danger. Now she was mere inches away. So I just had to put myself in a little danger.

"You think that's impertinent?" I stepped back from the being. "Try this one on for size. Godda will never, ever rejoin you, a woman who has betrayed every righteous dream you two once held dear, who has rolled over and done the bidding of the worst of the Huntsmen just to steal a few more years of miserable life."

Aspen lunged at me, hands wrapping around my neck and squeezing. "How dare you." I held her stare as my face reddened and my eyes bugged out of my face. The periphery of my vision grew blurry and I batted weakly at the hands around my throat, panic driving every thought out of my mind except one—had I misjudged Aspen's love for me?

The pressure against my throat released and I wheezed, sagging to my knees as the blood rush backed to my extremities. I swayed and my sister caught me. Just Aspen. Edeva was gone, blood-red eyes replaced with hazel. "Sissy, sissy, are you OK?"

I nodded, taking an experimental breath.

"I'm sorry. I was trying to keep you out of all of this. Do the dirty work so you could enjoy life. Have a future."

I laughed bitterly. "Aspen, you were...you *are* my future."

"I know. I'm not going to try to keep you out of this anymore. Come with us."

"What? No. Edeva literally just tried to kill me, using *your* hands. You're on the wrong side. Stay here in the castle—my friends can help you."

Aspen's face hardened like it always did when she sunk her teeth into an argument. "You know the grief you've been feeling for the last eighteen months? All-consuming? Disorienting? Reality-shaking? I've been feeling that for the last eighteen *years*. I decided I'd do whatever was necessary to stop the suffering. It's so much, Mira. I was ready to sacrifice everything I had and everything I wanted for myself, but I couldn't sacrifice you."

"What did you do, Aspen?"

"I snuck back. I bound us—it was easy, we were essentially already bound. Bonnie, our cherry tree, agreed to seal the bind while you were sleeping."

How *dare* she.

How dare she. My beautiful sister. All that sadness swirling in her heart.

And me. The one thing she couldn't let go of. I felt the force of her love like a hurricane. "Why didn't you tell me, Asp? I could've been there for you, could've gotten you the help you deserve. We could've been magpies together."

"We can still fight together, with Edeva. And maybe even Godda. We won't be enemies after today."

I let myself imagine it for a moment. Aspen laughing in a full-body hug with me and my motley crew—Kes, Ramaya, Adrian, Tai, Zo, Kate. The grief of that lost future pierced me like a knife in my side and I gasped. "I...I'm not sure—"

"The rootbound are not who they seem," Aspen cut me off, an edge of desperation in her voice. "We're the ones actually taking on the Huntsmen, tricking them into giving us their wealth and power. They wanted the song to bind the masses, but they didn't realize they'd be bound as well. Bound to The Confessor, and through him, to Edeva, the greatest animimicker the world has ever known, the true defender of people and planet."

I stared at Aspen, feeling the usual tug of her persuasion like a current lapping at my ankles.

"Capitalism is already sucking the souls from young people. The mindless swiping and consumption. The dead-eyed apathy. The skin hunger. We're doing them a kindness— dulling them to the pain. Speeding the collapse of this dying world to build something new and beautiful in its ashes."

"*Sis*. You're a full-blown ecofascist."

"And you're a full-blown Seven Sisters apologist, worshipping Godda like some lost little sheep!" Aspen spat. "We're at war. AT WAR. At least we're acting like it."

"Spoken like a true eco-fascist," I spat back. "I wish you hadn't bound us. I wish I'd been leeched to forget you ever existed."

"No you don't. I've seen how lonely you are without me. I tried to be there for you when I could, keeping you company, making you laugh. But imagine how much better it would be if we were together again, in the flesh. The two of us against the world."

I shook my head. "Wait a second, it was YOU? You've been in my head, *actually* in my head, this whole time?" I couldn't handle any more revelations. But my brain kept whirring, piecing things together, and realization dawned. "My God. You've been stealing our secrets, our vulnerabilities, our locations. That's how the Huntsmen knew Kes was at the party in Rhode Island. How The Confessor found Godda and Silverlight." Naomi's words came back to me again—*she'll kill us all. And you'll say I didn't warn you.*

"I did...borrow some info, but only enough to keep you safe." Aspen swatted the air as if she could knock the anger right out of my head. She reminded me suddenly of Naomi.

Always action first and thinking later. Absolute certainty over nuance. Somewhere along the line Aspen had gone from principle to dogma.

"Mira," a voice called.

Kes.

Twelve hours ago I would've leapt towards that sound, but now I froze. Aspen's expression had shifted, her shoulder lifting into the slightest shrug. Her preemptive apology look. The look she made before taking the last cookie or antagonizing our conspiracy-loving cousin at a family reunion. She was going to do something to Kes. I threw myself at Aspen and dragged her to the ground. "Run, Kes!" I shouted. "I don't have any treetalking powers. They're Aspen's!"

A root tugged me off of my sister easily, like a dog on a leash. Other roots lifted Aspen far more gracefully. My heart squeezed as Kes burst through the ceiling and into the dark, deep tomb.

Really, Mira? You'd choose your little crush over me? Aspen's voice in my head whispered.

Kes's face was calm but their chest heaved from the effort of the day. They were still recovering. Could Aspen see it? Could she sense how vulnerable they were? I felt a sudden sense of vertigo, clutching at a nearby wall as my world flipped upside down. I was no longer afraid *for* Aspen. Now I was afraid *of* Aspen.

My sister lunged at me, locking me in a vice-like grip as roots pulled us into the tunnel wall. Before we disappeared completely into the earth, Kes managed to grab my hand and mycelium spun up our arms, keeping me tethered in the space in some kind of deranged game of tug of war. My sister began to sing The Confessor's song.

"Stay with me," Kes commanded, binding me.

The song whispered, *Give up. Don't worry about Ramaya and*

Naomi lying still in the dirt, about your friends surrounded by Huntsmen, about your sister infected by Edeva. The others will manage. All you have to do is close your eyes and give up.

I felt the pull of the song and the pull of Kes's binding, dragging me in opposite directions like powerful currents. Desperate for anchor, I dropped into my breath, my body, felt myself exhale for the first time all day. I searched for the millions of threads connecting me to the two people trying to tear me in half. There was the same superconductor between myself and Kes—love. But not just our love—the love of Godda, who was deeply entwined with Kes, and Edeva, who was bound to my sister and me. Is that why we were so drawn to one another? Because of the love of the Sisters searching for each other across centuries and bodies?

And there, dozens of thick braided lines linked Aspen and me at every possible juncture, running thickest between our heads and hearts. I felt my way down those connections, probing for a way to break the power of the song, to help Kes win and pull me to safety. I'd expected to feel the lurking energy of Edeva, who had fused herself to Aspen in some way. But I hadn't expected the overwhelming nausea as I touched the tangle of threads linking our minds. The bundle was coated in something tarred and poisonous, like a bird's feathers after an oil spill. I probed the toxic substance, testing it, trying to understand it, and felt my stomach flip as if I'd fallen over the side of a pool and was plunging through the water.

TWENTY-FOUR

Dappled sunlight fell across a thick shag carpet and muraled walls, making me wince after the darkness of the castle tunnels. I was in Aspen's room. My sister sat at her usual spot in her window, calling softly to the family of ravens perched in Bonnie's branches. Her hair was different, short and spiky. She'd only worn it like that once, after she'd shaved her head for charity in junior year. So I was in a memory, Aspen's memory, from a few years ago. Touching the tar-like substance had brought me here. But why?

I studied Aspen carefully, taking in her sweatpants and favorite purple fleece, the one I'd refused to let my parents wash for an entire year after she disappeared. A poster for one of our high school divestment rallies lay unfinished on her desk, the shimmering paint still wet. I sat next to her on the window seat, putting my head on her shoulder, and getting an overwhelming whiff of peppermint essential oil. "Oh, we're still in your peppermint era, before you realized you smelled like a walking novelty Christmas shop."

Aspen didn't move or show any other sign that she was aware of my presence. The ravens swooped in to circle her room. She turned to watch them and I drank in her smile. She looked so young, so free, so unlike the creature who had just attacked me in the castle. The birds began to caw raucously at each other.

I'd never have recognized it if I hadn't heard it so many times in recent memory. But now that I did, the tune was unmistakable. Masked within the ravens' crowing was the rudimentary melody of The Confessor's song.

Many things came back to me at once.

Naomi's report that Seattle, my home, was a hot spot for the song.

The Confessor's admission that he used the song against his own people, his own allies, leeching them without their knowledge.

Horrible Hanna back at Salish Sea Hub taunting me, "That's how you *think* you think, but you've been exposed to hundreds of thousands of bits of Huntsmen propaganda."

And I finally understood. Aspen thought she served Edeva of her own free will. But the ravens had targeted my sister with the song for years without her knowing, planting the binding deep in her subconscious. They'd been singing to her since she was a junior in high school. That was the poison in her mind, which had begun to leak into me. Aspen didn't know she was Edeva's puppet, and thus the Huntsmen's puppet.

I had to tell her. But how to do it without waking Edeva's presence within my sister? Aspen had been forcing her way into my mind this past year and a half. Could I do the same to her? I stayed planted in the memory, grabbing seventeen-year-old Aspen by the shoulders and trying to turn her to face me. But I made no impact, no matter how much I tugged. I screamed and waved my hands in front of her eyes, breaking into a desperate set of jumping jacks but she never so much as blinked at my antics. I grabbed a book from her bookshelf and chucked it out the window. Then another. I sent one right into the heart of Bonnie's trunk, cursing the tree for her role in binding me.

I was closer than I'd been to Aspen in years and I still couldn't reach her. The thought felt unbearable, like a fever ratcheting up my temperature higher and higher until my skin began to melt and peel. I howled, an animal whine, and got a jolt of memory—the two of us scream-singing in the rain to Rihanna before Aspen knocked into me and took a bite out of my eyebrow so big I'd needed stitches.

I glanced at the giant hand-drawn calendar Aspen kept on one wall, locating the month and day—April 12th—and realized the collision had happened just a few weeks before this memory.

I warbled the first few words to *Umbrella* and swore Aspen's eyes darted in my direction. I sang louder and this time I was sure—Aspen was sneaking looks at me. "Remember when you bit me in the face? Your little sister? *Remember, Asp?*"

"Mom was so pissed." Aspen giggled. "But you have to admit the scar is cool."

I ran a finger over the half-moon scar bracketing my eye and beamed. "You're right. I should've been way more grateful you took a big old chomp out of me." I wanted to lose myself in the sibling teasing, in this perfect moment of togetherness outside of time and space, but I wasn't sure when Edeva would reawaken. "And do you remember this?" I gestured at the ravens, who had flown back outside to perch in the cherry tree.

Aspen followed the aim of my gesture and beamed. "Of course. The eggs hatched at the same time Bonnie's flowers blossomed."

"Can you hear what the ravens are singing?"

"Singing? They don't really sing, they're not robins." Aspen flopped on her bed, pulling a granola bar from under her pillow.

"Just listen."

She rolled her eyes but leaned her head towards the window. "Oh, you're right. I can hear it now, the same melody over and over."

"The rich man in his castle, the poor man at his gate," I sang in tune with the birds.

"What in the classist trash is that? A new RikRok trend?"

I tried again, more insistently. "God made them, high or lowly, and ordered their estate—"

Aspen made an exaggerated gagging sound. "Is this horrifying song punishment for biting you? I said I was sorry..." she trailed off, tilting her head.

I skipped ahead in the song, singing, "Sins and secrets untold, The Confessor knows. He'll bring this poisonous chapter of man to a close."

Aspen jerked upright. "They're singing The Confessor's song."

"ASPEN, you're here! Look how old you are in this memory —just a junior in high school! They targeted you with the song for *years* before you disappeared. Edeva's been whispering to you without you knowing, manipulating you at the deepest level. How can you be sure which decisions are yours and which are hers?"

"But if that's true..." Aspen's eyes widened. "Free me, free me from the song, Mira."

"I will—I promise." I pulled my sister into a quick hug and scanned the room for a way to exit the memory. I took a running jump and flung myself out of the open window, plunging towards the ground below. Just before I made impact, I opened my eyes.

The smell of damp and decay rushed back to me. I was still stuck in the tug of war between Aspen and Kes, roots lashed around my limbs like whips. "Aspen," I commanded. "Come back to yourself, COME BACK TO YOUR—."

"Silence," rasped my sister in Edeva's voice, grabbing my throat so that I choked on my words. "We returned for you, our sisters. Found a way past Silverlight's defenses slowly, spending weeks in the dark with no fresh air. Only our love to sustain us. You could've joined our cause, but you chose... them." Her eyes went from Kes to Ramaya. "How disappointing."

Aspen barked a harsh sound and the roots wrapping us together vanished. Still holding my neck, she hurled me backwards. I slammed into Kes and we both crashed into the ground, hitting our heads. As I lay groaning in the semi-dark, my sister walked through the dirt wall without a backwards glance.

"Mira," Kes whispered from below me. "There's something on your neck—"

I put a hand to my throat where Aspen had grabbed me, screaming as I felt something cold and metallic lodged in my skin.

She'd stabbed me with a siphon.

The tick creature nuzzled deeper, its legs vibrating as it gorged on my blood. A doctor had once told me the human body contains more than seven trillion nerves while explaining my pain syndrome. In that moment I swore I could feel every single one as my nervous system seemed to catch on fire, flames leaping from axon to axon until my whole body was ablaze.

I had an instant to look at Kes, their face pale but their gaze steady and full of love. And then the world faded away.

CHAPTER

TWENTY-FIVE

The pain chased me into the darkness. I wasn't safe from it, not even there. The siphon was a gauntlet of pain. A thousand gauntlets of pain. I felt twisted, consumed with it. Every time I thought I'd made it through, endured the gauntlet, it began again. Burning ice. Boiling heat. Stabbing knives. It would've been boring if it were not so endlessly *present*. The pain felt more alive than I did. I was so alone with it. Wandering through dreamscapes of people and places, but acutely aware that they were paper-thin facsimiles of actual love and care. No one could save me from the pain, which was like a five-bell fire alarm that would not cease. I could not sleep, I could not escape it. So I just stayed with it, stayed present with it moment by moment. And I wound through the maze of my memories, old and new.

I remembered a day when my Mom and I were at the doctor's and a fire alarm started going off, so shrilly that it made our teeth vibrate. The whole office building had to evacuate. Miserable people stood around staring at the building, hands clamped over their ears. Everyone except one toddler. She was just passed out in her mother's arms, mouth half-open, limbs everywhere, head tipped back in blissful slumber. I remember staring at that toddler with a jealousy that winded me, wondering if I would ever feel that safe again. And it came to me in a rush of emotion that the rootbound had begun to make me feel that safe. I wasn't sure I could ever be like that toddler, totally immune from the fire alarm of my pain. But at some point, a hundred, or a thousand, or a million moments later, I realized I could endure it. Even if it rang every moment for the rest of my life, I could endure it.

I had the distant feeling of pressure on my neck releasing and the pain finally began to ebb, draining from my body as if through a sieve.

I woke to Teddy—Godda—keeping vigil at my bedside. It was dark but I felt safe. My fingers traced the skin above my collarbone. The siphon was gone, replaced by a thick, raised scar. My arms were wrapped in roots spilling around the room, to Kes, asleep in the twin cot next to mine. To Tai and Adrian, slumped against each other and snoring. To Ramaya, head tipped back, new gadget fallen from her hands into her lap. I took a moment to savor those present before turning my mind to those absent.

I reached for the connection with Aspen. She was alive, but felt distant, cut off from me. "They're gone, aren't they?" I croaked. "Somewhere far away."

"Yes, your sister escaped with The Confessor, using her treetalking skills and Edeva's aid to outrun the magpie reinforcements on her tail. Silverlight tracked them as far as she could through the Rhiza but lost their whereabouts somewhere outside of Lima."

"Naomi?"

"She lives, barely. We don't know if she will ever...wake again."

I nodded at Teddy. "And Kes? Ramaya?"

"Ramaya's fine—Tai and Adrian sprayed the biologic compound she concocted to release the ants and she woke unscathed. Kes, not so much. They overexerted themself while still in a fragile state and collapsed, giving Silverlight and me quite the scare. But they'll make it. If only to spite the Huntsmen. They'll make it."

Her certainty eased me back into sleep.

When I woke again it was dark. I had no idea how much time had passed but the same group sat vigil at my bedside. They slept soundly, all except Teddy.

"You're back," she said, with that same gentle warmth of the first time I'd met her.

How easy it was to see her as the sweet, doting grandma, the invisible caretaker, and forget the steel underneath. "Do the others know? That you're...a thousand-year-old quasi-deity."

"Just this room. And Kate. I haven't told the Council. I don't want...it's hard for me to give up being Teddy."

"How did you...disappear yourself?"

Teddy laughed quietly. "Oh, that part was easy. The world disappears old women, all I had to do was let it. For centuries I lived a quiet life near here so I could be as close as possible to Silverlight. I never meant to live so long, but Silverlight asked me, begged me, not to leave her."

"And she fed you her life force through the Rhiza?"

Teddy nodded. "Eventually I found my way back to the castle, and for generation after generation I was the kindly, confused archivist."

"But they must've noticed you didn't die."

"I faked my death a few times. Sometimes quite dramatically." Teddy giggled. "And then I began the cycle again."

"Sounds...terrible."

"It's not the life I would have chosen. But at this point, I don't know where I begin and Silverlight ends."

I saw Teddy again that first night in the castle, roots wound thick around her calves, half woman, half tree. "Why not be honest?"

"I feared what the Huntsmen would do if they discovered the secret of my longevity. Do you see the steps they take to steal just a few more years on this earth, drinking the blood of their own children?"

I shook my head, not wanting to picture it.

"Ask it," Teddy prompted.

"What?"

"The question you actually want to ask."

"What will...what will happen to Aspen?"

"As you no doubt saw, she has been deeply infected by the song. Ramaya's new working theory is that Edeva and The Confessor targeted the strongest climate leaders early, turning them to their side before unleashing the song on the rest of us. Edeva always did love her minions."

"Aspen attacked me. With a *siphon*."

Teddy's eyes flashed with feral anger. There it was—the steel. After a moment, her face cleared, a cloudless sky after a rogue thunderstorm. "Aspen has done terrible things. But it is not too late for her."

"I leeched her...with my last breath, to come back to herself."

"She may yet, although it will not be quick, not with the poison of the song buried so deep. But you gave her the strongest chance you could, in a moment of chaos and peril." Teddy took a long sip of tea. "Thank you, by the way. It took immense courage for you to sacrifice yourself like that to protect the rest of us."

A branch unfurled through the infirmary window, pale yellow flowers bursting open from a vine wrapped around Silverlight's limb. Hundreds of them bloomed like a miniature fireworks show, filling the air with a sweet honey scent.

Teddy rolled her eyes. "OK, we get it, you're better at saying thank you than I am, Silverlight."

The branch poked Teddy, ever so gently, and the older woman grinned.

"Do you miss...your Sister?"

"Yes...and no. Many centuries ago Edeva saved my life. The courage it took to charge after me essentially unarmed when she'd fought so hard for her own freedom...it's still unfathomable to me. But Edeva chose a different path, long before this moment. She wanted revenge, and she did not mind inflicting violence to get it. But still, I loved her."

Memories of Aspen washed over me. She had chosen the wrong side. Intentionally hurt me. But still I loved her.

"That love almost destroyed me. It's how The Confessor bested me in the Test of Wills." Teddy shook her head, embarrassed. "Being a master willbinder is about conviction. A delusional belief in yourself. A burning need to achieve a goal. Hearing that Edeva, one who had saved me, who I thought was so deeply aligned with me, was alive and had once again chosen a different, terrible path unmoored me. I was right back at the bloody fields of Ceredigion, watching the roots pull my Sister into the Rhiza after the atrocities she'd committed. While I was lost to the trauma, the memories, The Confessor was able to overpower my mind. I thought I was untouchable with Silverlight by my side, but Silverlight too was drawn by the news of Edeva. If the birds had allied with her, why not the trees, as they once had? It is a terrible thing to watch someone you love do something you loathe, is it not?"

I pictured Aspen grabbing me by the throat, and shook the image away quickly. "Do we know more about the song? The new form of leeching? The Confessor called it a 'doombind.'"

"The Council has appointed Ramaya lead investigator of the bind. All of the magpies and owls will report to her. Even Kes." Teddy's eyes twinkled.

I couldn't help but twinkle back. "Finally. The Council should've been listening to Ramaya all along."

"No argument here."

I stared at my sleeping friends, my found kin, and tried to smother my longing for Aspen to be here in the nursery with us. "What do we do? What do we do *for* our sisters? *Against* our sisters?"

"Well, *I* must find the others. If Edeva lives still, they might as well. The Seven will rise again. *You*, you've done enough. It's time to rest."

"How do I rest when the world is..." I gestured. "On fire."

"The world has been on fire many times before. Millions who now slumber underground have taken up their small piece to tame the blaze and millions more yet unborn will do the same. As for rest—I'm sure this group will have some ideas. You know there are seven of you, including Zo and Naomi."

"My own group of Seven."

Eight, whispered Aspen, a note of apology in her tone. I thrilled at the voice, at knowing Aspen was safe, but I wasn't ready to answer. I wasn't sure I ever would be, not while she was infected by the song.

"Perhaps you could go swimming as the whales sing you lullabies? Or eat your weight in thimble berries on a sunny afternoon? Or sneak away to private hot springs in the dead of the night with a certain someone?" Teddy winked at me.

A warm hand found mine in the dark. I traced the callouses. "Steady Gaze," I whispered and felt a squeeze.

"I second the hot springs idea," Kes rasped.

"Trust *that* to bring you back to consciousness," Teddy said through a giggle while Silverlight's branch shook with silent laughter, raining flower petals down on Kes and me.

And there under the ache of grief I was surprised to feel it bubbling, like a spring stream waking beneath winter ice.

Hope.

AUTHOR'S NOTE

I've been a time traveller three times over. As a legal scholar, I've travelled to the past, poring over internal fossil fuel industry documents and imagining the small group of people willing to trade the lives of so many for a little extra profit. As a queer, neurodivergent dreamer, I've travelled to the future, imagining all the joyful possibilities for our collective thriving. And as a person who lives with chronic pain, I've learned to find and cherish the space between heartbeats. To love the world and my dear ones so fiercely, to be so grateful for the feel of warm sun and a cool breeze, that time slows like honey dribbling from a spoon.

As any good lover of sci-fi knows, time travellers are often chasing something across time and space—leaping from the Pyramids of Giza to the battlefields of World War II to catch an alien species or a villainous scientist. I've been chasing one of the most dangerous things of all.

A story.

A poisonous story, rooted deep in our public imagination. It is a ravenous, many-headed beast, this story. It was born into this world in the mid-twentieth century, fed first by the fossil fuel industry and then reared by a complex web of corporate actors and allies. As it grows, it devours alternative possible futures, one after the other.

The terrible (and magical) thing about stories is that they can shape how we feel and how we act, sometimes even more so than objective reality. As social scientist Albert Bandura writes:

> People's beliefs in their collective efficacy influence the type of social future they seek to achieve, how much effort they put into it, and their endurance when collective efforts fail to produce quick results. The stronger they believe in their capabilities to effect social change the more actively they engage in collective efforts to alter national policies and practices. Those who are beset by a low sense of efficacy are quickly convinced of the futility of effort to reform their institutional systems. [*]

If we feel helpless, we give up. If we feel powerful, we act. If we feel powerful as a collective, we act together. Our stories about the world *become* our world.

So join me in exposing and battling this many-headed beast of a story. It's an expert at hiding and blending in, slithering across newspapers, TV shows, books, school curricula, and social media. It disguises the fossil fuel industry's influence over our culture, our arts, even our very own thoughts.

---

[*] Albert Bandura, "Exercise of personal and collective efficacy in changing societies" in A. Bandura, ed. Self-Efficacy in Changing Societies (New York: Cambridge University, 1995) at page 35.

But its cries have a familiar cadence if you know what to listen for:

Don't. Don't. Don't.

Don't listen to the science. Don't trust the government. Don't be political. Don't vote. Don't care. Don't act. Don't work together. Don't blame us. Don't hope.

Give up. Give up. Give up.

Voices have been rising to challenge this story and stories like it for decades, for centuries. I'm inspired everyday by the people on the front lines, disproportionately young people, Indigenous peoples, and racialized folks, who are putting their bodies and lives on the line to push the boundaries of our collective imagination and create space for us to build a more just and vibrant future.

With *Rootbound*, I'm setting free a new story into the world and joining the countless other voices battling the many-headed beast. In part it is my story. How I've sought to hold space for grief and joy. For anxiety and *aliveness*. For resistance and play, and even for a little magic. How a body that experienced near-total apocalypse has been healing in wild and new ways, day-by-day over more than a decade, surprising countless doctors with its resilience. My climate sorrow was once so overwhelming that I could barely function. But in taking action on climate justice, I've found the best, most empathic, most *present* humans imaginable. And I've discovered that leaning in to fight existential threats arm-in-arm with my besties is the most gloriously meaningful way to spend my brief time on this planet.

It's a tiny, winged-thing, my story, like a hummingbird. I've filled it with so much love. Love for the people you'll see me thank below. Love for dozens more unnamed. For the trees. And the creatures. And the blue, blue sky. For vegan strawberry rhubarb ripple ice cream and sleepy dog cuddles. Others too have feasted it with care, helping it take flight in a life of its own.

My little hummingbird of a story, fueled by love and independently published, is no match for the many-headed beast fueled by billions of dollars and decades of covert corporate influence.

And yet.

And *yet...*

MY RESEARCH

For those of you who like a little less whimsy and a lot more footnotes (*you know who you are!*) my website has links to my research publications on climate misinformation and democracy: https://www.gracenosek.com/

Given the centering of youth climate protesters in *Rootbound*, two of my articles are especially relevant:

- Grace Nosek, "The Fossil Fuel Industry's Push to Target Climate Protesters in the U.S." Pace Environmental Law Review (Fall 2020).
- Grace Nosek, "Dear Gen Z, to protect your right to protest, you must exercise your right to vote" Grist (October 23, 2020).

WHERE TO START ON CLIMATE ACTION?

We need all the talents and skills and backgrounds and wild ideas in the climate movement—we need larks, peacocks, magpies, owls, and more! Climate action really can be anything we want it to be (like, and I'm just spit balling here... drawing from your very academic PhD thesis on fossil fuel industry misinformation and democracy to write a juicy queer young adult fantasy novel).

I'll share one little tool I created to help remind myself and my people that we can cultivate our power as members of a collective rather than as individual consumers, to turn outwards on climate action rather than inwards. When I get stuck in the grocery store for what feels like hours, reading fine print and spinning out over which light bulb is better for the environment, I chant the 3 Vs to myself. *Voice. Volunteer. Vote.* I remind myself to channel all that precious energy and care for the world into something more collective, more systemic, more justice-oriented than agonizing over a light bulb. That hour in consumer limbo could instead go to emailing all of my representatives about creating a robust Youth Climate Corps or calling my bank and requesting they divest from funding resource projects that infringe on Indigenous sovereignty.

THE 3 VS

Voice our climate concerns to friends, family, institutions, and government representatives. Social science says *we* are the most powerful climate advocates for our own communities.

Volunteer with groups and people that light us up inside, and in ways that feel joyful and generative and let us explore new skills. (And if you're a group with the capacity to do so, PAY YOUTH CLIMATE ORGANIZERS! They deserve it and it's a critical way to move beyond an environmental movement that has disproportionately centered whiteness and wealth).

Vote for climate justice champions and/or against climate arsonists, and get as many friends as we can to join us. (Check out my piece above on how voting can be critical to protecting our right to protest from corporations targeting dissent).

Publicly advocating for climate justice is a privilege, one that is being increasingly threatened around the world. Environmental dissent is being targeted, sometimes violently, by corporations and governments. For those of us who can, let's turn *outwards* on climate action, *towards* our sports teams, our book clubs, our schools, our governments, our grassroots movements, our unions, and more, to dream about and work together towards a more just and sustainable world.

CLIMATE ORGANIZATIONS

I crowd-sourced my wonderful community for what folks look for when deciding where to focus their time, money, energy, and support on climate justice work. We look for groups that are youth-led and Indigenous-led; groups that center disability justice, Indigenous sovereignty, racial justice, environmental justice, and queerness; groups that challenge corporate power and influence; groups that center art, storytelling, play, joy, and embodied community; and groups that engage in electoral politics and democracy in ways that build grassroots political power.

There are so many groups out there doing incredible climate justice and civic engagement work. Here are just a few I've had wonderful interactions with if you're looking for a place to get you started. And if you're a university student, check out your local fossil fuel industry divestment movement, PIRG, or other climate justice organizing club—that's where it all began for me.

<u>Environmental Voter Project</u>
<u>Shake Up The Establishment</u>
<u>Apathy is Boring</u>

Acknowledgments

Endless gratitude to my fearless editor, Andy Futuro. Your combination of incredibly incisive editing, gentle teaching, and wry commentary has helped me laugh my way into being a much stronger writer. (You'd tell me 'incredibly incisive' is redundant, but what can I say? You earned that adverb!)

Thank you to my cover artist, Rohina Dass—what a joy to reunite five years after our university climate organizing days and conspire around this gorgeous artwork. You've created a portal into another world, one that lovingly pulls readers into the magic of *Rootbound*.

Thank you to my sibby Em Jung Ng-Mittertreiner and my cousin Maya Kamoshita—our bond of chosen kinship inspired the rootbinding ceremony. It's a gift to move through this world with you both.

Legal academia is not always the easiest environment in which to take creative risks. But throughout my time at Rice University, Harvard Law School, the University of Victoria, the University of British Columbia, and the University of Toronto, I've been lucky enough to have an incredible set of mentors and supporters who encouraged my out-of-the-box thinking. They have modelled public scholarship in pursuit of justice in ways that I find endlessly inspiring. Thank you Professors Joel Bakan, John Borrows, Emily Broad Leib, Jon Hanson, Val Napoleon, Lynne Quarmby, Jim Blackburn, Laura Tozer, Joana Setzer, Calvin Sandborn, Liv Yoon, Amanda Giang, and Rebecca

Richman Cohen. And thank you to dear friends, classmates, and incredible scholars, Maira Hassan, Terri-Lynn Williams-Davidson, and Catherine Higham.

Deep gratitude to the University of British Columbia Public Scholars Initiative, and especially Dr. Serbulent Turan and Dean Susan Porter, for your incredible commitment to and funding of public scholarship.

I am profoundly indebted to the generous souls, many of you strangers, who donated to my crowdfunding campaign for *Rootbound.* This book would not exist without you. *Truly.* I promise to send your generosity forward into the world, supporting, amplifying, and lifting the next generation of climate organizers and storytellers at every opportunity.

Thank you to my dear friend Jessica Magonet—you've championed this story in every way imaginable and kept me going through the low points with your fierce and boundless belief in me.

To my wonderful sustainability literacy consultant Kiley Little—thank you for bringing me into the minds of students and teachers with your thoughtful comments.

Shakti Ramkumar and Mariana Martinez Rubio, thank you two wonderful humans (and icons!) for helping me type this story into being when my own wrists could not. And Ghabiba Weston, thank you for your brilliant feedback and warm encouragement.

Profound thanks to my early brain trust of amazing creatives who helped shape the vibes and the visuals of the *Rootbound* universe—Wongelawit Teka Zewde, Uma Le Daca Jolicoeur, Jazz Groden-Gilchrist, Jennie Zhou, Jess Wylie, George Patrick Richard Benson, Lindsay Borrows, Nina Rossing, and Anna Rossing.

Thank you to the amazing photographer David Markwei

for my author photo—you expertly captured the essence of *Rootbound* with your lens.

And to the many wonderful humans who feasted this little hummingbird of a story, offering your talents and energy like dozens of little gifts of nectar—*thank you*. To Mom, Dad, John Michael, Andrew, Jess, Ali, Tara, Flossie, Dulcy, Cate, Temi, Jenn, Tracy, Erin, Miha, Alex, Georgia, Sarah, Jen, Abbey, Margay, Britt, Amy, Joanna, River, Patrick, Meera, Swelen, Jinhwa, George, Pay, Joe, Barb, Charlie, Arlen, Jayne, Esmé, Ana, Joey, Liam, Rich, Marlis, Polly, Lilah, Johanna, Dani, Rivka, and last, but certainly not least, Adi.

Finally, to all of my dear ones in Toronto, Vancouver, New Jersey, Pennsylvania, London, Melbourne, and so many other places around the world—*thank you*. Everything I am and everything I do leads back to you and the ways you fill up my cup. You have laughed with me, danced with me, stayed up late into the night chatting about nothing and everything, carried my things when I could not, cancelled plans and lain in bed with me, moved me across cities and countries, and made me feel so deeply held and seen.

ABOUT THE AUTHOR

Dr. Grace Nosek is a sociolegal scholar focusing on climate misinformation, protest, and democracy, as well as an author and organizer. She centers justice, joyful community, story-telling, civic engagement, and systems change in her work and scholarship. As a Postdoctoral Fellow at the University of Toronto, Grace researched novel strategies to inoculate youth against climate despair, and co-authored the City of Toronto's Youth Climate Engagement Strategy. As an author, Grace has spoken to tens of thousands of people about how to spot climate misinformation and reclaim public agency in climate decision-making. Grace's research has been supported by Fulbright, Killam, and Pierre Elliott Trudeau Foundation scholarships, and she holds a BA from Rice University, a law degree from Harvard Law School, and a Master of Laws and PhD in law from the University of British Columbia. Her research, fiction, and non-fiction writing have been published and shared widely. She's never met a dance party she didn't want to join.

If you would like to contact Dr. Grace Nosek about speaking to your school or organization, please go to www.-gracenosek.com.

www.ingramcontent.com/pod-product-compliance
Lightning Source LLC
Chambersburg PA
CBHW031958050726
47590CB00006B/1955